I0669219

Divided We Stand

By

Kaitlyn Leyva

W & B Publishers

USA

Divided We Stand © 2014. All rights reserved by Kaitlyn Leyva.

No part of this book may be reproduced or transmitted in any form or by any means, graphic, electronic, or mechanical, including photocopying, recording, taping, or by any informational storage retrieval system without prior permission in writing from the publisher.

W & B Publishers

For information:
W & B Publishers
Post Office Box 193
Colfax, NC 27235
www.a-argusbooks.com

ISBN: 978-0-6923212-5-6
ISBN: 0-6923212-5-X

Book Cover designed by Dubya

Printed in the United States of America

Dedication

I would like to dedicate this book to my biggest supporters. Without their continued support, I would never have completed this story. My mother, who is my best editor and is always prepared with a good dose of honest criticism. My sister Morgan, who is my go to researcher when I need more information on a topic. My sister Jordan, being a fiction book addict is my hardest critic. My youngest sister Sophie, wise beyond her years she is the one who makes sure I stay tied to reality! And last, my husband Max. No matter what crazy thing I come up with next, he is always there to encourage me forward.

Thank you.

A note from the Author

The results of bad leadership have the potential for disaster.
I hope you enjoy my story...

Prologue

"Ace! Where are you honey?"

"Be there in a sec, mom!" Ace called over her shoulder. She climbed back down the cliff face and ran to the house. She had made it five feet farther than last time she climbed the dreaded cliff face and was interrupted by her mom.

Her parents didn't let her stay out after dark anymore; not since the last gun law passed. Everyone in town was on edge and her parents didn't trust anyone anymore. There had been talk of doing something crazy to get the Government's attention, to let them know these new restrictions and laws weren't okay, that they weren't going to take it.

It wasn't just in their small Arizona farming town that this kind of talk was happening either. Ace's parents didn't even let her watch the news anymore. Nothing in the media could be believed, the reports were too clouded with government influence. If you wanted to know what was really going on you had to listen to private broadcasts on an old antenna radio from some crazy-sounding guy who didn't care if the government disapproved of his message and came after him.

As she strolled into the house, her father looked up from his book and smiled. Her mother was in the kitchen washing dishes and her older brother was doing a crossword in the newspaper.

She had one other brother, Silas. He was away at a special boarding school, a college prep school in Washington State. But it also meant that she didn't get to see him much.

Her family had eaten dinner without her, as usual, because Ace didn't come inside until she absolutely had to and that meant eating her dinner separately. Her mother always put a plate aside for her.

"How is Dylan doing?" Ace asked as she put a forkful of chicken in her mouth.

"He is fine." Her mother said too quickly.

For only being ten years old, Ace was a lot more perceptive than her parents would like to believe. She knew Dylan wasn't doing fine. Ever since the latest gun laws passed, he had lost his business. There was a problem with owning a gun shop when the government passed a new law that made it illegal for private businesses or individuals to own or distribute guns of any kind. Dylan hadn't been able to find work since he had to close shop.

The gun law wasn't the only thing the Government took over. The control over the people had started out slowly some six years ago. But the signs were there all along. When the President and his family spent too much of the money on constant vacations, clothes, and other personal uses that weren't in any way related to running the country, it should have been a big enough red flag to get some attention. He spent more time out of the country that he did at the White House or even on American soil.

The laws started slowly and were buried in the guise of helping people who needed it.

To start with, they began by controlling healthcare, making it illegal to go without health insurance, even if you couldn't afford it. At first it seemed like a good thing but then the restrictions on it grew and were tied into other rights. They started increasing federal tax on guns and ammunition to the point that no regular citizen could even afford to buy it. If you were not in full compliance to the new laws, you were ineligible to vote. That way it was easier to control the voting outcome which made it easier to control which laws passed by taking away the rights of individuals who didn't agree.

When they started taking away the guns, it started slow. The first law made it illegal to possess assault rifles. Although several people and gun rights groups were upset with this, there was enough persuasive argument behind it that the majority of society supported the argument that the average citizen had no need to own an assault rifle. Then a second law made it illegal to possess semi-automatic weapons, arguing that the second amendment covered only hunting rifles and there was a list of approved hunting rifles. The reasoning behind that law wasn't quite as popular and they placed a heavy tax on any new sales that would go into a fund for families that were affected by gun related violence. This tax was very popular with anti-gun groups who put a lot of money into the campaign and got the law passed. After that, privately owned gun shops were shut down in an attempt to control the distribution of approved guns and eliminate any possibilities of a "black market" starting up. And then, any individual person couldn't be in possession of more than two guns that had to be registered back to the authorities and raised the age limit so you couldn't buy or own any type of gun until you were twenty-one.

Nowadays you couldn't even have .22 bullets without getting arrested and hauled off to jail for five or more years.

The newest law had only been in effect for a year and things were already getting tense. The President kept saying that as soon as things settled and public adjusted to the new laws that we would be okay. Society just had to get through a transitioning phase. But it seemed like things kept getting worse, not better.

It was announced that people had to drop all unregistered guns off at the local police station. The officers were still allowed to carry and handle weapons, especially while taking guns from unhappy citizens.

It soon became apparent that most people weren't turning in their guns. A lot of people did, but for every person that complied there were five that didn't.

The President decided he would send police into towns, going door to door, to retrieve unauthorized guns from their owner. Someone on the gun commission made the foolish choice to have the very first gun seizure televised to show Americans how easy it would be to just hand over your guns. Everyone would be all smiles and shake hands and pretend to be happy about it.

However, they did not predict the disaster that ensued.

Before the televised event, a specific family was contacted to be sure the confiscation would go quietly and according to plan. The police showed up to the first house in Polson, Montana and went over everything with the farmer and his family. The farmer agreed to all of the terms. But what the government didn't know was he agreed to this so he would have the chance to make his own public statement.

On live television, with everyone watching, the family refused to hand over their guns. The man claimed he needed his guns to protect his family and his cattle, that it was his right to have them. He made a big speech about the President needing to be impeached, that this law proved his incapability of leading our nation properly. He argued that the removal of our second amendment would bring destruction down around us all.

The cops told him if he didn't hand them over, he would be arrested and the guns would be forcibly removed from his house. The farmer held out his shotgun, and told them they could try and take his weapons but that he was prepared to die to protect his rights and his family.

The officials should have left, then and there to figure this out. The news crew should have shut off the cameras until they knew what was going on. But neither of those things happened.

The news crew got the whole thing on live television. The police telling the man to lower his weapon while drawing their own pistols; the farmer shooting the first cop who raised his gun; the second and third cops shooting the farmer. Then the farmer's son, all of maybe thirteen years old, came running out of the house. He knelt next to his father's body and lifted the shotgun to throw it aside.

But the remaining cops just saw him reaching for a gun and shot him before anything could happen.

Then the farmer's wife ran forward, sobbing. The third cop was expecting trouble now, he shot her as soon as she came into view, not a single weapon in her hands.

Then everything went silent. Not even the news people in the studio managed to recover. The only sound was coming from a crying baby somewhere inside the house. No one turned off the cameras, no one moved to see if any of the people who were shot were still alive. They all just stood there. The cameramen, the news broadcaster lady, and the two remaining policemen.

***

Ace would never forget what she just witnessed. Her father had recovered before anyone on TV. He got up from his chair and turned off their flat screen. He went through the house and locked all of the doors, unplugged the TV, and started putting all of their guns in the bomb shelter in the cellar.

It wasn't a real bomb shelter, that's just what the family called it. The room had concrete walls that were so thick it could probably would keep you safe from a bomb. If you didn't know it was there, you wouldn't know how to find it. It was hidden behind a false bookcase. Even if you did find it and tried to open the door, you would think it was locked or rusted closed. There was a secret way to open the latch that her father invented.

After a few minutes of watching their father, Ace's oldest brother Quentin got up to help. Quentin was almost twenty and he understood what their father was doing. Ace's mother had tears in her eyes, but they didn't fall. She got up and started cooking in the kitchen without a word. Ace just sat on the couch and watched her family. She wanted to turn the TV back on to see what was happening, to see if maybe the boy lived but she stayed where she was like she was in a time bubble and everything just stopped.

They had several guns so it took a while to get them rounded up and moved into the secure room. Her father was former military and retired early because of an injury to his leg. He could get around pretty well now, even though he had a noticeable limp.

Her father and brother got all the guns secure, except for a few handguns and two rifles which were cleverly hidden though the house. Her father made them memorize where each gun and where each piece of ammo was stored in case they needed one of the firearms. Ace didn't know why she would need one of the guns. She had her father and Quentin there to protect her from everything. But she listened intently.

After that, things went a little crazy around home. Her father and brother went to the store and bought so much food they almost didn't have room to store it all. Most of it was canned goods, but some was freezer food. Ace thought they were probably done grocery shopping until she graduated from high school. Her father had predicted all of this happening. Ace didn't know why at the time, but he had started preparing as soon as the first few laws came into effect. Maybe he didn't know exactly how or when things would happen. But he knew something bad would happen sooner rather than later.

They had the entire cellar filled with canned food, and several extra-large chest freezers which were now also full of food. None of them had cell phones and two years ago they got rid of the house phone. They had a battery operated radio to stay connected with what was going on, but only her father was allowed to turn it on.

They had the TV, but they only got a few channels off of the antenna and only turned it on when for news and when there was a special broadcast that her father wanted to see.

Ace didn't even go to public school. Her parents brought her home for schooling halfway through kindergarten when it became apparent that the school's curriculum was being altered by the government, dictating what could be taught and promoting social agendas.

At the time they told her it was because she was too smart for her classmates to keep up with her. But as she got older, Ace started to realize it had something to do with their way of life. Her parents were preparing for something bad to happen.

She didn't get the typical education. Sure she learned the basics in reading, writing, math, and history. But her focus was more along the lines of edible plants, treating wounds and sickness without a doctor, how to properly use a multi-tool to do just about anything, self-defense and physical fitness. Ace didn't mind, she thought it was a lot more interesting than regular school.

A few weeks after the broadcasted disaster, just when Ace thought she was going to lose her mind from being locked away in the house, her father unlocked the back door and told her she could go out. But only for an hour, she had to stay in sight of the house, and if she saw anyone she had to run back inside right away. They weren't too worried about her going to anyone's house since they lived far enough out of town and away from people. Ace was out the door before he could change his mind.

And that was the situation for a few more weeks. Her time outside gradually got increased as things relaxed without incident. It increased until she was leaving just after breakfast and returning just before dark.

And that's how it was the day everything went wrong.

***

Ace had just triumphantly pulled herself to the top of the cliff that overlooked her family's house and a few of the fields when she heard a vehicle drive up. She peered through the brush over the edge and watched a strange-looking van pull up to the house. Several men got out with big guns that she vaguely remembered her dad teaching her about. They were military weapons. Assault rifles.

They stood in front of the van, talking and gesturing to the house. One of the men didn't seem very happy about whatever they were doing. There was a lot of arguing and gesturing, and finally the upset man leaned against the front of the vehicle while the rest moved to the house.

A part of Ace wanted to run down to the house and see what was going on, but another part of her was too scared to move. She stayed at her vantage point and waited and watched. The doors to the house were always locked. Even Ace had to knock and have someone let her in when she went back in the evenings.

No one came to the door, not even her father. She was surprised by that. Everything about those people spoke of military, she had assumed they were friends of her dad or that he at least knew them.

After a few minutes one of the military men tried to kick the door open, but it didn't work. Their doors were reinforced with metal frames, and they didn't break open very easily.

But this didn't deter the men. She watched while they got a large black battering ram out of their van and, with two men on each side, they hit the door with it several times until the door finally broke open.

They weren't inside long before Ace heard gunshots echoing from all directions around her and down the valley from the town. There were so many so fast that Ace couldn't even tell if any had gone off in her house or not. She saw the man still waiting at the truck flinch when the shots went off. He covered his face with his hands, then got in the truck and just sat there.

She still wasn't able to move. Even her fear for her family didn't give her the courage to move so much as a muscle.

Some of the uniformed men walked out of the house and back to their vehicles. There were a few belated shots that rang out through the hills but they sounded far off. Ace waited there until the vehicles left and she was sure they weren't coming back, and then a little longer before she managed to convince her limbs to move and take her down to her house.

She had to go the long way down. Her hands were shaking too much to be trusted scaling down the cliff.

As she approached the broken door she slowed down and crept up to the threshold. Ace peered inside and instantly burst into tears at the sight of her parents and oldest brother laying on the floor, blood from their bodies covering everything. There was also two men in uniform lying there.

She ran forward and collapsed to her knees at her mother's side. She remembered everything her father had taught her about first aid. His lessons had increased greatly since the last day he allowed her to watch TV. Ace checked her mother's pulse and to see if she was breathing.

Her mother was dead.

Ace cried harder, but managed to pull herself over to her father and check him. He was dead, too. Before she managed to pull herself away from her father's side, she heard a weak cough and rushed over to Quentin's side.

"Quen?" She tried to roll him over but he was heavy and she had to struggle to get him to move. He was bleeding from two gunshot wounds; one in his chest and one in his stomach. Blood trickled down the side of his face from his mouth as he took strained shallow breaths.

"Quentin? What do you need me to do? I'll get the first aid kit or I'll go to town and look for help. I'll get one of the doctors. I can help you, just tell me how." She cried into his hand as he lifted it to her face. He had always been the cool older brother, allowing her to tag along with him and his friends, never acting annoyed by her presence or the fact that she slowed him down and limited his activity options. He taught her how to do things her parents told her she was too young to learn.

"Hey, sis. I'm not gonna make it." He glanced over just enough to see their parents. "You're gonna be on your own for now. I want you to take all of the weapons you can find, and run."

Ace started crying harder. "I can't, Quen, I can't go without you guys. I need help."

He shook his head slowly. "You are strong. Dad taught you how to survive. You just have to be careful and think. Do what Dad and I taught you. Remember Mom and Dad's beliefs, our rights. That is what we are fighting for. Just don't get yourself killed. Alright?"

He coughed, spraying blood across Ace's face. Her hands and knees were already covered in it from crawling across the floor to him but she didn't notice.

"Quen?" She sobbed, "Please don't leave me. I don't want to be alone. Please, Quentin! I need you." She cried into his chest, not caring about the blood on it.

It was almost an hour later when she numbly pulled herself away from his body and over to the hiding place of one of her father's pistols. She tucked it into her belt. Then she went outside, found a shovel, and began to dig.

She didn't stop digging as the sun went down, and she didn't stop when she was so exhausted she thought she would pass out and never wake up. She knew the graves weren't very deep and she wished she was stronger but by late afternoon the next day she had three shallow graves.

She thought the digging was going to be the hardest part. But she didn't think about how to get her family into their graves.

Ace drug her mother over first. She was a very petite woman and not very tall so she was the easiest to move. Once she was buried Ace moved on to her father, which took a lot longer. She managed to maneuver him onto a blanket and drag him outside. She saved her brother for last wishing that this was not really happening. Quentin was her hero. She looked up to him almost more than her dad.

She had never been that close with her other brother, Silas, but still she vaguely wondered if anything happened to him through all this chaos.

When all three were buried, Ace curled up on the ground between them and passed out.

***

The sun was in the middle of the sky the next day when she woke up. Ace had no tears left. She was numb, but she pulled herself to her feet and went through the house. She retrieved all of the hidden guns and the ammo and a few of her knives. She knew she couldn't open the bomb shelter because she wasn't strong enough by herself. Only her father and brother had been able to manage the lock and the heavy door.

She stuffed her duffle bag with food and filled every water bottle she could find. By the time she was done, she couldn't lift the bag. So she dug out her old wagon, hauled her bag onto it, and then started walking down the driveway.

Quentin had told her to leave. That meant he was worried something bad might come back to their home. Maybe he was worried about raiders or the soldiers coming back to look for guns. She headed out on the path that led into the hills, eyes forward. She told herself she would never come back.

Chapter 1

Nine years later...

Using her toe, Ace rolled the body onto its back so she could identify the cause of death. A tan nose peered around her to sniff the body and she flicked a hand towards it, telling the horse to stay where it was. With a glance around the deserted town, she whistled to her dog. She had saved the Irish wolfhound from being drowned in a sack when it was just a pup. She had to admit she considered killing it herself. It would feed her for another night and an extra mouth to feed was hazardous. But she couldn't bring herself to do it.

"Wolf, check it out."

The dog sauntered out of a nearby building and trotted down the streets ahead to look for trouble. The little town was quiet and looked totally deserted.

The body at her feet was a boy, probably not any older than twelve. He had a poor quality knife clutched in his right hand and a pink teddy bear in the other. Finding this odd, Ace squatted down and picked up the bear. On the back was written, *"Nina's bear"*.

With a sigh Ace set the bear down next to the boy and began searching the surrounding rubble for more bodies. The boy had been shot twice in the chest. He was old enough that he should have known to hide from armed men so he must have been desperate. Soldiers didn't usually shoot children. Quite the opposite in fact. They usually took them back to training camps. The only other groups out there were the Rebels and the Scavengers. The Rebels would have fed them and given them refuge. The Scavengers would have stripped them of anything that had potential value.

However, if someone put up a fight, the soldiers would not hesitate to shoot. And the pink teddy bear made Ace think there might be a girl somewhere. Maybe he was trying to protect a little sister.

After some searching there didn't seem to be another body around so Ace figured that the soldiers had one more to add to their numbers. It wasn't good to be a female of any age in their camps. Ace was thinking the dead boy was better off than the girl would be.

She tossed her blonde braid over her shoulder and strayed farther down the street. The town she was in now hadn't survived the Uprisings very well. A few had, but smaller ones like this one usually became a base for soldiers or a booby-trap zone for Scavengers. Most were fairly well picked over but sometimes Ace could find a few things to help her get by. She kept jewelry any time she came across it for trade. She had never actually come across anyone to trade with, but it was worth keeping on hand.

Some people would tell you if the Retaliation had been planned better, the bombings and Uprisings might not have even been necessary. The Retaliation was the first stand the civilians made against the government. If it had been better planned, the people would have already had militia formed and safe zones for children and elderly. But they didn't. They weren't prepared for the government to fight back so quickly and so forcefully.

The Government sent soldiers into the smaller towns that were uprising so they didn't have to waste bombs. Anyone who didn't swear in then and there to become a citizen for the UNA was shot. The large cities that were uprising were completely destroyed with bombs.

There were a few cities that had been protected during the bombings, ones that had been cooperative like Washington, DC and Olympia, Washington and other places where the

UNA government had a strong foothold. All of the politicians and their families had been safely hidden away in "safe zones" until the smoke cleared. There were a several cities all over the states that the UNA controlled, but they didn't have a full state under complete control yet. Of course, those cities didn't stay protected for long. DC was one of the first places hit by the initial Rebel movement. Now the only thing left of DC was rubble.

The Government said the citizens forced them into battle, but the citizens would say the government forced it on themselves when they started thinking they owned the people instead of taking care of them. The government was supposed to work for the people, but they started thinking the people worked for them.

It was a gradual change from American democracy but once they started to remove rights and the ability to vote, they were able to get their own politicians elected into office. That made getting new laws through pretty easy.

Soon they changed the name from the United States of America to the United Nation of America, UNA. They said that it showed more unity and less division. It is amazing what people will believe and follow when the message is buried with pretty words and eloquent speech.

It wasn't long after the bombings that the UNA set off some sort of electromagnetic shock wave that destroyed all electronics. It was designed to prevent rebel groups from forming and having any sort of organized resistance. The government misjudged how many more people would rebel after they recovered from the bombings.

However, people from all walks and occupations made up the Rebellion. They were able to repair equipment and create devices that they could get working. It wasn't state of the art, but it allowed them to communicate and organize.

Ace's father had prepared her well for survival, especially during the last few months before he was killed. He had wanted all boys, but when Ace came along after her two older brothers, he didn't change his raising techniques. She was taught how to fight, shoot a gun, and survive in the wilderness. He had taken his job of making her self-reliant very seriously. She had to wrestle with her brothers and learn to shoot as well as them, even some days could outshoot them. He knew something was going to happen; everyone did. He had always told her it was only a matter of time before the government did something drastic to get the people under government control which would lead to aggressive uprisings.

One day her father had gone all the way to taking her far out in the woods, so she didn't know where she was or how to get back, and left her. She hadn't been prepared for such an adventure and only had her belt knife with her but she had managed to find her way home.

Now those skills were coming in handy.

When the people had decided to rebel against the Government, all of the news reporters said everything would be fine and that it wasn't dangerous to be out and continue on with everyday life. The small population of people rebelling would get over their anger and the Government would find a way to settle the country and save us all, without any politicians destroying their pride. But it hadn't happened like that.

People didn't want to give up their personal protection, their rights that they had always had, and step into line like thoughtless lemmings. A lot of people were killed when they refused to just roll over and play along. That's when the first uprising against the UNA happened.

The people formed their own militia, mostly comprised of hunters and hobby shooters. When police came to take the guns out of small towns, they were ambushed. You think the government had a large army? Try adding up every hunter in the nation. The government army was severely outnumbered. Several of the army left their duty and supported the people that were fighting back. They felt that the new Government was becoming a domestic terrorist threat.

It didn't take long for the news to broadcast that the same thing was happening all over the Nation. That was before the electromagnetic shock took out televisions. Nowadays if you wanted to listen to government reports you had to listen to them over an old antenna radio. You could find a TV now and then that worked if you really tried but you had to pay obscene amounts of money for it, just like anything else electronic. Then you had to find a source of electricity and hope someone didn't kill you for what you had. If you thought buying a car was expensive beforehand, try it when they are scarce. And then you had to find fuel. The UNA controlled refineries that still produced fuel for the UNA cities but it was at a UNA price!

Peering into some of the abandoned stores, Ace noticed they had already been ransacked. That meant she wouldn't be restocking on her food supplies at this town. Luckily she had become proficient at hunting and didn't mind eating campfire meat with little flavor. She gathered several wild herbs to season with but had yet to find a replacement for salt, a lost treasure in her mind.

There were a lot of towns that had been abandoned like this one. Several of them now had people living in them again but they were guarded and fenced in against the Scavengers, the Rebels, and anyone who might cause trouble. You could go in to trade for or buy supplies. But it was best to have an eye watching your back at all times, lone travelers were especially targeted. The guards weren't very nice to young women, especially if you were pretty.

A little farther down the street she found a second body. The little girl was maybe eight or nine years old. Her old haggard yellow dress stained with the drying blood from a bullet in her back. She was better off dead than captive as far as Ace was concerned. She sighed at the death of two innocent children, but it wasn't her problem. This was just another average day now, and all that mattered to her was that she was still alive. That is how her days were measured.

The bodies were cold so whoever had killed them had most likely moved on and were not still around to be a danger. Ace figured it was probably a patrol squad because of the precise shot placement. They were supposed to bring in kids they found to be trained up as soldiers. Children were young and impressionable which made them easier to convert to the beliefs of the Government. It was a twisted system. But being taken in and brain washed and having a full belly was better than what she had to fear at her age. Soldiers weren't nice to young women. Nor were the Scavengers, and even many of the Rebels. Ace had encountered them all. And she was too old to be taken in and brain washed. Being caught by a patrol squad for her meant a whole different kind of trouble.

So she avoided everyone, even people like herself just trying to survive. She had even left a few others to be taken to the fate she herself feared with every fiber of her being instead of risking becoming a victim herself. Just like the day her family was killed.

She wandered for survival. Staying in one place too long was dangerous. You either ran out of supplies or someone found you. She wasn't sure which scenario would be worse. Originally, her only goal was to survive. But after she got a few years older, she tried to find Silas, her other brother. She headed north to his school but by the time she made it to his school there was no one left alive. There was a pile of bones and ash where it looked like bodies had been piled up and burned, but not even a trace of a living person.

Ace shifted the shoulder strap of her rifle to a more comfortable position and double checked the spare clips for both of her hand guns. Judging by the boot prints in the ground, she figured the troops headed out the southeastern road. It looked like there were about six people in the group. The prints were going the same direction she was wanting to go which wasn't a good sign. She hadn't been much of a tracker when she started out living on her own, but there was truth in the term *practice makes perfect*, because now she could follow almost any trail she set out on.

Turning. she got up on Flint, her buckskin gelding, and headed down the road. She had come across the horse by a stroke of luck. Traveling by horseback was the most efficient way to get around anymore. Learning that driving a car around drew far too much attention to herself the hard way, she had given up on them. The speed they could travel was hindered by the trouble they caused and attention they attracted. You had to be willing to kill to get one and then keep killing to keep it. Not a good survival strategy. Three years ago, Ace sought refuge in an abandoned barn on a stormy night and came across Flint who had also been abandoned. She had searched the barn and found a saddle and bridle to go with the horse. Ace had no idea how old the horse was, but he was sturdily built and seemed young enough in energy. It took her several weeks to learn how to ride and build a tolerance in her muscles for it, but Flint was well trained and tolerated her while she learned to stay on. It was the longest she had stayed in one spot since she had been on her own. She never regretted the time she spent working to ride.

When the sound of a struggle up ahead on the road reached her ears she stopped Flint and snapped her fingers, calling Wolf to her side.

She could hear some guys arguing and yelling and the sounds of a scuffle. She had hoped it wouldn't come to this, and hadn't expected them to be so close to the empty town still. She turned off the road to enter the woods, but one look at Wolf told her there were sentries in the forest. His eyes had a very focused look and the hair on his back was raised up. He had transferred into the hunter that he instinctively was. Even if she turned around now, they would be certain to see her. There was no safe route to escape. That meant she would have to hide out until they left and hope they didn't find her or she would have to kill them. If they were observant they were certain to see her hoof-prints on the road heading back to the town.

The noise was coming from a bend in the road and it sounded like there was a pretty good fight going on. She dismounted Flint, quietly led him into an alley, and tied his reins around the saddle horn. She had trained him to stand still until she called him and if anyone else tried to grab him, he would strike out with his front feet to keep them away. Then she moved forward at a crouch with Wolf.

"He's not worth wasting the bullets, take him!"

At least it was good to know they weren't in the mood to shoot. She found a big tree to hide behind and peered through the branches. There were three men standing casually to the side while a fourth held a captive and a fifth beat him to a pulp.

The man being held looked like he could normally hold his own but five to one was a pretty unfair match. One of the men—they looked government-hired—tossed a rope over his head and they bound the captive's hands behind his back and then forced him to his knees. He had blood dripping from his nose and a split lip. Judging by how hard he was breathing, he must have put up a good fight. Several of them were also sporting bruises and bloody faces. One of the men shouldered his rifle and shot the ground a few inches from the captive. They all laughed when he flinched and did it again. So they didn't want to waste bullets shooting this poor guy but it seemed they had no issue with wasting them for some twisted entertainment.

The captive man said something that Ace couldn't hear and then he was knocked to his side by the butt of one man's gun. If they would just have shot the poor guy and been done with it, she could have just continued on her way. But she felt a deep rage building against these soldiers. They were part of the new system that wanted peace and prosperity. If only the citizens in the UNA cities knew what was really happening out here. But they were happy to believe the sterilized reports that the media fed them. Ace had had enough of this injustice.

She un-holstered her pistol and aimed between the branches, then shot the man who had his gun shouldered before anyone even knew she was there. While they were still in a state of shock trying to figure out where the shot came from, she steadily shot one bullet per man before they could figure out where she was.

She waited and three sentries came out of the trees on the edge of town to see what the commotion was about. Apparently they weren't expecting there to be any trouble because they came out relaxed without their guns at the ready. They probably just thought it was their buddies tormenting the captive some more. Ace shot them before they could figure out what happened.

She waited several moments longer, Wolf at her side all the while. When she could hear nothing, she slowly walked out into the open.

All of the men she had shot were dead. She kicked over bodies and began to rummage through their pockets to scavenge from them anything that could be of use to her.

Ace caught movement out of her peripheral vision and swung around with her rifle shouldered.

The man tried to roll and meet her eyes as best as he could from his position on the ground with his hands tied.

For the first time in her life, Ace's finger hesitated on the trigger. He was a captive, not one of the soldiers. She just stood there staring at him. She had never saved anyone before.

"Please, don' shoot."

She tilted her head at his strange accent but didn't comment. Something in the back of her mind told her it was Scottish or Irish or something of that nature but it was too faint to tell.

She looked at her dog, but he didn't have his hackles raised. He just sat there with his tongue hanging out and waiting. That was almost as odd as her not shooting the second she saw that one of them was alive. Wolf just looked at her with a lazy look, yawned, and sat down totally uninterested in the current situation.

Ace didn't care if her dog had gotten lazy, she wasn't about to relax. She didn't lower her gun and she didn't move her finger from the trigger, but she didn't shoot him either.

"I don't s'pose you could cut a man free, eh, lass?"

She didn't respond. She hadn't really spoken to another human being in years. It just wasn't what she did. Oh sure, there was the occasional cuss word shouted out during a few close calls but nothing that could be considered real communication. She killed people that were a threat if she couldn't get away and she avoided most of them like they were the plague. She didn't know why today was different but she couldn't bring herself to shoot a defenseless man tied up and bleeding. What she didn't understand is why she didn't just walk away. She was good at that. There was no responsibility, no ties, no extra mouth to take care of.

She looked back to her dog. "Guard." Wolf yawned, not taking his job very seriously, but stood and showed his teeth in a silent growl just the same. The man looked at the wolf-hound, but didn't seem too concerned.

"I don't aim to attack my savior. Just cut me free, then I'll be on my way," he gasped tiredly. The position he was lying in must have been making it difficult to breathe because it sounded like he was straining to get his words out.

She knew she was going to regret this but she slung her rifle over her shoulder and holstered her pistol. It went against all of her rules. She stepped over to the man with a knife in her hand and quickly cut him free. As soon as her knife sliced through the ropes she jumped up and stood back several pace with her knife held out. The man slowly pulled his hands around and made an attempt to undo the knots around his wrists but he was too weak and beaten up. Instead he just plopped back onto the ground.

He looked over at her with half closed eyes and sighed. "I'll just make my way to the next town, there's one nearby to the west. There should be somethin' there."

"I was just there. Only bodies." She looked up at the sky, gauging how much time she had left before night fell.

The man tried to sit up, but slumped back to the ground in a heap and didn't move again. She wondered for a second if he died after all, but she could see his chest moving rhythmically up and down. Ace sighed in frustration. She didn't help people, she couldn't. She only watched out for herself and her animals. That was it. She was no savior, no heroine. She was a survivor and that meant one thing: to stay alive. Nothing less, nothing more. She had hidden away while people were taken, screaming for help, or attacked, and she had never done anything. So why did she feel obligated to help someone now?

Was it because no one else was around and he was alone? If she left him half-dead in the road, he would be completely alone. She remembered when she had been completely alone. She didn't like those days nor would she ever want to go back to them. It had been a long time since she was this close to a person and not fearing for her life.

Ace knelt down and looked at him. He lay there, dirty with blood running down his face but looked strangely peaceful. She pushed the hair back from his eyes. It felt strange under her fingers and she felt something that she hadn't felt in forever. It was something that was locked away deep inside behind layers of self-preservation. Something she didn't know was still there. It was an odd sensation, almost like she just ate something bordering on going bad.

After making an irritated sound at herself and the whole situation, she stood up and whistled for Flint. There was no way she was dragging that man on her own and she needed help moving the dead bodies. She needed to at least drag them off of the road. Once they were discovered, the other soldiers would do a search of the area to see if there was a danger still about. The longer it took them to find the bodies, the farther away she would be.

It took her longer than she wanted to get the job done, but she was only so big and these men were well fed. By the time she was finished, it was dusk and she still had to get the man who was stubbornly still alive to a safe place. Getting him anywhere would be difficult, he was twice her size. Dragging him behind Flint would be the easiest, but that probably wouldn't help his condition.

She finally decided to try to get him up onto Flint. She positioned her horse in a ditch so he was as low as possible, then she tied a rope around the mans's chest and under his arms. She drug him over to Flint and got him halfway up onto the horse, sweating now from her efforts, then got on the other side of Flint and pulled as hard as she could on the rope. After several struggling moments, she got him to the point where he was draped over her saddle on his stomach. She looked again at the soft lines on his face and turned his head to the side so he had a good airway. She brushed his hair aside again with trembling fingers. Again, she felt that queasy feeling down deep in her stomach. She shook it off and looked around for the best direction to travel. She tied him securely to the saddle, satisfied he wouldn't fall off, and led her animals into the trees.

***

When she found a suitable camp site it was totally dark and she was tired but she still had to eat and take care of her new burden.

"Wolf, we need some dinner."

The hound trotted off into the trees to do some hunting. Ace untied the man, and tried to gently lower him to the ground. Getting the man off of Flint proved far easier than getting him on. She collected some wood and started a small fire. She drug the man over near enough to the flames that she didn't think he would catch on fire, but wouldn't freeze either. She even gave him her blanket. She wouldn't need it if she slept in her jacket and stole some body heat from Wolf. It was still early spring and Idaho nights could get pretty cold.

She checked over the man's injuries. Mostly, it looked like he just took a good beating and for the most part to the head. He likely had a concussion and needed sleep. She remembered her dad saying that keeping someone with a head injury awake wasn't always good. The brain healed best with rest. But either way, he would make it through the night or he wouldn't and nothing else she could do would change that.

Then she began un-tacking Flint so the horse could be more comfortable. At night she left him loose so he could find food and water on his own. He never strayed far and he was always there when she woke in the morning. By the time she had camp settled and was sitting on the ground, leaning against her saddle Wolf trotted in with two rabbits hanging from his mouth. She fed him the entrails, skinned them out and put them over the fire to cook.

When the meat was done cooking she set one carcass aside and ate a small portion of the other. With all the recent events, her stomach was in knots with nerves. Ace knew she wouldn't be getting any decent sleep while the man was around. She checked on him one last time. There wasn't much else she could do for him now other than wait for him to come around so she settled back and closed her eyes to make an effort.

***

Ace opened her eyes when a cold nose touched her hand. This was Wolf's way of saying she had over-slept and he was getting impatient. She stretched and sat up with a glance around her camp and at the man who seemed to be still breathing. The fire was down to embers so she stoked it back to flames for the burden. She was wandering around camp, gathering her things when he spoke and made her jump. Instinctively, she drew her pistol.

The man raised his hands to show he wasn't armed, "Didn't mean to scare ya." His voice was scratchy so she holstered her pistol and tossed a water bottle over to him while remaining a safe distance away. He eased up to a sitting position and took several long gulps before setting the bottle down and turning his attention back to Ace.

"My thanks. For not lettin' me die and all."

Ace didn't say anything. She just stood her several yards away and stared at him.

"I don't suppose you have any food?" He asked. Ace noticed that his accent from the previous day was almost nonexistent now.

She tossed him the whole cooked rabbit she had set aside the night before. He took a few bites before clearing his throat to speak. "So what's your name, Love?"

She glanced over at him with a wary look. She wanted to leave and be on her way but she wasn't sure if he was well enough to be on his own. She was startled that she considered anything about his health or him at all. That didn't mean she wouldn't leave but for some reason she just seemed to be frozen in place.

He smiled without looking up from his rabbit, "I'm Bishop."

He noticed she was still just standing there staring at him. "You a mute?" he asked with a frown.

She glared at him. "What kind of name is Bishop?"

"It's a nickname. Long story." He replied with a little grin.

She nodded, then replied, "Ace."

He looked at her questioningly.

"Call me Ace," she said, irritation making her voice sharp.

"Don't like giving out your real name either, huh?"

"Not to strangers. And for all you know that *is* my real name." She replied, never taking her eyes off him.

"And do you know any non-strangers?" He asked curiously with a glance around the trees.

"Flint and Wolf."

Bishop raised a brow and tried to contain his smile. "Named a Wolfhound Wolf, huh?"

"Yeah, I lack creativity. Not exactly a concern in our world now, is it?"

"I suppose not. How did you luck into a horse *and* dog?" He asked, then added as an afterthought, "You don't look very old."

"Luck. Found the horse abandoned. Saved the dog's life. And I'm old enough." She moved over to her saddle bags that she had slung over a fallen tree the night before and picked them up, being careful and not to turn her back to him.

"Not fond of cars, huh?" He asked, watching her curiously.

"In a car I am targeted, and I don't like to draw attention to myself."

"Well, thank you for savin' me and everything." He said nonchalantly as he took another bite of the rabbit.

Ace frowned, she didn't like him thanking her for some reason. It felt odd and she wasn't really sure how to respond. This man frustrated and confused her. "If I had known you were still alive, I probably would have waited until they killed you outright."

He looked up at her with raised brows. "Why?"

She had moved to saddle Flint and was standing with him between them.

"Because . . . people get you killed so I avoid them."

"Or kill them." He added.

"I kill the ones that attack me or create an impasse. Better them than me killed." she said sharply, balancing her rifle on the saddle so she could tie her saddle bags on.

He studied her for a few minutes. She was obviously capable of taking care of herself. She was confident and yet seemed uneasy by his presence. "You really would have waited until they killed me just to avoid helping me?"

"You have already made my life more difficult. And yes, it's how I stay alive. And I prefer to stay alive."

"So then where are you headed? What awaits you?"

"East."

"Any reason in particular? Going to a place or meeting with some friends?"

"Because I've already been west."

Obviously she wasn't very interested in sharing information. He studied her as best as he could in the early morning light. She had blonde hair that went halfway down her back in a loose French braid. She wasn't scrawny and she had just enough curves that made an attractive figure. She was wearing a black leather jacket over a white tank top, blue jeans with a sturdy belt that held an assortment of weapons, and heavy tread boots. He thought her eyes were a light color but he couldn't tell from this distance and it didn't seem like she was interested in letting him get any closer. He was interested in this girl, young woman. Was she really traveling alone? How long had she been alone? He found himself wanting to get to know her.

"Well, I am headed east as well." She shrugged and continued with her bags. "Maybe we could travel together for a little while? Help each other out?"

This got her attention and she turned another suspicious look his way. "Why would we do that?"

"Because we are headed the same direction and having someone to watch your back never hurt."

"Unless that person has a knife and intends to stab it there." She muttered. What was he doing? She had never traveled with anyone. Why didn't he just go his own way and let her get back to things the way they were before. She wanted to just forget about this whole incident and pretend she never met him.

"You don't trust me, do you?"

This shocked her. "Of course not, why would I? You don't trust me."

"Aye, I do." He said calmly.

Again shock. "Why in the hell would you trust me? You don't even know me."

"Because you saved my life when you could have moved on your merry way."

"I told you I would have let you die if I had known you were still alive." She replied defensively. Oh, he was so frustrating.

"You could have still left me once you found I was alive."

Her look changed to one of agitation, "I work alone."

"Your collection of friends suggests otherwise." Bishop said with a smirk and pointed towards the animals. "Speaking of work, what do you do besides wander, Love?"

Ace frowned at him. "I have my things." Why was he still talking to her? Why was she still talking to him? This man was complicating things way too much.

"Like avoiding people and letting innocents die?" His tone was accusing.

She frowned at him and didn't like the feeling of guilt that settled into her stomach. A memory flashed before her eyes of watching a mother and child die while she observed from her hiding place, gun and ammo in hand, doing nothing to help. The mother had seen her when the Scavengers were spotted coming up the street. She had called for help before Ace had run for cover in the bushes. She had tried to send her son to hide with Ace before the Scavengers got there. The mother insisted on needing to go back in the house for something. The boy had been shot while trying to run to Ace. She had sat in the bushes and done nothing to help him while she watched the trucks drive in. The mother heard the shot and came running out of the house with a baby in her arms, her eyes had locked with Ace's in the last seconds before the bullets hit her. Ace had seen what was in those eyes: blame, accusation, hatred. The images for that day came to life, haunting her. How could he have known what she did or did not do?

"I have enough trouble keeping myself alive." She bit out at him.

He stared at her with those eyes. They looked just like all of the others she had seen, accusing her, saying it was her fault that she didn't help people she didn't know, people that weren't her responsibility.

"You haven't helped one person since the uprisings?" He asked quietly, judgment crinkling the corners of his eyes.

She didn't answer, just glared at him and walked around to Flint's other side. What did it matter what this guy thought? She didn't have feelings, she didn't have guilt. She did what she had to do and moved on. So why did she feel like she had a rock sitting in her stomach and a sour taste in the back of her mouth.

Bishop shook his head and went back to gnawing on his rabbit. Apparently this girl wasn't big on conversation. He could only imagine how hard it must be to just exist. Humans needed comfort and she seemed totally shut off from emotions. Yet she had helped him.

After tossing the bones aside, Bishop settled back against a log with his hands behind his head and looked up at the sky. He could feel Ace's eyes on him, but he didn't know how to break through the walls she had built up around herself.

Ace looked over her shoulder. Wolf had gone off to find himself some breakfast and should be back soon. She intended on leaving as soon as he showed up, and the sooner that was the better. The longer she was around Bishop, the more she felt . . . well, just felt. That was alien to her, she had suppressed all her feelings a long time ago in order to live. He made her remember things she didn't want to remember. Made her remember about how it was before.

Bishop took a moment while her focus was not aimed at him to study her in the light of day. He marveled at her figure. Perfect hourglass curves visible in her tight jeans. She had slung her jacket on the saddle in front of her and her tank top showed off a pair of strong sculpted shoulders. She had a thin belt that held up her jeans, then a thick utility belt that hung lower on her hips holding an array of weapons: two hand guns, three knives and a multi-tool. Her eyes were scanning the tree line.

"What are you looking for?" He asked, causing her to jump.

Ace glanced at him then back over to the spot she had been watching. "Wolf. We leave when he gets back."

"*We* do?"

She glared at him. "Flint, Wolf, and I do. I don't care what you do but it won't be with me."

"Why are you leavin' so quickly? It's barely dawn."

"I have my reasons. Those men yesterday were standard issue government type. They would have had a checkpoint or check-in time which they did not reach and someone will be looking for them. If they aren't already on their way, they will be soon. I'm clearing out. I have no desire to be here when they show up."

Bishop sat up and studied her for a few minutes. She had done a good job cleaning up her camp to the point where he could barely tell they had stayed there. He had watched the way she moved and the alertness she had. He thought he was beginning to figure some things out about her.

"You're on the run."

Her gaze flew to his face with another one of her famous frowns confirming what he thought. "No." She said a little un-convincingly. "But I don't like to be found."

"Is that why you ride alone and from dawn till dusk?"

"I suppose I don't have anything better to do." She said distractedly. Ace looped Flint's reins around the horn, moved over to him, and crouched down so she was at his eye level. She got too close to him for her comfort but she needed to get her point across. "If you tell anyone my name or description or any other detail about me down to the dust on my shoes, I will hunt you down and kill you. Do you understand what I am say-ing?"

Green, her eyes were a pale green that blended into a gold rim around the outside. They were a shade he had never really seen before, almost a sea green, pale and soft. Except for the menacing glare she was giving him in that moment. There was nothing soft in that glare.

"I believe you. And I won't say anything. If you do the same for me."

Ace rolled her eyes and walked over to her horse. "You are the first person I have spoken to that I didn't kill in years. I think you are safe."

"I don' think I can travel just yet." He said with a wince as he touched his ribs. "You gonna leave me defenseless out here?"

She glared at him, then took one of the spare rifles she collected off the dead soldiers and a clip of ammo. She tossed them into the trees.

"By the time you can get to that gun, I'll be long gone, and you won't be my problem anymore." Wolf trotted in and went over to Flint, sat and waited.

Ace got on her horse and left without another word, the wolfhound trotting at her heels.

***

Bishop presumed her rough manner towards him was out of discomfort of being around another person. She probably did not know how to react towards a non-threatening person that was still breathing. Again he wondered at what all she had been through and he hoped that he hadn't seen the last of her. It seemed that she knew an awful lot about the government, which both intrigued him and made him suspicious.

Most people that wandered freely didn't know about government hires having checkpoints and required contact times or anything of the like. So what was this girl involved in that had caused her to acquire this knowledge? She killed the men quite without thought so he figured she wasn't with the government. He would know if she was helping out the rebellion because he was high up in the chain of command and would have been notified of a girl like her wandering about that could take out small control groups on her own.

Besides, she didn't really seem to be the rebellion type. She had admitted that herself when she said she never helped anyone other than herself.

It was time that he made his way back to his headquarters and got an update on recent events. If he hadn't been distracted by her in the first place, he would have been back by now. He had seen glimpses of the girl when she was sneaking through the town and tried to get a better look at her. It wasn't often that he saw a beautiful female wandering around by herself. He was so focused on watching what she was doing that he wasn't paying attention to his surroundings. That almost got him killed by that group of men who were more muscle than brain. He should have been able to easily avoid the amateur soldiers. Thankfully she had saved his life.

He slowly pulled himself to his feet and gingerly made his way to the rifle Ace had left him. It was time for him to be on his way. As he made his way back to his camp, he spent his time figuring out the girl and wondering how to cross her path again. She was too intriguing for him to just move on and forget about.

Chapter 2

A few weeks later, Ace ambled down the road on Flint. She was headed toward Montana, mostly because she had never been there and she wanted to see it. She had read about it in a travel book she found in an abandoned house some time back and decided that she would travel there if she had the opportunity. There wasn't any other place she needed to be so she decided to head east from Idaho. She didn't have a specific town in mind to travel towards other than 'Montana.' When she had traveled to Washington, she had a specific goal in mind: to find her brother. She had made good time and allowed nothing to distract her. But now that her last living relative was most likely dead, she took her time. Not that it was a sightseeing trip, she had nothing to do except survive, which was easier said than done some days. There was no such thing as relaxing and resting for Ace. Even though there wasn't much for her to do she didn't often get bored in this life. In this life, someone could attack her at a moment's notice.

The day was quiet and a slight breeze blew across the dirt road. The sun warmed her back but quiet wasn't always good. The birds were silent and there was no wildlife around. That could mean nothing or it could mean everything. Ace was always checking over her shoulder and listening to her surroundings. On occasion she would get overly tense with paranoia. When that happened, her mantra was gallop it out.

"Let's stretch a bit," she said to Flint. With an adjustment to her seat, she sent him into an easy canter with Wolf loping effortlessly next to them. Flint's ears pricked forward, happy to be allowed a good run, and Ace fed off of his enthusiasm as he tossed his head and flicked his tail. She laughed, "Alright, but no more than up to the bend."

As she leaned down over the saddle Flint shot forward, stretching his legs as far as they would go and pounding the ground with his hooves. Wolf faded back, running as fast as he could but not able to keep up with the horse. Flint stretched his neck out and Ace felt the wind whip at her braid as tendrils of her hair were pulled free. They raced down the dirt road leaving a cloud of dust behind them. This was the only time that she could feel truly free and let her mind relax. She closed her eyes and inhaled a big breath of air. If only she could make this moment last forever. But then, as always, she remembered where they were and came back to present.

As they approached a sharp corner Ace sat up to slow her gelding so he wouldn't lose his footing. It was best to be prepared when your path wasn't in plain view. You never knew what might be hiding just out of sight. But as Ace was pulling him up around the corner, Flint slammed on the brakes and spun to his right. Ace had been so relaxed she wasn't prepared for such a sudden response and sailed over his left shoulder and crashed to the hard dirt road in a heap.

***

Ace coughed, trying to force air back into her unwilling lungs. She was vaguely aware that something spooked her horse and that she should be preparing to defend herself against the situation that caused her to make sure gravity still worked. Trying to push herself up from her facedown position in the road, she reached back with one hand to pull her pistol free.

"I wouldn't do that if I were you."

Ace stilled at the sound of a male voice and dared a glance up through her hair that fell across her eyes. She sucked in a ragged breath and spit out some dirt. She ground her teeth against the grit that coated them. She could see three pairs of shoes. Good! That shouldn't be too difficult of a number to deal with. Pushing herself up to her knees she was grateful she had on her leather cutoff gloves which protected her palms from losing their layers of skin, although her unprotected fingers got a little scraped up. She did a quick mental survey of her body. She hadn't been wearing her leather jacket, and now she had road rash that went from her left shoulder down to her elbow that was more than a little painful. She didn't think she had any serious injuries outside of some bumps and bruises.

Ace cursed at herself for her stupid thinking, or rather, lack of thinking. She knew better than to be galloping around blind corners without knowing what was around them and now it landed her on her ass in the dirt with guns pointed at her.

Sitting back on her heels she surveyed the people standing in the road. They were part of a road block that was set up with a large truck and plastic orange snow fence that was sloppily put up but still good enough that no one could easily pass. They weren't wearing government uniforms but the vehicle definitely looked government. That meant that the truck could have been stolen but that didn't happen very often. The government guarded their vehicles pretty well and pulled no strings to recover any that went missing. Most likely, they simply hadn't felt like pulling on their ugly jackets. The guns were definitely military, but that didn't mean anything either anymore. Hers were even military.

"Can I help you?" She asked with a grimace as she made to get to her feet.

The man standing in the middle of the trio flicked his gun in her direction. "What are you doing on this road?"

Ace glanced around nonchalantly. She honestly had no idea which road it was nor why it would matter to these men. It was simply a dirt road and people could still travel around on their own. It wasn't smart, but they could.

"Um, I would say traveling. Isn't that was roads are for? Going from here to there."

The man frowned at her. Then he turned to the man on his left and said something that she couldn't hear. The other man nodded, then turned away from her as he spoke into his radio, "Any sign?"

She raised a brow at this. They were looking for something, or someone, and she was pretty sure it wasn't her.

The radio came to life with a garble while someone from the other end spoke. "Got him. Headed to you. Any trouble?"

The man looked back at the blonde girl. "Small issue. We'll wait for you to arrive before we make any decisions."

The man standing in the middle seemed to be in charge and walked forward to Ace and began removing her weapons. She didn't stop him. How could she? All it would earn her right now was a bullet. So she handed them over. He tossed them into the dirt a few feet away. He sure seemed like a typical Government Issue meathead. Did he really think she couldn't reach them? Push come to shove, Ace would rather try to go for them and get shot than let these men take her anywhere. That wasn't the ideal plan but it was always the backup plan.

The man glanced at her face then he slowly lowered his eyes and gazed down her shirt, taking full advantage of the fact that he was standing a hairs width away from her. He wasn't even subtle about it. She followed his eyes down and then pushed him away as soon as she realized what he was doing.

Ace didn't have much experience with men other than to stay away and protect herself from them but she read about how men behaved in books. She had yet to meet one that didn't fit the profile. She took books whenever she found them, regardless of what they were about. It helped pass the time and several could be very educational. She read everything from crazy dystopian novels to technical books.

She had never really spoken much to men since the uprisings, but she remembered reading a book once that referred to them as dogs. Ace didn't understand the similarities. Wolf was much more respectful than most men she encountered. The man staggered back and pulled his pistol from the holster and held it loosely in her direction with a look of total astonishment on his face. The two men behind him gave each other wary glances, but made no move to stop their comrade. They did not appear to be very comfortable with his behavior either.

The man glowered at her, surprised that she had the audacity to push him away. Most free people that would be out traveling were timid and tried to avoid conflict with any officials. At least they were when staring down a barrel, yet Ace looked more like she was bored and irritated with the whole situation.

"You're just full of piss and vinegar, aren't you?"

Ace frowned at him. She was not sure what that term meant but was pretty sure it wasn't a compliment. "Do you really need something from me? Or can I be on my way?"

"You have places to go, wench?"

She *did* know what that meant. She had been called that before, and it definitely wasn't a compliment.

"Actually, yes I do. So if you would give me back my weapons and step aside I promise I won't hurt you or report you to anyone for your behavior. And then I will just be on my way."

"Are you a spy or something? You seem to be in a bit of hurry to snake out of here. I know how strict your check-in times are when you work for the government. Don't want to be late, huh?"

Ace frowned. Could this guy really be any more dense? "I don't work for the government." As soon as she said it, she wished she could take it back. She still didn't know for sure who this guy was nor who he worked for but she was beginning to suspect it wasn't the government.

"You got some high end government weapons there." He gestured to her discarded guns.

"So do you. I got mine the same way you probably got yours, from a dead man. Now let me pass."

"Fine." He said too easily. "But I get to keep your guns . . . and you have to earn your free pass."

Her frown deepened. She knew exactly how he wanted her to earn her pass and it would come at a high cost. "No deal."

"I wasn't aware we were negotiating, Goldie Locks. The way I see it, you are my prisoner. What I say goes, because I have the gun. See?"

Goldie Locks? How original. Even before the uprisings she knew who Goldie Locks was. This guy was getting more obnoxious by the minute. She just needed to bide her time and wait for the perfect opportunity. She took a deep breath and sighed out.

"How about this: give me back my guns before I kick your ass and take them and then continue on my merry way."

She didn't even have time for a sarcastically sweet smile before he hit her in the face with his pistol. She prided herself on managing to stay on her feet, but she knew it wasn't going to look pretty in the morning. She could taste the familiar tang of blood on the inside of her lip and feel it puffing up.

"Bitch! You will pay for your smart mouth."

Ace wiped at the blood dripping down her chin, "Wasn't that hit kind of a payback? Or was that just another ego stroke for you?"

Just as she braced for another hit, the roar of an engine became audible and the man frowned. He reached out and grabbing her braid, he wrenched her down to her knees and held his pistol to her forehead. He leaned in close to her ear and whispered, "Looks like someone else will get the pleasure of dealing with you. Hopefully he is in a sour mood. Boss don't like wenches with smart mouths."

Ace suppressed a shiver and glanced over at her weapons. With more men arriving, her chances of escape were greatly reduced. She was afraid to so much as flinch and risk getting shot by the Neanderthal standing above her. She could feel the fear flare in her chest. Her heart rate went ballistic and she started to feel like there was no oxygen in the air she was sucking into her lungs. Silently she reprimanded herself for losing control and slowed her breathing. She needed to get control of her brain! She had avoided being captured for so many years. There had been so many close calls; this could not be the end.

The truck rumbled up close behind her, then stopped and turned off. She heard mumbled greetings, then the sound of someone jumping to the ground.

***

"Well, if my eyes don't deceive me. You have a prisoner for me, Welch?"

"We found her on the road while waiting for you, sir." The man holding the pistol at her grumbled in response.

"I see. And I can also see ya've roughed her up considerably."

Ace wasn't sure, but his authoritative voice sounded disapproving as well as familiar. She couldn't believe what she was hearing. The man had the same slight accent only wrapped in authority. What was he doing here of all places?

"I didn't do that to her, Sir. She fell off her horse."

Ace could almost feel the man smirk behind her. "Thought I recognized that bundle of attitude all wrapped up and easy on the eyes." He walked around to stand to the side of her. "Hard to tell under the dirt and blood though. God sakes, Welch, let her up."

Ace got to her feet and slowly turned. It was unbelievable but before her stood Bishop, all in clean clothes, bathed and looking much healthier than the last time she saw him. He was clean shaven and had a confident air about him.

He sure hadn't looked this good before. And why was she noticing how his hair curled lightly around the tips of his ears? Everything about him seemed different. She wouldn't have pegged him as simple wanderer if he had held himself like this before. Now he looked like a boss and an official of some sort. But maybe that was the point. If she had thought him important, then he might have been at risk. She wasn't very happy about the deception and cast a challenging look at him. Not that she would be able to put up much of a fight against him in close combat, she noted with a glance to his biceps.

She raised a brow, "Interesting running into you again. Bishop, was it?"

He smiled, "You have made a decent amount of travel in a short time. Where are your animals?"

"Waiting to tear out the throats of your disrespecting man." She said bitterly while tipping her head to the men who held her on the road. Bishop frowned and glanced at a pale Welch. "Just how disrespecting?"

Ace waved a dismissing hand at him and turned to search for signs of her animals. "No more than most men, I'm guessing."

She gave three loud, short whistles. And waited a few seconds before a bark came in return. She smiled, they were safe. Turning back to Bishop her smile turned to an annoyed frown. "Am I allowed to go or is this some kind of hold up? I am pretty sure you guys are not with the government."

Bishop smirked, looking quite entertained, "It's not a hold up, we are not with the government, but I do think you should come with me."

"What on earth would I do that for?" She asked as that trickle of fear started to rise in her chest again. She wasn't sure what he wanted, and why he made her feel things she didn't quite understand, she most certainly did not trust him.

"Because I need to ensure that you're not a spy."

Ace let out an exasperated breath. "I am not a damn spy."

"I don't think you are either but I would still like to be sure. Besides, I can't let you roam this road unprotected."

"What is wrong with this stupid dirt road?" She exclaimed.

"Do you know where you are?" Bishop asked her seriously.

"Heading east and that is all I care about. You are interfering with my meandering." She said angrily, all the fear dissipating. This was getting old and all she wanted was to be on her way. It had been a long time since she had talked this much with anyone and she was more than ready to leave this man and all this confusion behind.

"Yeah, well, I am going to interfere because I'm serious when I say you shouldn't wander this road unprotected. I don't even wander this road unless there is reason. Call your pets, let's go." His voice rose in his frustration. He didn't understand why she couldn't see that he was just trying to help. She was so irritating and he just wanted to see to her safety.

Ace crossed her arms and gave him a daring look. She barely managed to hide a cringe as her movement pulled on the drying blood of her wounds from her unwelcome contact with the ground.

Bishop smiled challengingly back at her, "Oh, Ace, don't dare me to make you. I just might be tempted." Everything about her intrigued him.

She paused at his words, but wasn't about to go easily with a truck full of strange men to who knows where. She glanced back at the trees, then to Bishop. She needed to think fast and a plan was beginning to form.

"I have no intention of going with you. I have my own plans."

He raised a brow and started to respond just as she dove for her guns, rolled, and came up with the pistol in her left hand and a fraction of a second later had her rifle to her right shoulder. The men reached for their weapons but Bishop moved his hand out to his men telling them to stand down with a small smile on his face. "A bit challenging, aren't you?"

"I told you not to get in my way. I left you with your life and ammo three weeks ago. You owe me the same curtsey. Payback time and then we are even."

"Yes. I am offering you that and more. You can keep your guns *and* come with me. I am protecting you, not taking you hostage. Look, you can get cleaned up and have a decent meal. These roads are regularly patrolled by government men that are well armed and not very understanding. Currently, they are searching for someone who killed a group of patrollers three weeks ago. So get your panties out of whatever twist they are in and start thinking logically."

He gave her a knowing look and she hesitated. If she was found there was no way they would know it was her that had killed those men, but she had killed many government men before. They were already searching for her, it didn't matter if they thought she killed those me or not. If they found her she was as good as dead.

But was going with this strange man any better? How was she supposed to know? She was pretty sure that he worked for some sort of rebellion, maybe even *the* rebellion. But that didn't make her safe. She wasn't on anyone's side but her own. All she did was help herself. Now that didn't even get her close to being a good person, but from the stories she had heard, the rebellion wasn't very merciful either.

Ace frowned, not sure what to do. Preferably she would just leave without any trouble but this foolish man didn't seem to want to allow that.

"I will travel off-road if it will ease your foolish concerns. Now let me go."

Bishop leaned back against the faded green military jeep and folded his arms across his chest with an entertained smirk. "It sounds like you're daring me to make you come along."

Ace was getting really irritated with this man. He was so at ease, teasing her nonchalantly while she had a semi-automatic rifle aimed at his thick skull.

"I like a challenge." She taunted with a sultry grin. Then added with a straight face, "I could easily kill you right now."

He narrowed his eyes in thought. "I don't think you will though."

"And what on earth would stop me? You are standing be-tween me and freedom."

"Yes. But one, my men would shoot ya' the second you pulled the trigger. Two, they could kill you just as easily as you could kill me right this very moment."

Ace shifted uncomfortably glancing at the other guns around her.

Then he added, "I don't want to do that, but it will be out of my control if you shoot me."

She cursed under her breath at him. She should have let him die on the road three weeks ago!

She cast a calculated glare in the direction of Welch, whom she noticed was no longer in possession of his own weapon.

Turning back to Bishop she spoke in an irritated tone, "And if I do get in the jeep with you, how do you expect my animals to follow?"

He smiled. "I think they follow you well enough. We will drive slowly, you can lead the horse from the back of the jeep if you like. Look, we just want to talk and make sure you are okay. It really isn't a big deal."

He motioned to her with a wave of his hand to the jeep as he pushed himself away from it and walked over to her. He stepped right up to her, much closer than she liked and stared into her eyes. Her breath caught in her throat and she ventured a look up at him. He reached out to her gently as if he was going to touch her face. She could barely think. What was he doing? Then he moved his hand to hers and removed her guns. "You can have these back when you are no longer a threat to Welch here."

Ace glared at him. She could feel the heat rising through her face. Then one of the other men walked up to her. "Sorry, Miss. Rules, you know. Nothing personal." He searched her for any hidden weapons. Ace looked over to Bishop and contemplated how many ways she could kill him with just her hands. Bishop didn't seem to care about the threat in her gaze. He did, however, push the man searching her away when his hands got a little too wandering. Ace was grateful for that but not grateful enough to suddenly jump into his jeep and follow him to unknown locations.

He still stood in front of her and reached up to wipe a little trickle blood from her face. Her gaze hardened and her hands tightened to a fist. She hadn't been touched by anyone in a very long time. Her whole body tensed up and she sucked in a small breath. Bishop noticed, but didn't care. He looked hard at her split lip and the bruise that was starting to color out on her chin. "This happened when you fell from your horse?"

"No," was all she gave him for an answer. She was pissed off and the last thing she was going to do was stand there and play along with him. He had taken all her weapons, except for a hidden knife in her boot, but she could still fight without that.

She waited for him to glance down her shirt or to his men, knowing one or the other would eventually come, and did. But she was shocked that it was him looking over his left shoulder to say something to the man driving the jeep. This gave her the perfect opportunity and she drove her fist into his stomach. She had to admit it hurt her hand more than usual. This guy had some serious abs! Then, when he bent forward slightly to absorb the blow, she swung with her other hand and connected him in the jaw, and then kicked his hip while he was off balance.

There was only one man holding a gun at that moment. Everyone had relaxed and tossed their weapons into a vehicle to prepare for travel. As that man swung his gun for her she pulled out her hidden knife and threw it, hitting the gun less than an inch from where his hand was resting which caused him to drop the gun and leap back just as she hoped.

She whistled once, then bolted for the trees. It was only about fifteen feet from where she was standing. She could hear people moving behind her, scrambling to get organized. She sprinted hard knowing that Flint had heard her and was on his way to find her when she whistled again. As he came into view she changed her direction of travel slightly so she was running to him.

She had to slow somewhat so she could grip the horn of the saddle and swing onto his back. It was something she had remembered seeing on movies when she was little, earning several bruises during the learning process, but could now do in her sleep.

But as she jumped up to grab the saddle something slammed into the side of her, tackling her to the ground. She threw her elbow back and successfully contacted whoever was trying to get a grip on her. She heard him curse as he pulled away slightly and rolled, giving her a chance to rotate so she could face him. She was slightly surprised to see Bishop, but resumed her attempt to flee.

He was straddling her now, pinning her legs down under his weight. When she swung another elbow at him, he caught her arm and pinned it above her head, then did the same with the other, successfully pinning her beyond escape.

The position he pinned her in required him to lay his weight completely on her, so his face was only a few inches from hers. They were both breathing hard from the struggle. She looked up at him with a glare, which he answered with a smile.

"You know how t'fight." He said between breaths, voice thicker than normal.

She struggled slightly beneath him, trying to find any weakness in his defense. "It's a necessity for survival. How do you think I have stayed alive this long?"

"I could help you, you know. If you would just let me."

She glared up at him, "Bite me."

That made him smile again. "Careful, sweetheart, I might take you up on that offer."

His comment made her very aware of how close they were, and she wondered again what his intentions were. He was clearly stronger than she was and could overpower her. But it also gave her an idea. She adjusted her struggling slightly so she could grind against his groin. It was seemingly innocent but she knew it had gotten his attention. If she could just distract him a bit, maybe she could still get herself out of this mess. She glanced up with a glare. As her eyes met his she paused, the glare slipping from her face.

He noticed how her glare faltered, and all of her movement paused, and he wondered if she was aware just how her struggling had been affecting him. He was most certainly aware of it.

His face was about an inch away from hers. It didn't take much for her to close the gap as she brought her lips to his.

She had never kissed anyone before, although she had read about it in plenty of books, so she didn't know if she was any good at it. But it seemed to get what she wanted. His grip on her wrists relaxed and as he tried to deepen the kiss, he slid one hand down to grip her hip and used the other to brace against the ground for balance.

Ace moved her hands down to his torso, then wrapped one leg around him as she pushed so they rolled and she was on top of him. The movement made Bishop smile and he went to kiss her again, but she punched him hard in the jaw. She reached up and used the hand cuffs she had pulled from his belt to bind his hands after she pinned them together while he was recovering from the blow.

Bishop realized what was happening the second she hauled back to hit him, but he hadn't been prepared enough to stop it. He had to admit that she hit him harder than he ever guessed she could have. And then before he knew it, his hands were cuffed and she was on her feet, readjusting her clothing from their wrestling match.

She smiled sweetly at him, "Thanks for the offer, but like I said, I travel alone."

He cursed at her as he pulled at the cuffs on his wrists.

She looked back at him as she reached her horse, "Oh I'm so sorry if you got the wrong impression, I just couldn't resist that chiseled jaw of yours."

She didn't really know if his jaw was chiseled, she wasn't sure what a chiseled jaw looked like, but she thought it might look like his.

With a wink she was on her horse and cantering away from him through the trees. She wished she was as cocky and confident as she acted but she felt like she was going to lose her breakfast all over the forest floor. That would make her seem really bad ass. Instead, she took a deep breath and steered Flint deeper into the woods.

* * *

Bishop just sat there in the dirt trying to figure out how she slipped away and how he managed to make such a mess of things. His men walked up to assist him. They tried to resist the urge to laugh, but weren't doing too well by his standards. "Get these damn things off me and get after her, now!"

The man who had been driving the jeep walked over to him and started sorting through his keys.

"How did she manage to get the best of you?" He asked. When Bishop didn't reply, he glanced up and saw the blush. "Don't tell me you seriously fell for an act of that sort." He looked back down to his task at hand shaking his head. Bishop couldn't believe he fell for it either. But he had to admit to himself that all it did was elevate her in his mind. He had to break through and figure her out.

"Now what do you plan to do? Hunting her down sounds like way too much effort and a waste of resources."

"We need her, Jayce."

"She is dangerous." Jayce said grimly, "She nearly took off my hand when she threw that knife and didn't even think twice about it. I am pretty sure she could have just as easily put it through my chest."

"We need her."

"Why? Because she bested you? Took advantage of your blatant attraction for her?"

"Because *they* want her. And I want to know why." He said with an irritated glance at his friend. He did want to know why and he really didn't want the government guys to get her. They would not go easy on her. Bishop didn't think that Ace understood the amount of danger she was in.

"You don't have enough government-wanted criminals in your command already?"

Bishop looked his friend in the eyes, serious now. "Because every single patrol squad or government hired goon I have come across in the last three weeks has a description of her written on the dashboard and again in their pockets. I want to know why they want her so badly and I don't think she is aware of the bounty on her head. She needs protection."

Jayce rubbed his jaw in thought. "The only other person I know that is wanted that badly is you. That might even be worse than you. But why do *we* need to protect her?"

"Because she is the kind of people we try to protect. If she is wanted that badly and they still haven't caught her, then she is good. She doesn't have any help. We need her."

"Maybe she's not alone. What then? And what if she isn't admittedly a part of the rebellion because she doesn't like the rebellion? If she's that good, she could likely kill you to clear the bounty on her own head."

Bishop shook his head. "She wouldn't do a single thing for the government. I have no doubts about that. When I first met her, she saved me from that patrol squad, and killed every single one singlehandedly without another thought."

"Sounds like someone who is very dangerous. Think about what you just said! She isn't a damsel in distress." Jayce repeated.

Bishop became irritated again. "She sounds like someone who knows how disgusting the government is."

Jayce raised his hands in surrender. "Fine. We will find her. But it isn't going to be easy. And I am not sending everyone out after her. You can have this and one other squad. I can't risk the whole camp just for her."

"Keep an ear out for reports, attacks without leads progressing east. Look for that pattern and let me know right away."

Jayce nodded as they headed back to the jeep. The squad reported back to him an hour later that they had lost her but she was leaving a good trail that they could follow. After gathering some supplies they went back to the trees to track her.

Chapter 3

Ace still remembered kissing Bishop. It was a few weeks later and she was riding on Flint alongside a road. She had been traveling in the safety of trees but currently there was a shortage of those in the area. She hated the plains. They made her feel vulnerable. The good part about them is that she could see far around her for danger. The bad part was that danger could easily see her. But her thoughts often drifted back to Bishop, distracting her, and she hated that too. She had been expecting the kiss to be completely non-exciting, nothing special in any way, maybe even a little on the gross side. But she had enjoyed it, and had to force herself to remember it was just an attempt to get away. A very successful attempt, and while she didn't want to use it again, it was a good last resort.

Descriptions of kissing in the books she had read over the years seemed fairly accurate, of course she didn't hear any fairytale music and the birds didn't start singing, but it felt nice. After years of being alone she had convinced herself that she didn't need anyone. When she got lonely, she could always talk to Wolf or Flint. It was a bit of a one-sided conversation but all-in-all she thought she really was better off. So now that this man kept popping up in her thoughts, she wasn't sure how to get him out of those thoughts.

It was her annoying thoughts of Bishop that were keeping her distracted to the point that she wasn't aware of the vehicle coming up behind her until Wolf signaled an alarm with a low throaty growl.

Her head snapped around. It was definitely a government vehicle and she had no trees to hide in. With a jolt of adrenaline, she sent Flint into a headlong gallop. Wolf was already about a half mile ahead of her scouting. She yelled at him to hide and being that far ahead, he had a better chance at getting away. Getting away from the road in this area was pointless. The ground was flat enough that they could still chase her if she went off road, but then she would have to slow down to keep Flint from tripping up on the numerous tumble weeds and varmint holes, or they could always just shoot Flint. If the tables were turned, that is what she would probably do. It sounded horrible but it was effective.

Flint stretched out in surprising speed, but she knew it was impossible to outrun a car. Still though, they tried and when the armored van pulled alongside them with guns pointed at her and warning her to stop or they would shoot, she pulled him up to slow. The van pulled in front of her and started to slow, Ace signaled Flint and he slammed on the brakes, then wheeled around and bolted in the opposite direction.

To deter them from shooting her, she pulled her rifle off her shoulder and shot behind her. She didn't bother to aim, just shot in their general direction to keep them from shooting at her. These government guys aren't usually sharp shooters nor are they very brave when lead is flying their way.

She thought it was working and then suddenly she felt a sharp pain in her arm and Flint's head jolted to the side in a flinch. Fear gripped her that Flint had been shot. She heard more bullets whizzing by, so she pulled him up harshly and stepped off into the dust cloud. While the van was driving towards them she quickly scanned Flint for any injury. He had some blood running down the side of his face and he held his head a little tilted. She traced the source of the blood to his ear. It looked like the bullet had gone right through his ear.

While it would hurt and be sore, it wasn't a lethal injury. She quickly pulled off his bridle and tied it on the saddle horn, then shooed him away and waited for the men to pull over. The reins wouldn't get in his way or pull on his face this way. It was miles to the nearest cover. It was her they were after so hopefully they would just ignore Flint and let him go. She could still see Flint galloping away and if she squinted she could see Wolf standing a distance away, watching and waiting. She whistled once loudly to get his attention and then pointed at Flint. Wolf watched her for a few seconds before she saw his form begin to move toward her horse. Good, at least they would be safe. All she had to worry about now was getting herself out of this mess. She had gone months without any incidents. But it seemed like that was all she could find these last few weeks.

"Toss the guns to the vehicle!" A voice from inside the protection of the van shouted.

She threw her gun, knowing how hard it would be to replace if she escaped. Then pulled off her pistol and threw it as well. If they wanted her knives, they would have to get close enough to her to find them. They were not obviously visible.

When the doors of the van opened, she put her hands up in the air to show she wasn't going to try anything. They held guns on her and crept forward, looking around for backup to appear. "Are you alone?" Ace sighed and rolled her eyes. "Nope, I have a whole army hidden in my pockets." These guys were genius. You could see for over a mile in any direction. Just where did they think she had any help stashed?

"Keep your hands where they are," said the man closest to her, who was sporting a bullet wound on his left arm. She obeyed, praising herself mentally for actually hitting something while shooting over her shoulder without looking, letting the corners of her mouth creep up with a little smile. But the man didn't look too thrilled about it.

They searched her, finding the few knives she had managed to acquire since Bishop's men took her weapons a few weeks ago. She hoped they would just take her weapons, do a quick field interview, and leave like usual. But they didn't.

"This is our lucky day! You match a description of someone that our Sergeant is desperate to get ahold of." He sneered at her.

Fear rose in her chest. She couldn't believe they were still looking for her. There was no way they had an accurate description. No one alive had detained her in years, except for Bishop and his little group. But she had a pretty good feeling he was in with the Rebels, and that meant he didn't sell out to government soldiers.

"I don't know any Sergeants. Just let me be on my way please."

"Now why would I do that without at least bringing you in to be sure?" He looked at her weapons. "Those are government issue. Which means you stole them from someone."

"Yes, I did steal them but that doesn't mean I stole them from a soldier. It means they were stolen from one at some point and then eventually made their way into my hands. I don't know how many people stole those weapons before I took them. But if you are so attached to them, I will let you keep them," she said irritated. It was true that she had stolen them from a soldier, one she killed, but this man didn't have any proof to accuse her of such and she certainly wasn't going to admit to it.

The man made a motion to his men and they quickly moved in to bind her hands before dragging her to their armored vehicle. She sent a prayer up that this wouldn't take long. She honestly didn't have any knowledge of an encounter with any Sergeant, so it couldn't be her they were after. Hopefully they would do an interview and send her on her way. The nice thing about a war was no ID, no one knew who you were unless you told them.

Flint and Wolf would hang around as long as they thought it was safe, but eventually they would need to seek out food and better shelter.

* * *

Ace let them roughly shove her at every chance they thought warranted such treatment without complaint, but the fear had a cold grasp on her chest. She had been captured before, and lost a few years of her young life because of it. There was no way she wanted to go back to that, go back to the cruelty they put her through. She probably never would have been recaptured if that stupid Bishop guy hadn't interfered with her. Helping him is what kick started this whole series of recent events. This was just proof to her that she should stay alone and away from people. People get you in trouble or killed.

She knew she wasn't who these men were looking for, but that didn't necessarily mean that she was safe. They still might torture her until they were certain she wasn't who they wanted, and that she didn't contain any useful knowledge of the Rebellion. Torture for information on the rebellion would actually be the least of her worries.

She didn't need to hear the stories from other people; she had seen it herself out in the streets. The soldiers would often drag the women to a semi-secluded place, not caring who could still see, and do whatever they wanted. Some were unlucky enough to live through it. The fortunate ones were the ones that died right away from the beatings. If someone there figured out who she really was, it was possible that she might never see the light of day again.

Once the van started moving, a bag was placed over her head and she was wishing she had been wearing her jacket after all. She felt far too exposed at the moment and couldn't readjust her tank top with her hands tied as they were. She was jammed in the corner of the van. Her hands were tightly tied behind her back and she was sitting on her ankles. It was not a comfortable position at all.

They traveled for a decent amount of time before they pulled up into their camp. It wasn't long enough for her muscles to get cramped up so she knew they couldn't have gone too far, just far enough for her to start getting motion sick. They drug her out of the van and tossed her onto the ground. She fell to her knees and face but managed to sit up and onto her ankles. When they pulled off the bag obstructing her view, she blinked a few times to let her eyes adjust to the light. It was still early afternoon. She saw that this was not a simple camp for patrollers, but a full station buzzing with activity and people in uniform coming from every direction.

There were soldiers everywhere. She wondered how she had been so near this place without knowing it was here. It had to be pretty well hidden. Most stations this size had a lot more traffic and activity for miles around them.

Ace remembered seeing places like this. She knew that her chance of escape just diminished to zero. And she knew this was bad news. At a simple patrol camp there might not be anyone who cared enough to find out who she really was. But here, there was likely to be at least one person who knew or could find out. This time she did not follow compliantly. She struggled at every turn, trying every move in the book to get away knowing it was pointless. Even if she managed to escape those that were holding her, she would have to get past a hundred more to escape. And she just wasn't that good, no one could be.

Still she remembered everything she knew about survival. She took in every detail she could manage: where the exits were, how many rooms, what was in those rooms, the people and where they were stationed. They took her through a series of hallways, the layout was fairly standard and she thought she would be able to find her way out again if the possibility of escape arose.

But the room they finally took her to, that seemed to be a bit more of a challenge.

It had steel walls, floor and ceiling with no windows, and the door was solid with multiple locks on it. It felt like a cage. The air was stale and chill. At first she thought the lack of window was a design flaw. What if she was able to set up an ambush inside, but a quick survey told her there wasn't anything to use against them. Maybe they knew what they were doing after all. That didn't give her any comfort and she did her best to control the fear that was invading her thoughts.

In the center of the room there was a single steel chair bolted to the floor, which she was forced into and secured. They tied a bandana around her mouth to gag her. Luckily she was still in ropes and not chains or zip ties, but she wasn't sure that was a big enough blessing to help her.

Once secured, the soldiers silently left her alone in the room. Not a single word of what she was to expect, what they wanted, or who would be questioning her. Ace took a few deep breaths, trying to get the cold fear making her breathing ragged to release its grip. She strained to hear anything that might assist her or give any clue about anything but was met with total silence.

She flipped some hair out of her face with a flick of her head, tendrils escaping her French-braid and sticking to her forehead with the beads of sweat that were starting to form. With a glance down at her chest, she sighed with more irritation. Then began the attempt to pull the top of her shirt back up to where it covered her a bit more modestly without the use of her hands. It ended up being pointless, but that didn't deter her. At least it gave her something to focus on.

Her attempts were interrupted by the clank of all the locks being opened. The door was pushed open and a man she instantly recognized came into the room. He hadn't changed much these past years: still tall with a muscular frame. Same black hair and just a spattering of grey starting to show up at the temples. Same face with no emotion at all, just a cold stare that brought back all the pain of the past.

She shifted back into the chair as far she could get and sank down into it trying to make herself smaller. If this was the man that was looking for her, she was in a lot of trouble. She hadn't known he was a Sergeant, maybe he wasn't back then. She just knew he was an evil man that she had escaped and apparently pissed off. The only bit of light in her current situation was that she was fairly certain this man didn't know for sure exactly who she was, aside from some girl who escaped him on a lonely road. That night was a few years ago. She had been erasing her trail from the road to her camp so no one could follow and attack her in her sleep. She was walking down the road when an SUV full of soldiers pulled over next to her. She had heard them coming and would have ducked into the woods but knew they had seen her. It was better to just stop and wait. Chances were if she had run they would definitely chase or shoot her.

When the vehicle slowed down, the man standing before her now was driving the vehicle and he leaned out to talk to her. They assumed she was on foot and alone. He kept asking her if she needed a ride, or a safe place for the night. She ignored him and just kept walking slowly down the road, not looking back towards her camp. Finally he jumped out of the SUV and threw her against the vehicle. He told her that he demanded the respect she owed him for serving his country. She made something up about just heading to her friends, they were waiting for her and weren't far. It was true enough, Wolf and Flint were at her campsite. It was right after she had found Wolf; he hadn't been old enough to take with her for protection. This man had attacked her there and then; apparently he had just wanted to make sure she was alone at the moment. His two friends watched from inside the SUV as he bloodied her face and tore her shirt. She tried to fight back but he managed to get her pinned to the ground. The two men in the SUV also watched as Ace got the upper hand. She pulled her knife from her waist and stabbed him in the side. It was a shallow wound and wasn't enough to kill him, but it was enough for him to scream and pull back in shock. She kneed him in the groin, and then ran for her life.

She supposed getting beat by a sixteen-year-old girl when you were a soldier was pretty embarrassing, and his comrades didn't bother to help him, just laughed. She remembered hearing their snickers when he was attacking her and their laughs as she ran away. Her nose was gushing enough blood she was surprised when they didn't follow the blood trail and finish what they started, but they must have had a checkpoint to get to or decided she just wasn't worth the hassle. She escaped with a broken nose that she had to straighten herself, several bruises, and a new stockpile of emotional scars.

Ace had thought about that night several times. It wasn't the first or the last time she had been trapped beneath a man with evil intent, but it was the only time that had witnesses and he was the only man who survived.

Still though, she hadn't expected him to be hunting her down like this. Did he really have patrols out looking for her for revenge on a random attack *he* started that happened three years ago?

"Nice to see you again, miss. I want you to know that I haven't forgotten you in the least, although you are a lot prettier than I remember. That might be because the last time you left me you had a little blood on your face."

It was more than a little. She had almost been worried for her life with the amount of blood that came from the injury to her nose. But her training kicked in and she remembered nosebleeds often bled a lot and rarely caused death. A little blood can look like a lot when it is all over your face and the front of your shirt. She tried not to look at him.

"Not in a talking mood?" He asked while stepping closer to her. When she shrank away from him he smiled. She hadn't meant to show any weakness but her body reacted instinctively. "Oh, I am going to have some fun with this. You really thought you could just sneak away? Make a fool of me in front of my men and just walk away without worry that I'd chase you down? I am going to make sure I have a lot of fun this time, and you aren't going to get away. I can take all the time I want." He caressed his fingers down the side of her face. His touch gentle and light, but she flinched away from his hand. She felt nauseous and like there was no more oxygen left in the air.

She never understood why people started interrogations while the prisoner was gagged, it was pointless. While she was thinking over the gross bandana in her mouth, he swung out and backhanded her across the face. He hit just as hard as she remembered.

The tangy taste of blood filled her mouth, but she straightened herself again and waited for the next blow, trying to fight down the panic that was almost choking her. She wasn't getting out of this as easily as she did last time.

Chapter 4

"We found something you're not going to like," Jayce said with a frown as he approached Bishop.

Bishop glanced up. Upon seeing his friend he put down his papers and hopped out of the jeep. "What is it?"

A few of Bishop's men came forward leading a nervous looking horse with a very unhappy dog at its heels. The men seemed wary of the dog, but it was coming of its own will so there wasn't much they could do about it.

"You found her?" He asked, knowing the answer wasn't going to be that simple. He looked at Jayce and waited while his friend took a deep breath.

Jayce knew Bishop wasn't going to like what he was about to tell him.

"No. We found them. The problem is when we found them, they were less than ten miles from a soldier base. We couldn't do much of anything that close to the base but observe. Fortunately we have a contact inside that particular one. When we checked with him, he said they had a new prisoner. Their sergeant had been looking for a certain young blond woman, and it seems he found her. I think this is more than a coincidence."

Bishop cursed, then started to pace on the edge of the road. He wondered how much trouble that woman could get herself into. He knew that base and the rumors about the sergeant there.

"We need to get her out of there."

Jayce sighed. He knew that would be the answer. "I let our contact know that we will be sending someone in as another captive, to get to her, then would need help escaping. He said that would be easier than getting her out alone. However, because the Sergeant spends every spare moment he has in there with her, it will be a little tricky. He needs to come up with a reason to get her alone long enough to get her out. And they only have one prisoner room in this base because it isn't set up to hold anyone for long. It is mostly set up for communications and training."

"Perfect. I'll be ready in ten minutes." Bishop said as he headed back over to the jeep.

"Whoa, whoa, whoa," Jayce held up his hands to stop Bishop. "Who said that *you* were going to be the prisoner?"

"I did."

Jayce knew by his tone that Bishop wasn't going to be talked out of this. It wasn't the first time these two didn't see eye to eye on a situation. Bishop could get very passionate about a cause while Jayce was indifferent and more calculated. Together they made a good leadership team but occasionally their different approaches would collide head on.

With a sigh, Jayce relented. "Fine. But if you don't follow my order to the letter I'll happily let you rot in there, ok?"

Bishop smiled, "Why wouldn't I do as you say?"

With a frown Jayce began laying out the plan.

***

The large metal door squeaked slightly as it was opened and Bishop was tossed to the floor inside. With all his defense training, he had to work really hard to pretend his hands were still tied when he hit the ground and not catch himself. If they even suspected he wasn't secure they would trade rope for metal and that would make his job a lot harder. The soldiers didn't give him a second look. They did walk over and double check the bindings on Ace. It didn't look like she was moving. They walked out and he could hear them lock the door and walk away. Bishop slid the ropes off his hands and scanned the room.

As he stood, he looked over to the chair Ace was tied to. She was wearing just her bra and jeans. Her head was tilted back, unconscious. Her breathing was steady, if shallow. Dried blood was smeared across her face. It looked like it originally had come from a cut that was surrounded by bruising on her left cheek.

Bishop rushed over and gently searched her for additional injuries. Her wrists were raw and crusted in blood from her fighting the handcuffs. She had a large discolored bruise on her right shoulder and a shallow cut on her arm.

A large mug of water had been put in the room which seemed pointless since she was strapped to a chair. He brought it over and used her shirt, which has been discarded to the edge of the room, to get her a little cleaned up.

He had finished with her face and moved to her wrists when she started to come to. It was slow and with the amount of groaning she was making, he assumed she had been knocked unconscious instead of falling asleep of her own accord. As soon as she was able to register that someone was touching her, she tensed and tried to wrench her arms away, scraping her wrists newly raw in the process.

"Would you quit it? I just got these clean." He ground out at her.

At the sound of the familiar voice Ace hesitated, though she didn't relax. Her head pounded as she tried to think. She couldn't believe she heard his voice. "Bishop?"

He smiled, though he was still behind her. "In the flesh, love. I've got to say the damsel in distress angle is not the one I expected you to use to get my attention. Next time just wink or something."

She snorted at that comment. As if she would ever use this angle to get *anyone's* attention.

"What are you doing here? I assumed you had crawled under a bush and were patching together your ego."

Bishop t'sked at her. "I may be prideful but I am not egotistical." He moved around to face her and frowned at her unfocused half-open gaze and slurred words. "How you feelin' Love?"

She grimaced. "I hate it when you call me that."

"Well, if I had a real name to go on, I might be inclined to use it." He said seriously. He sat on his heels and looked into her eyes. This managed to get enough of her attention for a more focused look.

"That's a two way street, *Bishop*."

He studied her for a few minutes. "Maybe another time. For now, we have to think about getting out of here."

"Good bloody luck with that." She muttered.

He held up his hands to show that he wasn't tied, but her shocked and blushing expression landed on her tank top that he held, not his unbound wrists. With a quick glance she realized her current state of undress and moved to cover herself a little better but with her bound wrists it proved useless.

"Sorry, didn't have a rag and you were in a right mess when I showed up."

She glared as he let his gaze linger a bit on her exposed flesh. Her sports bra had a bit of modesty but not enough for her comfort.

"Breathe easy, lass, I've seen plenty more than that before." His comment was an effort to make her more comfortable. True as it was it didn't mean he certainly wasn't enjoying the view. Her stomach wasn't as tan as the rest of her but it was flat and taught. And the pathetically thin excuse of an old sports bra showed more detail than not.

"Give me back my shirt." She said with a blush.

"Oh, because you think I am skilled enough to get a shirt on someone whose hands are bound behind their back? Besides the fact that I *can't* put it back on you, it is covered in blood."

It was her black tank top, not her favored white ones, but she would have taken any shirt at that point.

"I don't care what it's covered in. It's all I have." She muttered to herself. She looked over to him. He had a concerned look on his face and was kneeling on the concrete in front of her. He reached up to brush a lock of hair out of her face. She couldn't help thinking back to the woods when she kissed him, which made her blush all over again.

"So what's the plan? I find it hard to believe that you are here by coincidence," She asked trying to change the subject and give herself something else to think about.

"Simple, we escape."

She looked at him dubiously. "Right. Let's just walk on out the front door and ask for keys to my cuffs while we're at it."

He gave her a disapproving look. "That's a horrible plan. It's that kind of thinking that got you here in the first place. We really need to work on your tactical planning skills."

She sighed in exasperation. "Obviously! I want to know what *your* plan is because I am hoping you didn't just rush in here hoping to be named hero of the day and figure the rest out as it unfolded. Please tell me that you know what you are doing."

He gave her sideways grin as he rocked back on his heels. "Good to see your focus is back. I was worried about how hard 'e knocked ya' for a minute there." He had been studying her pupils to make sure they were working correctly but the realization that his face was a mere inch from hers gave him pause. She had large doe eyes with a light blue-green color to them. Their kiss came back to him and he thought for a moment how delightful it was that their roles were reversed.

She noticed his sly lopsided grin start and her brows furrowed but before she could give him a tongue lashing for whatever thoughts were going through his mind, he kissed her ever so gently.

She thought about pulling away but the sting of her wrists reminded her she had nowhere to go, and who was she kidding? It wasn't like she wanted to move away, kissing him was nice. Without thinking she discovered she was kissing him back. Her heart pounded through her chest and a warm, alien feeling seeped through her body. She had never been kissed before and she never thought she wanted to be kissed before but this was gentle, warm, and made her feel safe. She began to think maybe it wasn't so bad after all.

He pulled away a fraction, satisfied by the blush in her cheeks. He took a deep breath, "I have a man on the inside who is going to help get us out of here."

She raised a brow. "The rebellion has people everywhere, huh? Hope I haven't accidently killed any of your men."

She had meant it sarcastically, but it came out sounding more like regret. Bishop just shook his head. "No chance of that, Love. They are never men who are out in the field. Those ones can't be trusted."

She rolled her eyes at the term he used when speaking to her. Damn foreign men thought they were so charming with their little nicknames and accents.

"Well if you have a plan then let's get on with it. I'm itching to get a move on and out of here. I never stay in one place for very long. And I really don't want to be here when that sergeant comes back in."

"How long have you been in here?" He asked with a glance at the door.

"Now, how in the hell am I supposed to know the answer to that? Not exactly able to see the sun from this particular suite. I asked for one with a better view but between the lavish hospitality and me taking involuntary naps, we just never got around to it." She replied with an irritated tone.

He gave her a bemused look and walked over to the door. He knocked in a specific pattern, then stepped to the side and smiled back at Ace. After a few long minutes of absolutely nothing happening but them looking at each other, the door opened.

A man in full uniform walked in and Ace's eye narrowed. She looked questioningly to Bishop as he took the key for Ace's handcuffs from the soldier. He spun them on his finger and sauntered over to unlock her wrists. As he knelt down behind her to free her from the cuffs he stroked the inside of her wrist.

"I thought your men didn't work in the field? Couldn't be trusted you said." She said it quietly, hoping it was quiet enough to keep it from the soldier's ears.

Bishop answered distractedly. "They don't and they can't."

"Really?" She asked, getting more and more worried by the second. "Because if that is your inside man, we have a problem." She said the last part in a whisper, never taking her eyes off the soldier.

"Why is that?" Bishop huffed sounding slightly exasperated.

"Because the man in the doorway is the one who brought me in."

Bishop glanced up, then spoke quietly. "That's not possible. He works on computers. He is a tech, nothing more. And he would have known I was looking for you."

"Well, he is the one who got out of the damn car and pointed a gun at me after running me off the road."

Bishop slowly stood, leaving Ace to rub life back into her hands.

"What's the plan, John? Jayce told me you had it all taken care of." Bishop said with an ease to his voice that made Ace wonder if he even listened to her.

"We will all be free of this convoluted mess soon enough. This is a time for action, THE time for action, but we don't have much time so let's go." The man seemed a little on edge. It was more than just enabling them to escape. Something seemed a bit off about the way he was suddenly looking everywhere with a fanatical shine in his eyes.

"Ok but first, I need your help with something. Can you come here real quick?"

Ace wasn't sure what made the man believe in such a simple and obvious ruse. There wasn't much in the room that could possibly warrant such a request, but maybe it was to keep up some guise that he was on Bishop's side. As soon as the man was in reach, Bishop grabbed him by the shoulder and slammed him face first against the wall. Bishop pinned the man's hands behind his back and cuffed them with handcuffs from the soldier's own belt. Then he turned the man around and shoved him to his knees.

"Tell me what the hell is waiting for us outside of that door, or I'll kill you right here and get away while they're distracted by your dead body."

The man was shaking his head. He had wild look in his eyes that made Ace uncomfortable. "I am sorry. I look up to the rebellion. I do! But I had to do it. I had to!"

"Do what?"

"The only way to get the upper hand is to cause more bloodshed than the government. We must get their attention! That's what the rebellion was doing until YOU took control of it! We need to send them a message. They need to fear us!"

"Tell me what you did or I'll let them have you alive." Bishop growled.

No threat seemed to get through to the young man. "It doesn't matter. It's too late. You can't get away. Your death will set the Rebellion into an outrage big enough to be worth all our deaths. The leader of the rebellion killed at a government base? Do you know how much fight that would give your men?"

Ace threw her hands in the air, "I don't give a rat's ass about the Rebellion so my death means nothing. Now tell me how to get out!"

Bishop ignored her outburst and spoke to the soldier, "I am not a suicide martyr and your death won't mean anything to anyone. Now tell us how to get out of here and maybe I will take you with me."

The man shook his head. "I won't leave. I refuse to leave. The bombs will go off any moment now, best say your good-bye prayers and ask the heavens for forgiveness for your sins. The cause is just and we will be exalted!"

Bishop grabbed Ace's hand and pulled her towards the door. "We have t' go, lass, now."

"What about him?" She asked with a glance in the direction of the handcuffed man on his knees muttering prayers.

"He won't come and I don't have time to save a man not wanting to be saved. Let's go!"

They ran.

Right past the baffled soldiers who started to chase them. Suddenly though the soldiers were distracted by a blast that went off and shook the entire base.

Bishop and Ace didn't hesitated for a moment while another and another blast went off. Bishop recognized the timing between the blasts. It was typical government destruction. They would set off a series of explosions throughout an area. They would start at one end of a location and scatter the bombs in a random pattern so that there was no safe direction to flee and would ensure the entire base was nothing but ruins by the end of the last blast.

If the man went through all of the trouble to kill himself and the Rebellion leader in some twisted message, then he likely was going to make sure the whole base went down with them and that meant using more than enough explosives to ensure no survivors.

They sprinted for all that they were worth. Debris started raining down around them as they exited the building and Bishop knew they weren't going to get out of the base in time. They had been heading for the shortest route to freedom which was a timbered section of the complex not far from where they were being held and it put them in a less occupied portion of the base. None of the soldiers in the base paid them any attention because they also were busy running for their lives in every direction.

The next explosion went off right on time. Bishop had been timing each explosion and he was as prepared for it as he could be. When the blast sent them flying, he had a good grip on Ace's hand. They both slammed into a building, hard enough to knock the air from their lungs, with seconds to spare before the final blast.

"Inside quick!"

Ace stumbled after Bishop as he drug her into the building and down a set of stairs that took them below ground. They both dove for the farthest corner possible. Just as the final bomb detonated Ace read a sign on the wall; "*CAUTION! Unstable structure.*"

"Bloody hell, Bish-" was all she managed to get out before they felt the final blast. The building groaned, then collapsed.

***

Dust was still falling as Bishop coughed and groaned as he tried to move. His leg was pinned under something heavy but the bone didn't feel broken. It was too dark to see much of anything, and after a few moments of feeling around where he could reach he concluded that there wasn't much space either.

"Ace?"

He was surprised he had let go of her in all of the commotion, but he vaguely remembered her pulling away from him when the heavy concrete building came down. It wasn't a large room so she shouldn't be too far away.

"Ace!" He called again. There was still no response. He tried again to lift the chunk of wall or ceiling off of his leg but it was no use. He was at the wrong angle with no leverage. He felt around on it. It must be almost two feet thick and covered his whole leg. He pounded his fist into the ground just before he heard a faint gasp, followed by a hollow cough.

"Ace? You there, Love?"

"Yeah." Her voice was rough and weak.

Imagining the worst he called out again.

"Are ya' hurt?"

After the longest seconds of his life she replied, "I think I'm faring pretty well for having a building fall on me."

He was happy to hear she was in good enough shape for sarcasm. "Can you get to me, lass?"

There was a hesitation, then he heard a few scrapes against concrete and loose rubble as she moved around.

"I can't see a damn thing." She said, sounding just as far away as she had before.

"Just come to my voice. I'll guide you as best as I can." After a pause he spoke again, "That didn't go quite the way I imagined it going."

The sounds of her movement got slowly closer until her hand reached out for a grip on something solid and came in contact with the toe of his boot.

"There ya' are, lass. Come up here so I can be sure you aren't hurt."

"Um, there is an awfully large piece of building on your leg." She said in a matter-of-fact kind of way.

"Is there now? I hadn't noticed. No wonder it was a wee bit difficult for me to move about."

Even in the complete darkness he could picture her un-amused expression.

"Do you want me to try and move it?" She asked uncertainly.

"That would be a grand plan if you think you can. Want to give it a go?"

He could tell by her hesitation that she wasn't so sure about trying but she moved into a braced position and got a good hold on the object. "Ok, I'm ready."

He got as good a grip on the piece of concrete as he could and counted to three. They both lifted and pushed with every ounce of their strength for several seconds before it finally moved. Once they had a little momentum going, the concrete rolled awkwardly off of Bishop's leg and to the ground. The building groaned and both of them froze as they waited for more concrete to rain down on them, but just pebbles and dirt fell.

Ace coughed for a few seconds, recovering her breath as best as she could in this dust-riddled environment. She moved closer to Bishop's face, helped him into a more comfortable position, and then settled down herself.

"Just so you know, you are not very good at this whole rescue thing." She muttered.

Bishop chuckled at first, then it evolved into a roar of laughter. Ace sat quietly staring in his direction even though she could see nothing, her expression confused.

"You done? It wasn't that funny, Bishop."

"Aye, it wasn't. But I did get you away from the cell and those soldiers are taken care of."

"Did not!" She said indignantly. "That crazy suicidal guy did. Credit where credit is due, mister." He shifted beside her, "Was there any light coming through over where you were?"

"None at all." Realization dawned on her, though they may have survived the bombs and building collapse, they wouldn't survive down here long. They needed to get out or get rescued.

"I think we should explore a little bit, see if we can find a way out," he said quietly.

"And what if all our crawling around makes something collapse even more and we slowly get crushed to death? I think I would rather suffocate or starve or whatever method is going to kill us down here rather than from being crushed."

"Afraid of small spaces, lass?"

"So what if I am?" She asked a little too defensively.

"Aye, so what. We are only stuck in a very small space with no lighting and no escape-"

"Stop it, would you? Tell you what, next time I am captured and being tortured for no reason other than a personal vendetta, stay out of it! I would have found a way out. He wasn't going to kill me."

"He might not have, but another might. Are you aware that your description is pinned to the dash board of every government vehicle I have come across since I met you?"

He could feel her pause, then a sigh. "Not exactly, I suppose. I knew they were after me. I just didn't know how aggressively they were pursuing the matter. I'm fairly confident *you* didn't give them my description, so that only leaves so many options."

"No it wasn't me. What did ya' do to piss off that Sergeant anyways?"

"None of your business." She retorted, feeling her walls come slamming down.

"Yer a bit of a wee lass to have so many enemies."

She noticed that his accent seemed Scottish. It wasn't always there, but at times it came out clearly. In his last statement it was clear enough that she could pin it down.

"Aye and ye' be a bit of a youngin' yourself, eh?" She muttered in a mocking tone.

He wasn't sure if he was offended by her mocking his accent or impressed at how well she was able to do so. "You know a wee bit of the accent, Love?"

She shrugged. "Not really. Though I think it's Scottish? You don't always have it though, that's why it confused me for a while. There are just hints of it in the way you speak. Calling me 'lass' and 'love' was a big give away."

"After the Uprisings I had to learn to blend. Having an accent made me too identifiable. So I learned to drop it and I guess it's just faded over time. Still comes around once in a while when I'm distracted or really tired, though."

They settled into a comfortable silence. After what Bishop guessed to be an hour, he heard Ace start moving around.

"What are you doin'?"

"Looking for a way out. Unless you want me to sit here idly and wait for death."

"I thought you said that was better than the possibility of getting crushed?"

"Well... I changed my mind. I'm not good at waiting."

He wasn't surprised by that, since he got the impression she was always going somewhere. "How long have you been traveling?"

"Since the bombings."

"The first bombings? Where were ya' when that happened?"

"Why do you care?" She asked as she squeezed between two solid slabs of concrete.

"Just creating conversation, the solid blackness is bad enough I don't need it deathly quiet as well."

She sighed. "Fine. I was in Skull Valley, Arizona."

His brows raised. "Skull Valley? They went through that town with soldiers, not bombs. And killed pretty much everyone on sight. It was a rancher town, lots of guns still in there. They didn't want the farmers to organize and rebel. Didn't even let the children live unless the parents swore in then and there. How did you get out?"

"You know a lot about a small town," she said loudly. She had crawled about twenty feet away.

"I lead the main rebel group. I know about most of the initial attacks."

"Well you're not wrong. I wasn't at home when the attack happened. I was on top of a cliff that overlooked our place."

He stayed quiet for a minute, listening to her move around. "How old are you?"

She didn't answer right away. ". . . Nineteen."

"You were around ten or so when the attack happened? And you were away. So you came home to your family . . . to what the soldiers did." He thought out loud. He tried to imaging being that young and coming home to that sight. There was the sound of some rubble falling but Ace didn't make any sounds of distress. "You are assuming I had a family."

"Well, I am pretty certain you weren't livin' alone at that age."

"Fine. But I didn't just come home to it, I saw the soldiers arrive and everything unfold from my vantage point."

He could tell her voice was strained, but he couldn't stop his prying. "And what happened?"

He was shocked when she answered. She had silently maneuvered closer than he thought she would be.

"What the hell do you think happened? I watched the soldiers go into my house and I heard the gunshots ring all over town. When I went inside after everyone left I found my family slaughtered. I buried them, packed my things, and left."

He thought about that for a few minutes. It is not what most young girls would have done. Someone had to have taught her some things that most girls wouldn't know. "Your father was a former soldier?"

"Yeah, so?"

"He trained you on how to survive?"

"Yes."

"Did your family call you Ace?"

He could feel her look at him, even though he couldn't even make out her form.

"Yes."

"So it's a lifelong nickname then? Not one you just created for yourself to avoid using your real name. Which means there's a story behind how you got it."

She sighed in annoyance. "Tell ya' what, I just shared plenty. I am not telling you a word more until you tell me something about yourself. And I most certainly am not telling you about my real name until you tell me yours."

"Well, I guess we most certainly may be sittin' on our death beds currently. I don't hear any signs of rescue. And I don't think we are gettin' out of here on our own."

"I couldn't find a way out." She said quietly.

"Well then, might as well tell someone my life secrets."

"I'm sure plenty of trusted people already know them."

"No, actually." He said quietly. "Only Jayce, my right-hand man." She could feel him trying to look at her. "Come closer, I can't see a damned thing."

"You wouldn't be able to see me no matter how close I was so why would I do that." She asked defensively.

"Because I asked nicely."

She snorted, but moved closer none the less. Since she couldn't see, she didn't know exactly where he was, so she just moved towards him until she could feel him. He clasped her hand tightly, and it was only then that she realized how tense and strained he was.

"Is your leg okay?"

The question took him off guard. "It's fine, why?"

"Well, you seem really tense. I was just making sure you weren't in pain."

He snorted. "Seriously, lass. We're about to die slowly and you want to know why I am tense? I am tense because I do not want to die. I most certainly do not want *you* to die. And there is nothin' I can do to prevent either one. I am not normally so helpless."

His words made the atmosphere somber and quiet. Ace was trying hard not to think about the fact that they really could die down here. She preferred being distracted from those sorrowful thoughts.

"You were going to tell me all of your secrets, remember? I get that it's only because we will mostly likely die here, but I would still like to hear them."

He took a deep breath. "As for my story, here goes . . . I didn't have the misfortune of comin' home to a family. I didn't have one. I was eighteen when the bombs hit. And they actually saved my life. I was in the middle of a bad situation with bad people that I thought I could scam. They didn'a take too kindly to discoverin' I played them for fools. So I was about to be killed for not havin' the money I owed them. The bombs went off, distractin' everyone while I ran. I wasn't sure what was goin' on but I ran for an abandoned car in the street. The driver had gotten out to see what was goin' on, and I jumped in and sped out of the city.

"I don't know what happened to any of the people that were there that I knew, but I wasn't on friendly terms with any of 'em so I wasn't too keen on goin' back to find out. It didn' take long t'find out what was happenin' all over the country. And after a few more bits of thievin' and conning, I pickpocketed Jayce. I hadn'a seen him since we were wee lads. He was involved in the rebellion, and instead of beatin' me to hell for stealin' from him, he recruited me. I worked my way up the ranks fairly quickly. None of the rebels know my past, they wouldn'a trust a thievin' con to lead them. Only Jayce knows. And he wouldn'a tell a soul."

She noticed his accent also got thick whenever emotion was involved and made a mental note to keep an eye out for the change in his speech.

"I adopted the name Bishop when I was conning. I used to carry around this little chess piece all the time, the bishop piece. Me real name is Grant." He laughed lightly. "I haven't said my own name in a long while. It sounds kind of strange."

"Why did you carry around a chess piece?" She asked, confused. She had never really played the game, but she remembered it.

He shifted into a more comfortable position. "Ya' see, when I was a wee lad, my mom could barely afford the food on our table. Some nights not even that. So birthday presents were something that other kids told you about. Before she sent me overseas to this land at sixteen years old on my birthday, she gave me that chess piece. As a gift. Said it was to remember her by." He was quiet for a few minutes. "She probably pulled it out of someone's trash or something. But it was my most prized possession. Anyways, it always calmed me when I was pullin' my schemes to have it in my hand, so people started callin' me Bishop."

"Why did you start scheming and all that?" Ace asked quietly.

"I was sixteen in a strange country with no money. What else was I to do?"

"Your mom sent you over without any plan?"

"There was a plan. It fell through. My mom would never put me in danger knowingly. She gave up everything to try and give me a better opportunity."

"What about your dad?"

"He wasn't around much. He would show up at random, but he and me mom didn't always get along."

"Why not?"

"She was a bit of a free spirit. It drove him mad, but he still loved her. So he came around now and then until she made him so mad he had to leave."

He wished he could see her face. She was too quiet.

Ace felt a little odd sitting next to him while he held her hand. It was a completely foreign to her. She never spoke with people, she killed them. She kept herself and her animals alive and left everyone else to their own fate. Hearing Bishop talk about his past made her think about her own family, something she hadn't done in a long time. Her father wouldn't be proud of her. He had always helped the helpless, always did good for others, and thought of others before himself. She didn't do anything unless it was to benefit herself.

The last time she sat down and spoke to anyone casually was before the bombings. Several years had been spent wandering alone. Most of her conversations during that time were with a dog and horse. Before them, she spoke to herself just to get rid of the quiet.

He shifted his position, then pulled her over until she was leaning up against him.

All of her muscles tensed, "What are you doing?"

"Relax, lass. Just gettin' more comfortable." He chuckled.

Ace didn't relax in the least. "You can be comfortable without me this close. Let go of my hand."

He didn't listen. She put on a pretty tough act but he had yet to meet a person who truly didn't need anyone else. She had put up some really strong walls around her heart but he was determined to chip away at them.

"You aren't used to having company around, are you?" He chuckled when she didn't answer and stiffly sat beside him.

"Your turn, Love." She still didn't answer. "We have a deal, lass. Don't leave me hanging."

Ace rolled her eyes. "Fine. It's a nickname. It's from my real name because my youngest older brother couldn't pronounce it when I was a baby. So he called me Ace."

He was quiet for a few moments, waiting for her to continue before he said, "That's it?"

"There isn't much more to tell."

"Och, that is bull an' ya' know it. You didn'a even tell me yer real name."

She stifled a laugh at how thick his accent got.

"That's because I don't want to."

"You're gonna die in this rubble without speaking your real name one last time? When was the last time ya' heard it said, huh?"

She thought about that, unsure. It would have been a long time ago, longer than her brain wanted to remember. Those memories were locked away deep inside. She wasn't sure she wanted to revisit them. What would happen to her if she allowed herself to remember?

"I'm not sure. A while ago, I guess. My dad used my full name, but eventually he got used to the nickname, also."

Bishop waited for her to continue but instead of telling him her real name she spoke very quietly, "Bishop?"

"Yeah?"

"I don't want to die." She whispered. She had been faced with death several times but it had been sudden and her responses automatic. Just sitting here, thinking about it and waiting for it was a totally different thing.

He didn't want to die either. He couldn't believe that he finally had some time with this girl that stirred him like no other person had before. It was not the dreamy scenario he would have liked. He wanted to plan several tomorrows unlocking her secrets and protecting her, earning her trust. His grip on her hand tightened and his left arm went around her shoulders. He snuggled her closer and feeling him against her bare skin reminded him she was still without a shirt. She pulled back from the contact, but he didn't let her move away.

"Look, Love, I am not dying sitting here by myself so just relax your muscles a wee bit, would ya'?"

"What's the difference between dying two feet apart?" She scoffed.

Bishop snorted, "You are the most stubborn lass I have ever come across. Don't you remember what it was like to have people close to you? Don't you remember anything before this God-awful world fell upon us?"

"Of course I do-"

"Then why the hell have you not learned to seize the damn moment?"

Keeping his left arm around her he let go of her hand with his right and placed it on the side of her face and pulled her into a tender kiss.

He had a point! But she instinctively stiffened against him. Years of telling herself she was strong and didn't need anyone or to feel any real emotions started to crumble down around her. This man was unlike any she had met. She wasn't ready to ride off to the sunset with him but she really wanted to have time to figure and sort all these feelings out. However, it didn't look like they had very much time. She pushed aside her fear and tried to trust this man beside her, just a little. With trepidation, she kissed him back. Bishop forgot about the pain in his leg as he deepened the kiss, happy that she was no longer resisting his touch.

A few moments later, they were interrupted by the sound of a blast and then a light blazed into their dark rubble strewn grave while dust rained down around them. Bishop pushed Ace back against the wall and instinctively put himself between her and the possible threat. He was guessing that some of the surviving soldiers were finally starting to look for any-one else alive. Being in the dark, his eyes were taking a second to adjust. All he could see was the bright daylight and a figure moving towards him.

Bishop looked quickly to the side of him and found a bro-ken length of rebar that was long enough to do some damage and still able to wield. He grasped the bar, then jumped up and swung at the man coming towards them.

Chapter 5

"Damn it, Bishop!" The figure said as it ducked beneath the swing.

Bishop shielded his eyes with a hand. "Jayce?"

"Damn you, Bishop! Can you never listen to a simple set of instructions?"

Still not able to see very well, he squinted his eyes closed. "It was *your* damn informant that blew the place up."

Bishop turned his attention to Ace who was still sitting on the ground with her hands over her eyes. After everything that had transpired in the last few hours, he wasn't sure if she would throw her walls back up and bolt or if she would trust him enough to continue with him. "Ace? You alright, lass?"

"I'm blind. I can't see a damn thing. And who the hell is Jayce?"

Jayce reached a hand down to help her to her feet, but she pushed it away. He just looked at her with a smirk and stepped away, shaking his head.

As her vision started coming back she looked around at how lucky they had been. There were cement chunks plenty big enough to kill them everywhere in the building. Looking at it now it seemed impossible that they both survived. The rest of what she could see hadn't fared any better. All around was endless rubble and destruction.

"Need help gettin' up, Love?"

"No. Go on out and I'll be there in a few minutes." She had some minor injuries from being beaten by the sergeant but she was also pretty sure she had gotten hurt during the building collapse. She wanted some privacy when she got up so she could figure out how serious it was. She had fully expected they were going to die in that hole. Now she had to figure out what her next step was going to be and she didn't want an audience while she figured it all out. When neither of the men moved she glared, "I don't need a babysitter."

Bishop narrowed his eyes at her. "Not sure I believe that. At least let me help you to your feet."

"I can stand on my own, thank you." She snapped a little too harshly.

"Then do it." He said as he crossed his arms.

She glared up at him, and then used the wall to steady herself as she stood. She teetered and caught herself as a wave of nausea and pain washed over her.

Bishop swore and Jayce pulled a bag off his shoulder then called, "I need one of the medics!"

Ace rolled her eyes. "Oh, please. Leave me the med bag I will take care of it myself."

Jayce started putting alcohol on a rag, "I'm sure you are one tough son of a bitch but right now you have a piece of metal sticking out of your leg."

Ace looked down. "I know. These were my second most favorite pair of jeans, too. You have no idea how mad I was when I realized they had been torn." The men gave her disbelieving looks. "What? You tellin' me you find it easy to find a pair of good fitting jeans? It's not like I can just run down to the local boutique." She looked back down to her leg. "I suppose I could stitch them."

Jayce snorted. "You sure you don't just want me to have the medic stitch them along with your skin to save on supplies and time?"

Ace couldn't help it with such a good opportunity, she put on a seductive smirk, "Now, that would make it mighty difficult to take my clothes off, Mr. Jayce."

She waited a few seconds for her words to sink in and sure enough both men looked slowly down her exposed torso to the top of her jeans, all the while a lovely blush creeping into their cheeks. Ace's smile widened. "Didn't think y'all would care for that particular scenario."

She walked past them, moving carefully so as not to jar her leg. It also gave them time to recover and then catch up. As she crawled over the last bit of rubble she looked around at the disaster that was left from the base. She turned to Jayce, who was still climbing over rubble. "Any survivors?"

Jayce came over the last piece of concrete, turned to help Bishop, then they both approached her. "I think we should get your leg taken care of before we talk about-"

Ace reached down and ripped the piece of metal out of her leg with a wince. She wasn't too worried about the wound. She had been through worse and it wasn't really very deep.

"God damn it, woman! What the hell is wrong with you?" Jayce exclaimed as he nearly fell in his rush to get to her.

She ignored Jayce, but allowed the person with a large medical bag to rush over and try to stop the bleeding.

"Now are you going to tell us what really happened here? We were a little too busy staying alive to take notes." She glanced around, noticed the men in the immediate area gawking at her, then cursed under her breath, "And would someone get me a damn shirt, please."

Jayce smiled, "Well, while I'm sure just about every man here would do just about anything for you, I'm afraid they aren't going to jump right on that one."

She blushed as she glared at him and crossed her arms over her chest. Bishop shoved him out of the way, walked over to a vehicle, and pulled a shirt out of a bag. He tossed it to Ace, "This will have to work for now."

She pulled on the white t-shirt, which was several sizes too large. She didn't really care: it covered all the important parts and made her feel better considering the large amount of people present.

Jayce told them everything that they could piece together about the situation while Ace got her leg got stitched. As soon as the medical personnel were done with her she turned to Jayce and Bishop. "Do you know where all my stuff might be?"

"We have everything we could find including the horse and dog back at our camp."

"Well then, let's go."

"Right now?" Jayce asked.

"Yes, right now. I haven't been away from my animals for more than a few hours at a time. You going to tell me that they have been difficult to contain?"

Jayce looked at Bishop, who nodded. "No, they have been fine." Then he looked around, shook his head and said to everyone, "Get everything cleaned up then we head back to camp. No more than twenty minutes before I want no trace of us being here. We need to get out before any of them come back."

Bishop put his hand on Ace's elbow, led her to the jeep, and climbed in behind her. Jayce got in the driver's seat and they drove away. It was less than an hour before they pulled into a very secluded camp buzzing with activity. Ace had no idea how they hid so much in such a secluded space. She could have ridden right past this place and unless she just happen to turn between two big rocks and drop down into a little valley she would have never known it was there.

She looked around as she stepped out of the jeep, taking in as much as she could in those few seconds. All of a sudden she was sprawled face first in the dirt. Bishop and Jayce were out of the vehicle in seconds, but Ace was laughing and trying unsuccessfully to push the dog's face away so he couldn't lick her. The guys just stood there and stared at her rolling around with her dog.

"Wolf! Down." She giggled, but the dog didn't listen. When she finally managed to push the large dog off of her, he bounced around in circles like a giant puppy. "Settle." She said to him with a smile, then she turned to Jayce. "Where's my horse?"

Jayce looked around with a blank expression searching for someone to ask, which told her that he didn't know. She turned back to the camp, put her fingers to her lips, and whistled loudly.

A frantic whinny answered her, then came the sounds of cracking wooden boards.

She cocked an eyebrow at Jayce and said, "We will address this later." Then she smiled and jogged towards the sound with a slight limp. She ended up at a storage shed on the outskirts of the camp. Obviously they hadn't been outfitted to keep a horse and improvised. Her horse hadn't been locked up since she freed him from the barn when she found him all those years ago.

"Easy, Flint." She said calmly while unlocking the latch. Wrenching the door open took some effort, but she finally got the opening wide enough for the gelding to fit through. He bolted out and took off for the nearest escape. Ace leaned back against the wood of the shed and watched him gallop away as Bishop approached.

"Don't worry. He probably won't run very far and we can send our best tracker after him."

"No, don't. He will come back when he's done being upset. He doesn't like being held in one spot."

He gave her a look like he didn't believe her, but said nothing more on the matter. He was surprised she wasn't upset and demanding to go immediately after the unruly horse. "We have your things in my office. If you want them come with me, I'll show you around. It's a nice place here. I think you will like it."

She followed him back through the camp as he pointed out different buildings and what they were for.

They came to one at the far side of the camp. It looked pretty much like all the others. Bishop swung the door open and stepped aside. "After you, Love. This building is mostly for my use. Your stuff is in my office at the end of the hall on the left."

The building had a central hallway with rooms coming off each side. She walked down, found the door and sure enough her things were piled in the far corner. Relieved, she walked forward to make sure nothing was missing. As she knelt down she heard the door click shut and she rolled her eyes at the ceiling while keeping her back to the door.

A slight smile played on her lips. She was going to have to figure out what the situation was between her and Bishop now that they were out and not awaiting their deaths. She wasn't just going to hand over a roll in the sack.

She turned and saw that she was alone in the room. Confused, she walked back over to the door and tried to open it but the handle wouldn't budge. Her entertainment instantly turned to annoyance. "Bishop?"

"It's not personal, Llove. Try and understand." he said from the other side of the door.

"Bishop, open this door right now."

"I'm afraid I can't do that."

"Why the hell not?" She yelled.

"Because the second you have the chance you are going to leave."

Oh she was good and mad now. She understood perfectly clear what the situation between them was. Obviously his words of endearment and gentle touches were nothing more than opportunity and not given out of any real emotion. How could she be so gullible? She knew better than to trust another person. She put her protective walls solidly back in place.

"Yes, I am leaving! That is my right! I am not one of your people, Bishop. I am not one of your anything! Just leave me alone!"

"I'll send someone in with food and water in a little bit. Again, just try and understand a little."

"Open this door, you bastard!" She called after him.

He laughed from the other side of the door. "Make yourself comfortable, Love." He would give her some time to cool off and calm down. He was sure she would see that he was doing this for her safety. She got so headstrong and if he could just get her to relax, he was sure she would want to stay with him.

"Bishop!" She yelled through the door. "Just do one thing for me. Leave my animals be! If you lock Flint up again I will kill you the second I get out of here."

He didn't respond, but she knew he heard her. Turning around she decided she might as well do some snooping. She couldn't believe that she was being held prisoner, again. Years without real contact with people and now it seemed as if she couldn't get away from them. She needed to form a plan. She took a deep cleansing breath and surveyed the room. Bishop had said it was his office. She was surprised he chose such an important room to lock her in. She was certain there were documents on all of the rebellion activities in here. Maybe there was even information on government locations. The information would be helpful so she could avoid any more confrontations on her trek to Montana.

Sitting in his chair, she propped her feet up on the desk and started working on the locks on the drawers.

***

A knock at the door woke Ace up from her nap. She was sitting on the floor leaning back against her saddlebags. She had changed into her own shirt but decided to keep her torn jeans on to prevent rubbing over her stitches. Not bothering to move or answer, a few minutes passed before the door finally opened. A young woman peered around the door and then stepped inside. Behind her, the door closed and clicked as it was locked again.

She held a tray of food awkwardly, not sure where to put it. Ace slowly sat up, then got to her feet and pulled out a knife that was hidden in her boot. The government soldiers hadn't been very thorough when they searched her.

The girl looked warily at the knife and backed up until she was pressed against the wall. She wasn't much of a girl. She was just a young teen and seemed terrified. "M-M-Mr. Bishop told me to bring this to you." She held up the tray.

Ace raised a brow. "And how does Mr. Bishop know I won't harm you? Or hold you hostage in exchange for my release?"

Her words made the girl nervous, but she answered. "He, he told me you might seem scary but wouldn't harm an innocent person."

"So he sent the most innocent-looking girl in camp. Yeah I've played that ploy. You could be the greatest assassin and I wouldn't know it."

The girl flinched at the words and looked around nervously. "My name is Gwen. I am not an assassin, I promise."

Ace hmphed and took the tray. "I still might hurt you, if it benefits me. And then I'll hurt him."

Gwen flinched and her eyes got as round as a full moon. "You can't threaten Mr. Bishop, ma'am."

Ace took a bite of the sandwich after checking it thoroughly for obvious poison. She smelled it, looked for any powdered substances. "Well, I just did. And I have before. I didn't poof into dust then. And I have escaped and beaten him before."

The girl stood in the middle of the room with wide eyes. "Why do you dislike him?"

Ace rolled her eyes. "I am locked up against my will- after saving his life *and* his leg and you want to know why I dislike him?" Her tone was biting, making the girl flinch again.

"I didn't know you did all of that." She was quiet for a minute. "The dog and horse are yours, right?"

"Yes. Are they locked up?"

"No. The horse won't come into the camp but he is standing just inside of the trees. And the dog is staying with the horse."

"Leave them alone. They are doing what they are supposed to. The only way they will come anywhere near a person is if I tell them to. I'm surprised you guys were able to catch them to begin with."

The girl relaxed just a bit. "It took a while. The horse really was difficult and we all were afraid the dog might eat someone. How come they won't leave?"

"Because they know I'm here."

Gwen stared at Ace while she ate. Ace tolerated it to a point, but irritation began to set in.

"Do you want something?" She snapped.

Gwen jumped, then looked around wringing her hands. "Umm, I should go."

She went to the door, knocked a few times, and then squeezed out quickly. Ace just shook her head as she finished her food, then went back to reading papers.

***

"I dare you to come in here and let me have a shot at you, coward!"

Bishop walked up behind the man standing guard outside of his office door. The man was facing the door, yelling back at his little firecracker inside.

"Yeah? You couldn't handle me, honey."

A laugh came through the door. "*Honey*?" She laughed again. "Sorry, little boy. I only deal with experienced men." She wasn't quite sure what it meant, but she knew it would affect him in a negative way.

"You little-"

"Peter."

The young man swung around to face Bishop and instantly straightened. "Yes, sir."

"What are you doing?" He tried to keep the mild entertainment from his tone.

"The prisoner is being difficult."

"She is not a prisoner. We are just checking into her background."

"It's been two weeks, sir."

Bishop gave him a look that stopped the questioning. "Gwen will be by with food soon. I was just warning you since you don't normally guard the door. Gwen usually stays in there for a few minutes. Oh, and don't engage Miss Ace in conversation."

The soldier nodded and tried to look competent as Bishop walked back outside.

***

Ace wasn't sure when she was going to get out of here. She was certain now that anything between her and Bishop had all been one-sided. She couldn't believe that she was so stupid. She gets kissed for the first time and she instantly assumes it means something other than a way to pass the time. She was staring out the small window watching the movement of people. She took mental notes on where people were, where they went, what they did. She was watching Bishop talk with some of his men when something squealed, high pitched and excited. Ace glanced around and saw a woman bounce excitedly over to Bishop and jump into his arms, kissing his square on the lips.

Ace wasn't sure why, but this bothered her. She felt her chest tighten and she scowled at the big-chested young brunette in her little spandex shorts and belly showing tank top. So much for the feelings Bishop claimed he had for her, he really was just like the men she read about in all of those books and magazines. Just like every other man.

She was furious with herself for kissing him as much as she had. Actually seeing it, having proof that he was a player made her feel like she just took a punch to the stomach. That feeling slowly evolved into a hot burning anger. She couldn't believe she allowed herself to be used like that. Again she thought about how she should have just let him die that day she first saw him. Ace was angrily pacing the small office when Gwen entered a few minutes later with her lunch. She set the tray down, then took a seat.

"You seem on edge today." Gwen mentioned timidly.

"I have never been in one place for so long. I am going insane!"

Gwen looked at her hands. "You are going to leave as soon as they let you go."

"Yes, at top speed! As far away from here as I can get."

Ace looked at Gwen and saw the impact of her words. Gwen had been hanging around longer and longer when she stopped by with food. Ace decided to try to be pleasant to her, she was good enough company. But she would still use the girl to get away if she had to. Over the two weeks that Ace had been locked in the office, Gwen had kept her company during meals. It was amazing what you could learn by just getting someone to talk and listening.

Ace had learned that Gwen didn't really have any friends in the camp. The girl was so timid and she was starting to trust Ace. "You could come with me you know," she suggested awkwardly to the girl. She wasn't really sure she wanted Gwen coming with her, but she could at least get her out of here and get her to another place. Maybe it would be all she needed to get Gwen to help her escape.

Gwen's eyes widened. "I could never leave."

"Why?"

"Because I know too much about the rebellion. You are lucky they haven't told you anything. If you grow up here you can't leave, you could create a problem if you were ever captured."

"So you're a prisoner."

"No!" Gwen shook her head.

"Let me see, you can never leave and you have to do what they say?" Ace just looked at her.

Gwen furrowed her brows. "I am not a prisoner."

"Whatever you say. Just doesn't seem to me like you have your freedom if you can't do what you want."

Gwen stood. "I have some chores to do. I will see you in the morning."

"Before you leave, did you check on Flint for me?"

"I did, he is at the north end of camp."

Ace smiled her thanks and waited for Gwen to leave. She knew it would be a risk asking Gwen for help and she was done waiting around. As soon as she heard the lock click, she rushed around to get her things ready. She put all her clothes in the saddlebags. She had saved some of the apples that came with her meals and put them away for travel food. As soon as darkness fell she was going to escape.

Gwen's words about no one being allowed to leave after they know too much decided it for her. They would eventually discover she had picked the locks on the desk and gone through all of the papers. She would be a prisoner here for the rest of her life seeing Bishop every day reminding her what a fool she was.

They were idiots for having the kind of information that they did in here with a prisoner, and she was an idiot for reading it. But there had been nothing for her to do while she waited for weeks. At first she was just after information to help her escape. But now she knew their next few attack plans, which recent plans they were responsible for, the numbers of occupants for this camp and a few surrounding camps, and who several of their inside guys were by name.

There was no way she would let them keep her here for the rest of her life. And she was never getting caught ever again. Ace tested the window, knowing it would be locked, but needing to know how much give it had. If necessary she would just break it and make a mad dash for the tree line. But she would prefer to make a soundless exit.

As soon as it was dark, she started working on the window using her small hidden knife to cut out the hinges since she was unable to undo the lock. The hinges come off with a little effort.

Opening the window she lowered her saddle bags to the ground as quietly as possible, then crawled through.

Her weapons weren't here and she had no idea where they might be, but she knew her saddle and bridle were at the shed on the north end of camp. And, according to Gwen, so was Flint.

The camp must have a lights out time, because the entire place was dead except for a group of guards at the central fire. She easily avoided the guards who were more interested in their card games than anything, and made it back to the shed. As quietly as she could, Ace whistled for Flint to come to her. After checking him over for any injury she tacked him up and tied on her saddle bags.

Swinging into the saddle, she looked back at the camp with a smile then rode into the trees with Wolf scouting the trail ahead. She was buzzing with excitement, almost difficult to contain. But with the thought of the camp still nearby she managed to contain her enthusiasm at her newfound freedom. Now her only concern was regaining some weapons. Luckily she still had her heavy weapons belt, all that was needed was some restocking.

She meandered east for several hours staying in the cover of trees but still near the road looking for campsites. If she could just sneak in and swipe a rifle or two she would be ready to put some distance between her and the past few weeks.

***

"How the hell did she escape?!" Bishop yelled to the guard who was supposed to be stationed outside of the room Ace was in. "Did you leave your post at all?"

"No sir."

"Then how did she get out of a locked room with a full time guard right outside the door?"

"Bishop, enough." Jayce said in a distracted tone from inside the room. Bishop glared at the young man, then walked into the room to deal with Jayce.

"She got out through the window."

"It doesn't look broken and no one can pick that lock!" Bishop said in extreme irritation.

"It's not. She cut the hinges out of the frame. Your little pet has some skills."

Bishop raised his brows. "Where did she get a knife?"

Jayce walked over to the desk and pulled out every drawer. "You will need to replenish your office weapons. She took both knives and the revolver."

"She got into the desk?!" Bishop sorted through all of the papers. "None of them are missing, but she has definitely been through them."

Jayce sighed. "You know what this means right? We have to go after her." He ran a hand through his hair. "I don't *want* to. If it were up to me, I would have forced you to leave her alone to begin with. But you just had to try and tame the little shrew. You know that we can't let her leave with this type of information. Even if she has no intention to sell it or use it, if she is captured and tortured for the information, she has no reason not to give it to them."

"She is not a sellout, Jayce. She would keep a candy bar from the government simply because they asked for it. But I agree we need to take some precautions and bring her back."

"And this time put her in a cell that could hold Houdini. And I don't think she is as righteous as you think. She is more the type to do whatever is necessary for her own survival."

Bishop glared at his friend. "We are not putting her in a cell. We will figure something out but we are not putting her in a cell. Maybe if we hadn't locked her up to begin with we wouldn't be in this situation."

"Or if you had just gone and spoken with her once or twice after locking her away she wouldn't have so much re- sentment for this place. You say she isn't a prisoner but she was most certainly treated like one," Jayce mumbled. "I don't know what happened between the two of you while you were trapped in that building, and I don't want to know, but you need to deal with it by the time we find her."

Bishop ignored him. "Get a team together to start the search and bring me Gwen. She might have some knowledge about where Ace headed when she got out."

The team was gathered, briefed, and sent east to begin searching. They were sent with orders to call for backup once spotting her and to just observe, avoiding contact with her until Bishop was there at all costs. After talking to the team, Bishop found Gwen waiting in his office.

"Gwen, thank you for coming."

Gwen was a girl that had grown up in the rebel camps. She was an orphan that was just raised by whoever was in camp. He didn't really know much about her other than she was very shy and timid and somewhere around fifteen years old.

"Did I do something wrong sir? Where is Ace? Did she leave already? She promised she would say goodbye after you released her.-"

Bishop held up a hand to signal her to stop talking with a kind smile. "She wasn't released, she escaped. You did nothing wrong I promise, I just needed to know if she ever mentioned somewhere she was going after she got out or someone she was going to visit?"

Gwen thought for a few minutes while wringing her hands in her lap "I don't think so. She just said she was going crazy because she had never been in one place for so long. And that she had never been away from her animals for so long. And that she really hated being a prisoner. She said she was going east, but that was all."

"Did she say why she was going that way?"

"No. All she said was that she traveled to a specific place north because she was looking for something. When she didn't find it she wanted to leave. So she just travels all of the time by herself. It sounded like a really lonely life. But she seemed eager to get back to it."

Bishop thought to himself for a few minutes. "Did she say what it was that she had been searching for? Or where she expected to find it?"

"All I know is that it was north from where she used to live."

"Hmm." Bishop wondered what would be so important for someone to a travel alone to at such a young age. She said she used to live in Skull Valley so north could be a variety of places. But he had found her here in Idaho, so maybe it was around here.

"She didn't say anything else? No conversations that caught your attention?"

Gwen shook her head. "I don't think so."

"What was the last conversation you had?"

"She told me when she left . . ." Gwen looked nervously up at Bishop.

"It's okay, you're not in any trouble. I just want to know so I can help to keep her safe. She is in danger out there alone."

"She told me I could go with her if I wanted. But I told her that once you know as much as I do about the rebellion you don't just leave. And then she went on this rant about freedom and how I wasn't really free even though I told her it wasn't how she thought, that I wasn't a prisoner or anything. But she seemed upset about it and wasn't listening to me so I left."

"Thank you. That will be all for now." She got up to leave but stopped at the door when he spoke again, "And Gwen, if there is ever anything ya' want, or need, or somewhere you would like to go...come straight to me. I'll be sure to do what I can."

She smiled, brightly enough that a pang of guilt went through Bishop, then left the room. He put his face in his hands, too tired to deal with guilt on top of his stress at the moment.

***

"Jayce!"

Jayce appeared in the doorway. "The team left. They already found her trail and are following it."

"Good. Are we doing the right thing here, Jayce?" Bishop said while rubbing his temples.

"You can't be a perfect leader. Let go the guilt from the little girl who has had a tough life. She's had it a lot easier than most children growing up. You kept her safe. A lot don't have that much."

"Thank you, Jayce. You are right. What do we do while waitin' for a report from the search team?"

Jayce put a bottle of whiskey on the desk. "We drink."

Chapter 6

Ace trotted along the side of the road. The sun had set and the light was quickly fading away. There was a fire up ahead and now that she had been traveling for a few weeks with no more than the weapons she stole from Bishop, she was getting nervous.

She only had two bullets left in the revolver, one of the reasons she hated revolvers was because they didn't hold much ammo. They were also limited in how far you could shoot. She would feel far more secure if she could pick up a rifle and handful of ammo to go with it. She hadn't made as much distance from Bishop as she wanted but she was being careful not to leave too much sign of her passing. She had learned her lesson on traveling too fast. While she might be being overly cautious, she was still free and hadn't plunged headfirst into any dangerous situations. She considered that a good improvement.

A quarter of a mile from the camp, she stopped off Flint and left him to continue on foot. She was hoping the owners of the fire were soldiers. They were usually the only ones brash enough for a fire all night this close to the road. It was basically a homing beacon for trouble.

To avoid as much bloodshed as possible, she was hoping to wait until they fell asleep and simply sneak in and steal their weapons. As she came up to the camp she found a con-cealed area under some brush where she couldn't be seen easily but could still keep an eye on the activities of the men. She confirmed there were nine soldiers. If all went as planned, she would have a good haul for the night.

Ace settled in and got as comfortable as she could. This was not a new experience for her. Stealing weapons from sleeping soldiers was much easier than taking them while the soldiers were awake. The hardest part about waiting for a camp to fall asleep was avoiding falling asleep yourself. The options for self-entertainment were limited since she was trying not to move but she had developed several small tricks to keep her mind busy.

Just as Ace was running out of things to do, a soldier jumped up and called out, "Drop all of your weapons before coming any further forward or you will be shot!"

This got her attention. None of the soldiers were looking her way. She shifted her position so she could see the entire camp but she still couldn't see the visitor.

"I have no weapons, just lookin' for a little bit of info on a missing lass."

Ace gaped, she knew that voice anywhere. She could not believe that he would not just let her walk away. This man was going to be the death of her in more ways than one.

"Come forward," one of the soldiers said.

Bishop walked into view. He had his hands raised up and didn't have any obvious weapons although Ace was certain he had some hidden on himself somewhere. The soldiers eyed him warily.

"We have seen a few female travelers recently. But before we help you, we need to be certain you have an honorable reason for hunting her down. We are out here to protect the innocent and keep peace, after all. So do you have an honorable reason?"

"Och, I wish I didn't." Bishop said, faking his resentment easily. "If the wench wasn't my damn wife, I would say good riddance. But she is and she has some really big brothers back at home that already don't care for me so much so I feel I should track her down."

The soldiers laughed. "Well, why did she leave? Maybe she doesn't want to be found."

"Oh trust me, she does. Other words she wouldn't have left such an easy trail for me to follow. She is a silly headstrong lass that likes to play these little games just to keep those brothers all riled up. I just need to know if you've seen her through here and when."

"What's she look like?" A different soldier asked.

"Blonde hair, average height, early twenties, easy enough on the eyes to make you overlook the scowl she always has on her face."

The soldiers laughed again. "I'm afraid we haven't seen anyone who fits that description." The lead soldier said while the others moved until they were blocking Bishop's exit. "You, however, match a description regarding someone involved in the Rebel movement."

Bishop looked around himself cautiously. He was completely surrounded and he really didn't have a gun on him in preparation for not wanting to give the soldiers a reason to get upset. He figured that would back up his story about searching for a lost wife.

Ace cursed under her breath. As much as she hated Bishop, she couldn't just let him get killed while she sat by and watched. She might have been able to if he was a complete stranger, but this was different. Besides if anyone was going to get the pleasure of shooting him, it was going to be her.

The soldiers knew that they had the upper hand. There was nine of them and just one stranger so they left their weapons leaning up against their SUV. She hoped Bishop had been working on his hand-to-hand combat.

Ace's last two bullets went to evening out the odds slightly as she burst out of her hiding place. Now it was seven to two. She grabbed the knife from her boot, jumped down into the fray, and grabbed the first one she came to. While she was engaged with him, another clamped a shackle around her right wrist. Before he was able to attach the other end to anything solid, she reversed the hold on her knife and slid it into his shoulder. She gave a downward pull and was certain she managed to sever the main artery that went through there. He wouldn't be back in the fight.

It looked like Bishop was holding his own against two while one lay still at his feet. That left five to still fight against.

The problem with a situation like this was that, at this point, no one could be allowed to get away. If any of the soldiers managed to escape they would head straight for the nearest base and get a description out. Ace and Bishop would be at the top of the most wanted list with an accurate description and their latest whereabouts. So much for staying out of sight and laying low.

She stabbed another soldier in the leg right across the femoral artery, but then was ripped off her feet when someone grabbed the free shackle dangling by her wrist. As she hit the ground, Bishop suddenly loomed above her and sent a hard punch into the man's nose. Blood sprayed and the man went down.

Ace scrambled blindly in the direction her arm was being pulled for lack of wanting a dislocated shoulder, but the pulling wasn't stopping. Reaching up she grabbed the chain with her free hand and pulled hard.

Bishop stumbled over and fell on top of her. "What the hell are you doing, Ace?!"

Ace shoved at him so she could get up. "Me?! Get off before we get killed!"

Bishop rolled off of her and jumped to his feet, yanking Ace's arm again in the process. Just as she was about to yell at him, he ducked out of the way of a knife that was thrown from one of the remaining soldiers and tried to dive for a gun. His attempt was cut short as his arm was wrenched backwards.

"Dammit, Ace!" He yelled as he glanced down to his left wrist and discovered the problem. They were cuffed together.

He grabbed her arm and pulled her towards him as he rolled and grabbed the gun, then shot the man that had thrown the knife. When Ace and Bishop got to their feet, both of them had guns aimed at the three remaining soldiers who were also now fully armed.

"Any ideas, genius?" Ace asked Bishop bitterly.

"Maybe." He held up his gun and addressed the soldiers. "How about we agree to go our separate-"

Ace shot two of them before he even finished his sentence. Good reflexes are the only thing that made Bishop shoot before he himself got shot by the one remaining soldier.

"You couldn't have shot the last one too, Love?" He demanded as he looked at her with a shocked look on his face.

"My gun only had two shots." She said with a shrug. "Come on, they flipped their emergency beacon. We have less than five minutes before reinforcements show up."

"Their what?" he asked. Ace went to move forward but hit resistance. She glanced angrily at the chain on her wrist.

"How does the Rebel super leader not know about their emergency beacons? Every soldier has one. If they think they can't handle a situation, they flip a switch on their wrist contraptions and it alerts the nearest base to send reinforcements immediately. They flipped theirs as soon as I fired the first two shots."

Picking up guns as they headed out of the camp, she practically had to drag Bishop out of there and back to where Flint was waiting.

"Would you come on? We are going to get caught." She turned to her animals, "Wolf, watch the road." The dog turned and loped off. She yanked on Bishop's arm to get his attention. "Hey! Can you ride?"

Bishop looked at her horse uncertainly. "When I was a lad, a little. But not since coming here."

"Well hopefully you remember at least how to avoid falling off. Keep a leg on each side, your butt down, and your head on top." She looked down at her right wrist, chained to his left and lowered her voice. "If you pull me off, I will beat you bloody. Understand?"

He frowned at her, "How are we supposed to ride one horse while chained together?" he asked, obviously uncomfortable with the pending situation.

"I'll explain after we're on the horse. Right now we just have to get out of here!" She was glad Flint was a big horse. She wasn't concerned at all about him carrying both their weights at a decent speed to clear out of the area. He wouldn't be able to go forever but they should be able to get some miles behind them if they were careful. She had Bishop stand at Flint's right shoulder while she got into the saddle, then moved her foot out of the stirrup so he could put his in.

"Now, put your right foot in the stirrup, grab the horn, and pull yourself up behind me. I'll do my best to counter balance your weight so you don't pull my saddle to the side."

He gave her a doubtful look but positioned himself to give it a try. His first attempt was so pathetic that he had to wait for Ace to stop laughing because she was in such hysterics that she was doubled over and completely useless. Once she sobered and caught her breath, he tried again. He slowly, painfully managed to pull himself up behind the saddle and packs without pulling Ace or the saddle off. It wasn't pretty but he was up.

With how their hands were cuffed, Ace had to have her right hand behind her back to Bishop's left one. It might have been more comfortable crossed in front of her but that felt more like an embrace. She didn't want that. She was used to riding one handed, but it was awkward having her arm pinned behind her, so after a little more awkward maneuvering she gave up and moved her right arm in front of her resting on her left hip. Bishop could still reach a good handhold with his free right hand and would just have to understand this was a necessity and nothing more.

For sake of Bishop and Flint's back, she decided to avoid trotting altogether. If she needed to pick up speed, she would have Flint go straight to the canter so her passenger didn't bounce off.

"Where are we going?" Bishop asked after an hour of intermittent walking and cantering.

"Far away from the camp we just slaughtered. Thanks to you." She grumbled.

"How is this my fault?"

She turned and stared at him. She could not believe he actually said that. "Because you just walked into a soldier camp like it was the city park. What on earth would convince you that was a good idea?"

"I was looking for a woman who bolted after reading all of my desk material," he said in frustration. "What were you doing at the camp in the first place?"

"I was waiting for them to fall asleep so I could restock on my weapons. Just let them fall asleep, sneak in, pick up a few rifles since mine got a little misplaced. It was all going according to plan until you barged in looking for your *wife*."

Bishop laughed a little, glad she couldn't see his blush. "I was trying to appear inconspicuous."

"If I hadn't been there, the government would have their hands on the Rebel leader right now. How smart was that?"

"You're right, and I thank you for that, but it doesn't change the fact that I was searching for you for a reason." Ace didn't respond. "I know you went through my desk and I know you read all of my documents."

"So what? You gonna take me in and torture me for what I learned to make sure you're safe?"

"I would never torture you, Love. You should know that. But I do have to take you in. For what it's worth, I am sorry."

"Yeah, I'm sure you're all sorts of sorry."

Bishop snorted in frustration. This was not going at all how he pictured it. He was getting a picture of how angry she was with him. He knew she was headstrong and wasn't going to just fall into his arms but he didn't think she would want nothing to do with him. He hadn't handled things well at all when she was at his camp.

He had some serious smoothing over to do. "I'll admit a part of me is very happy to have a reason to keep you around. But I am also seeing how much you despise me. I won't force myself on people who don't want my company. So yes, I am sorry- for everything."

Ace was quiet for a few minutes, considering his words. She really wanted to hate him but having him so close against her back made her think again. She felt that pull on her feelings again and some of the anger melted away.

"I don't hate you," she finally offered. "And I don't despise you. But I am not going back with you."

"I'm afraid our current arrangement makes it difficult for you to do anything else. Unless you want to risk going back to that camp and frisking those bodies for a key, you will have to wait until we get back to my camp and one of them can unlock it."

Ace growled her frustration. "Then what, Bishop? I doubt you are going to take me back to your little office, we have a little chat, and then you will just let me be on my merry way?"

"You could join us. Then there would be nothing left to discuss."

"I work alone, I already told you that."

"We could send you out on solo missions. I am sure we could work something out," Bishop offered.

"No."

"Why not? You don't even want to think about it? Or is it because then you would have to do something for someone other than yourself?"

"Seriously? I've saved your sorry ass at least twice now and neither time did it do anything for me but cause more trouble!" she retorted.

"Well, then I am afraid I can't help you. Jayce will have to do this his way."

"Which involves what?"

"Lock and key until further notice."

"Why would you want me back there anyway? I have no information or reason for you keeping me a prisoner. You keep trying to tell me that you care for my company yet the second I'm locked away you have big brunette all over you."

"I have what?" he asked.

Ace rolled her eyes. "You mean you don't remember spandex underwear, big boobs, and brown hair?" All the pain of that moment crashed back in on her.

"Chastity? When would you have even . . . oh."

"Yeah oh, so I don't buy the whole 'please come back because I have feelings for you' act," she said bitterly.

"I do have feelings for you."

"Yeah, and any other remotely attractive female in the vicinity apparently."

He could feel her tense up but she didn't say anything else, just signaled Flint to canter again. He knew she only did it as a guarantee that he wouldn't talk anymore since he was too focused on not falling off. Soon she pulled Flint up. She couldn't let her anger afflict her horse. It wasn't Flint's fault that she was in this predicament.

They traveled the rest of the night at the walk. Ace was concerned about overtiring her horse. Bishop managed to dose now and then for a few winks of sleep. But as soon as his head would lean against her shoulder, she would shrug him off and wake him up.

It was late afternoon of the next day. They were both half asleep with their guards down when they stumbled onto the edge of a camp. Ace's head whipped up immediately at the sound of footsteps and she cursed herself for her foolishness.

There was a small camp with one guard stationed out about forty yards away from her. About half a second after Ace saw the guard, he saw her and raised the alarm. She instantly signaled Flint to a gallop, forgetting momentarily about her passenger. Flint shot off and Bishop, still half asleep, hadn't been hanging on and flipped right off the back of the horse, dragging Ace with him.

She came up full of curses and a flying fist which contacted Bishop directly in the jaw sending him right back to the ground. Knocking him down didn't exactly help her, because as he fell he drug her down with him, which caused her to curse him all over again. Bishop was in the process of trying to stop Ace from assaulting him again when the sound of laughter made them both pause.

"This is an interesting technique for bringing in a prisoner. Even for you, Bishop."

"Jayce!" Bishop said with a smile. He was still on his back with his arms crossed straight out in front of him and one of Ace's fists in each hand as she was half laying half leaning over him in the midst of taking out her frustrations.

"You've got to be kidding me." She grumbled as she stood up.

Jayce walked forward and helped Bishop to his feet. "This is the second time I've seen her beating you."

Bishop grinned, "She's got a little fire. Give her red hair and she would be the complete package for sass."

He winced as Ace kicked his shin for his comment, then held his wrist up for Jayce to examine while keeping a wary eye out for more attacks. "A key would be nice, before I lose my hand."

"Mind explaining how exactly you ended up like this?"

"Your boss is an idiot. That's how," Ace bit out with a glare at Bishop.

"Hey, you didn't have to save me," Bishop shot back. "If I had known it would come with this amount of trouble I would have gladly taken the soldiers instead."

Ace rolled her eyes, then shook the chain emphatically in front of Jayce's face. "Hello? Could you hurry up, please?"

Jayce gave Bishop an amused glance when he shrugged, "I can't help you, sorry."

"What?" they both exclaimed in unison.

Jayce pointed to the chain between them. "That is the highest level government issue set of cuffs I have ever seen. We don't have any keys that will open them and I don't have the materials for cutting through them."

The color drained from Ace's face. This could not be happening to her. All she wanted was to get out of here and be on her way. "How long until we can get our hands on a set of keys?"

"Not a clue. We would have to start attacking random soldier camps and bases in hopes that they have these exact cuffs and the keys to unlock them."

Ace set her shoulders. "Fine. Let's get started."

Jayce held up his hands, "Slow down there, we are *the* Rebel movement. We can't just drop everything to go hunting down a key. We already wasted enough time hunting you down." He sent a pointed look in Bishop's direction.

Ace couldn't keep the look of bewilderment from her features. "Well, what the hell am *I* supposed to do? I am not a part of your stupid rebel movement and I refuse to be stuck within five inches of *that* twenty-four/seven!" She gave a pointed motion towards Bishop who looked rather insulted by her comment.

Jayce just shrugged. "Sounds like a good way to keep track of someone I am sick of hunting down all the time." Then he walked away from them, headed back to camp and motioned to the collection of guards that had gathered to follow him.

"If you leave me stuck with him, I'll just kill him and chop his hand off!" she yelled at Jayce's retreating back. The man waved a hand in acknowledgement but didn't seem too concerned for he didn't even look at her.

When her angry gaze fell on Bishop he put a hand up to ward her off. "What? It's not like I planned this. I don't exactly want you this close to me every second of the day either. Especially not if every time these things tangle us up it results in you pounding on me," he said in exasperation.

She just glared at him. "Now I do hate you." Then she started walking to the camp, half dragging him behind her. Wolf followed her into the camp at a crouch, watching everyone just as warily as they were watching him.

Ace glanced around. There were nine men and two women, one of which was the spandex lady with big boobs, who came running over squealing and jumped into Bishop's arms. When he went to catch her, he jerked Ace's arm up which earned him her best death glare.

Chastity kissed Bishop with just as much enthusiasm as she had when Ace first saw them from the office window. Ace blushed and yanked as hard as she could which pulled Bishop's arm out and caused Chastity to almost fall. She glanced around and seemed to notice Ace for the very first time.

"Oh, hi!" she said enthusiastically, seemingly unaffected by Ace's seething glare. "I'm Chastity."

She stuck her hand out with a big smile on her face. Ace sneered at her and walked away without shaking the woman's hand. The bouncy girl was dressed just as much, or as little, as she had been the first time Ace saw her except this shirt might have been even lower cut if that was possible. She was in danger of falling out of it with all hopping around she was doing.

Much to Ace's disappointment, Chastity seemed set on following Bishop, who was attached to Ace. When Ace glanced over her shoulder she noticed him noticing the heaving cleavage that was bursting forth from the brunette's shirt. Ace yanked on the chain again, hard.

Bishop cursed and glared at her. "What is your problem?"

Ace stopped and glared at him. "Not even a full day ago you are trying to convince me of your genuine feelings and you already have your tongue down someone else's throat. Forgive me if I don't quite buy the story." She hissed. Chastity was still hovering a few feet away waiting for Bishop to pay her more attention.

"Are you telling me you're jealous, Love?" he asked with a mocking smile.

Her glare hardened. "No. I'm just glad you are proving me right-"

"Who's your friend?" Chastity interrupted with a bright smile. If the girl got any perkier, Ace was going to pop her right in the face just to feel better.

Both Ace and Bishop turned to her, but Ace responded first. "I would be not a slut."

The woman's cheerful expression hardened into a scowl.

Bishop turned onto Ace, "I understand you don't have a lot of social skills but you don't talk to people that way. Especially not people who are just trying to be friendly." He growled at her.

Ace couldn't stand the satisfied smile on Chastity's face. There was no way anyone could be that clueless. Ace had enough of this.

"I don't need any help. I don't want any friends. And I'm not staying here long enough to care!" She tried to stomp off but Bishop didn't move a single step. When she looked back at him he was watching her with a mocking smirk.

"I swear if you do not move your feet right this minute I will kill you in your sleep."

Chastity's eyes widened at the threat and she seemed to decide she was needed elsewhere. Bishop rolled his eyes but relented. "Fine. Where are we going?"

"I need to check on Flint, and Wolf is uncomfortable with this many people."

The hound was still at her heels watching the whole human exchange with canine interest. He was no longer slinking around but was standing at his full height, which meant his back came up to Ace's hip.

Bishop eyed him warily, "Would he attack me or my men?"

"Yes. If I tell him to or if he thinks that I am being threatened." She gave him a pointed look.

"If he endangers any of my men, he will be shot," he said matter-of-factly. He didn't want to put any more of a rift between them but she needed to understand what could happen.

Ace stopped dead in her tracks. "You injure my dog in any way and I will kill you as slowly as possible."

Bishop actually blanched at the menacing tone in her voice. She had managed to threaten to kill him several times in the past fifteen minutes but this time she sounded perfectly serious.

She sighed and looked around the camp. "What exactly are we supposed to do until dark?"

"Well, it's too late to move camp now, so we will eat and get some sleep and figure things out in the morning," he said mildly, studying her expression. He was hoping that once she got some food and rest and discovered that she was safe, that she would calm down a bit and they could have a reasonable conversation again.

Ace frowned but nodded. "Fine, we'll get food after I check on Flint."

She walked to the edge of the camp and whistled once. She had different whistles for Wolf that meant different things, but Flint had only been trained to one whistle and that meant to come to her. Training the dog to multiple whistles was far easier than training the horse to just one had been.

Flint came trotting through the woods, anxious and flipping his head whenever he stepped on one of his reins which were dragging on the ground.

Ace cursed at that. She gently took the bridle off his head and checked his mouth. Bishop watched with interest as her features softened and she inspected the horse's mouth. Flint's gums were bleeding a little from the bit and bruised but not too bad. It would heal up quickly. She set the bridle over the saddle horn then pulled off the saddle. It was a little more difficult than usual with Bishop's hand tied to her, but she managed. As soon as Flint was unburdened, she let him wander off in search of food and water. He'd had a long night, too, and he deserved a rest.

Ace didn't blame him for running away whenever she fell off. She learned shortly after she found him that a horse's first instinct when spooked was flight, not fight. Wolf always stayed near, unless she told him to go elsewhere, but Ace accepted Flint's natural instincts in spite of the fact that she found them annoying. In a way it was a good balance. She couldn't imagine a thousand pound animal that had fighting as its first instinct. That was why she trained him to come to her whistle. If he ran off she was always able to get him to come back to her.

Bishop offered to carry Ace's saddle back into camp for her, but she refused. She still wasn't sure what was going on between them. All she knew was that they had shared a moment kissing and, she thought, getting close. She was gullible enough to believe his words of sweet nothings. Now that they were out of danger however, it seemed he didn't really care about her at all. They walked back to camp in an uncomfortable silence. She deposited her burden beside Bishop's tent, then they went in search of food.

By the time the pair settled down to enjoy their meal it was dark and Ace was exhausted. She fed half of her meal to Wolf, so he wouldn't have to go hunting. She knew he was tired too. He had ran all night beside Flint and he wasn't wanting to leave her side with all these strangers around.

Bishop gave her a look when she slid half the food off her plate to the ground for the dog but Ace ignored him. Wolf wasn't just a dog to her, he was her family and she wasn't going to let him go hungry. She ignored Bishop's look and picked at a roll.

***

She was almost asleep when her hand jerked out from under her chin and she startled to her feet.

Bishop was smirking at her. She realized he had pulled her arm away. Really funny man he was becoming. She couldn't wait to get these cuffs off and it was getting easier by the moment to figure out how she felt about him.

Despite the fact that the man was decent looking and something deep inside wanted to like him, she didn't want to. He was arrogant and he had a temper. She had seen bits and pieces of it. Any time she contradicted him or argued with him she saw it flare a little. It reminded her of all of the other men she had encountered. Still though, a part of her really did like him for some reason she didn't comprehend.

"I'm going to bed," Bishop said as he wiggled the chain connecting them, a sign that he wanted her to follow him. Ace stood up, uncomfortable with the smirks the men sitting around the fire were giving them as they walked away towards Bishop's tent. He held the flap open, but Ace didn't go in. She just stood there with her arm across her chest, holding onto her opposite elbow.

"No way. I'll sleep out here." She motioned to the ground.

Bishop made a face at her. "Oh, come on. I can't be that repulsive to you."

Ace blushed, which made Bishop grin. The thought of being alone with him terrified her. Things had changed and there was no life and death crisis going on this time. "I am not sleeping in there with you."

Bishop raised his hands in a show of innocence, which pulled Ace's arm up awkwardly. "I'll behave. I promise."

She shook her head. "I don't care what you think you'll do or not do. I'm not taking the chance of you changing your mind. I'm sleeping outside."

He scowled at her and grabbed her arm with his free hand. "Sweetheart, I have more self-control than that. Don't insult me."

Ace winced. "You sure about that?" She looked down at his hand which was digging into her skin and would leave bruises.

He cursed and let go, then took a deep breath.

"You infuriate me sometimes, sorry. I have never met another human being like you. Fine sleep outside, but you'll have to go in and crawl out under the wall."

Ace glanced nervously at the tent. She had been drug into one just like it a year ago. If it hadn't been for Wolf, she probably wouldn't have made it out again.

"Fine." She said tightly, trying to control the shiver that raced down her spine. Ducking down, she crawled in and moved over to the side as quickly as the chain would allow while Bishop came in behind her. She got down on the ground and wiggled under the wall. There wasn't very much space and even though she wasn't very big, it was still a tight fit. She came out right next to her saddle.

Ace adjusted her tack so she was laying on the saddle blanket and her right hand was tucked just under the wall of the tent, she was sleeping on her stomach so she could rest her head on her forearm. It was a warm night and Wolf would give her all the body heat she would need to be comfortable until morning. The stars were twinkling overhead. It would get chilly towards morning with no cloud cover but the nights were still tolerable. Once she was settled, Wolf curled up next to her and they both drifted off for some much needed sleep.

***

A cold nose woke her as it brushed her cheek. Ace glanced at her dog and saw his hackles raised in a silent growl. That sign had alerted her to danger so many times before that she knew there was someone nearby that he didn't like. It would be hard to tell who was upsetting him with a camp full of people but it was late enough that no one was obviously moving about.

Just as she was about to reach under the tent and alert Bishop, she heard whispers coming from the inside of the tent she was currently chained to.

"Chastity, stop." Bishop whispered quietly.

"Why? Is it because of that new girl? I don't like her," Chastity whined.

Ace rolled her eyes. Good, she didn't like the spandex princess, either. This was such a cliché move for a girl like Chastity to pull. At least Ace thought it was.

"Yes and no. It's complicated."

Chastity whined. "Please? I promise I'll make it worth your while."

Ace felt a blush flushing her face. She couldn't believe she allowed herself to kiss this guy. They were seriously going to get intimate with her right there and chained to him?

"Chastity, that new girl is sleeping right outside this tent. I really need you to go back to your own. Now."

"Why is she sleeping outside your tent, anyway? Is she like a guard dog? Your new pet?"

"Look, she is here because our hands are cuffed together. She helped me escape some soldiers but in the process we got handcuffed together. So, I really need you to leave," he whispered in a rush.

Ace felt someone touch the chain lightly.

"*Don't touch* that! You'll wake her up."

"What do you care if we wake her up? Even though I don't like her, I guess we could include her," Chastity replied in a naughty voice. "Whatever floats your boat, Baby. She could probably use a few lessons. She seems a little rough around the edges."

Ace bristled but stayed quiet. She was pretty sure that Chastity was saying things to get her riled up just to see if she was listening. She wasn't going to give the bimbo the satisfaction of a reply.

"Because she is important to me. Now, get out of my tent," Bishop ordered quietly. Bishop looked at Chastity with pleading eyes. He was never going to get Ace to talk to him again with this girl around.

Ace heard some more rustling and then heard footsteps as Chastity sulked back to her side of camp. Ace had to admit that it felt good hearing Bishop order the spandex princess to leave, but that didn't mean she was happy that the girl had visited in the first place. It made her wonder what was going on between those two before she showed up. She wondered what kind of a guy Bishop really was. She had no desire to just be another girl on a list. First thing the next morning, she was getting her hand free of the cuffs.

Chapter 7

Ace woke the next morning to pre-dawn light slowly brightening the sky. There was no movement in the camp nor in the tent next to her. Ace wasn't one to sit around all morning. She had to get going, there were people to avoid, roads to travel. She tentatively lifted the tent wall and glanced inside.

"Bishop?" she whispered. He didn't stir.

"Bishop," she said a little louder and shook the chain connecting them. He still didn't move. With a frustrated sigh Ace wiggled under the tent wall and crawled over the slumbering man.

"One of these days I hope sleeping in gets you in trouble," she muttered as she sat back on her heels.

"Hey. wake up," she said as she lifted his left arm and shook it by the cuffs. He mumbled something incoherent but still didn't wake up. Ace scowled down at him in frustration. She sat there in the dim light thinking for several minutes before she finally just grabbed his shirt and lifted him up as high as she could, then let go. When he hit the ground, he flew back up into a sitting position so fast Ace instinctively went to hit him before she caught herself. Bishop stopped himself from lashing out at her as soon as his eyes focused.

"Ace?"

She sat back up and frowned at him. "You sleep like a dead person. I have been trying to wake you up for ten minutes."

He blinked a few times and looked around. "It's still dark out."

"Only for another half hour or so. It's almost dawn. I need to get moving."

Bishop laid back down and put his hands under his head, pulling Ace's wrist forward so she was leaning over him.

"We don't get up until at least dawn around here. Besides,-" he jingled the chain, "-you don't have anywhere to go just yet."

"Well, give me some grease or oil, anything slippery. I don't even care if it is butter. I will get out of this damn cuff and be on my way."

Bishop snorted. "You may think it sounds just that easy but trust me, it's not."

"It is if I don't care how much flesh I take off as long as I get this damned thing off."

"Am I really that horrid of company?" he asked with a yawn.

Ace thought back to the previous night and Chastity crawling into his tent, but decided not to comment on it. It was too early to have that conversation.

"I just don't like being restrained. So can we please go find some oil?"

"Not until it's daylight out there," he mumbled. Ace scowled. "Well, what am I supposed to do until then?"

Bishop grabbed her wrist and pulled her forward fast enough that she wasn't able to catch herself. Instead, she flopped on top of him. He wrapped his arms around her so she couldn't get away, and it pulled her right arm behind her back so she had even less leverage for escape. She thrashed around a bit while he just giggled. After a few seconds she stopped struggling and peered down at him.

"Fine. What do you want?"

"You to lay down with me and relax. Just for a bit."

She stiffened. "Why would I lay down with you?"

"Because it's warm and comfortable." He loosened his grip and shifted her so she was lying next to him, cradled between his torso and his right arm. The position pulled her right hand over so it was resting on his stomach. Bishop turned his head and kissed her forehead. He was hoping that a good night sleep had helped to temper her mood a bit.

"Just relax."

Ace rolled her eyes. Instinctively she wanted to chew her arm off just to get away but if she put that fighting response aside she had admit that she enjoyed this attention more than just a little bit. After a few minutes she did relax. When he felt her muscles soften, leaned over to give her a kiss.

A million thoughts went through Ace's mind. She really did enjoy kissing him and on a level it felt kind of right. What was the worst thing that could happen? Maybe she would relax for once in her young life and just enjoy this moment. She would still leave as soon as she could. She figured that once she got on the road and put some miles between them that would make it easy to get Bishop out of her system. She quite enjoyed these new feelings she was experiencing. Except maybe the feelings she got when Chastity was around him. But when his hands started to roam she stopped him instantly and frowned. Kissing and snuggling were one thing but she wasn't ready nor willing to go further than that.

"Can we get up now?" she asked as she sat up and brushed her hair out of her face.

Bishop sighed. "I suppose. Although, I was sort of enjoying that."

He sat up and gently cradled her face with his free hand, then placed a gentle kiss on her lips.

"I care about you, Ace. I'd really like it if you let me keep you safe. I can take care of you."

Ace didn't say anything. She just sat there as far out of his way as she could while he got up. She felt those internal walls slide back up a bit. She wasn't looking for someone to be her caretaker. Her parents were the last people to take care of her and they were murdered. She had survived just fine on her own for the past ten years.

When they emerged from the tent, they found Jayce sitting at the fire drinking something hot out of a metal mug. Bishop walked over and sat down, leaving Ace to stand and scowl.

"You could take a seat you know." Jayce said as he looked over at her.

"I'd rather get going. Do you have any oil or grease?"

Jayce looked at Bishop, who shrugged. "She thinks she can pull her hand out if it's lubed up. I don't think it will work but she doesn't seem to want to take my word for it."

Jayce took another sip of his drink before handing it to Bishop. "Aright, I guess we can get something. But we would have to go to the next town. It isn't too far from here as the crow flies but it would take about a day and a half by car, maybe."

Ace frowned. "A day and a half by car? There has to be a closer town than that."

"Maybe remnants of towns. But for an actual established town that has a store and supplies and that we can sort of safely walk into, that's a day and a half from here. That is where we will go to get those damned things off."

Ace's scowl returned. "I understand why I am eager to get this done but why are you so eager? Can't wait to lock me up and interrogate me alone?"

Jayce shot a look at Bishop. "Gee, thanks for trying to make me the enemy here." He looked back at Ace. "We aren't going to lock you up. It would make my life easier if you would just agree to travel with us for a little bit while we figure out what to do."

"I just want to be on my way. I was doing fine before your stupid leader tried to get himself killed. Since then, all he has done is create problems for me." She shook the chain for emphasis.

"Hey now. I haven't done anything except try to help you out a little."

"Really? That's why you tried to capture me, then you drug me into the basement of an unstable building that collapsed on top of us, then you locked me in a room for two weeks? Then you hunted me down and got us chained together. Thanks for the help," she exclaimed.

A sleeping men from a tent complained about the noise. Ace didn't really care too much. The sun was up now and there was no reason for them to be asleep.

"I didn't do anything with the intent of you getting injured or harmed or upset. I locked you up so I could figure out why every patrol squad in the area was searching for you."

Ace hesitated, but she managed to play it off with a roll of her eyes. "Why didn't you just ask? I would have told you. The stupid Sergeant who captured me had a personal vendetta. He probably died in the explosion which means that my problems are solved."

"Actually our reports say he got out." Jayce interjected.

Ace paused for a few seconds, absorbing the news. "What? But how?"

"I guess there was a bomb shelter installed in the base somewhere. He and a few others managed to get in it in time. They weren't able to get out right away because of the debris, so they had to wait until reinforcements came to dig them out."

"Well, that doesn't matter because I plan on clearing out of the area as soon as you all decide I'm free to go. When do we leave?"

"I suppose we can start out this afternoon." Jayce said with a glance around the camp.

"Where is the town?" Ace asked out of curiosity.

"West from here. We usually try to avoid it, it's a common area for soldiers to pass through. But we have kept a low profile in this area. They think we are continuing east so they shouldn't expect us over in that area at all." Bishop said as he handed the empty cup back to Jayce.

"I suppose we are going to have to have one of the boys take your animals back to one of our larger bases while you are away. We won't have room nor time for the dog and there is no way to getting your horse there."

Ace frowned, she hadn't thought about that. Another three days without her animals.

"Fine. But take them to Gwen and have her take care of them. I don't trust anyone else in that base of yours. She will be at the main camp, won't she?"

Bishop and Jayce both frowned but said nothing further on the matter. They reassured her that Gwen would take care of the animals as if they were her own.

"Oh, and tell Chastity she will be going back to the main base," Bishop said to Jayce as he stood and then he motioned to Ace. "Come on. We need to get your animals ready to go."

Ace wandered out of the camp with Bishop in tow. When she had gone under the tent wall, Wolf must have headed to the woods for hunting. He wasn't going to be very happy that she was leaving him again. In the last month she had been separated from them more than she had in all the years they had been together. She knew Flint would be okay. He was a little uneasy around strange people but Ace thought Gwen's gentle nature would help him settle in. Even Wolf should take a liking to the girl.

Bishop complained a few times about how far they were traveling, but Ace ignored him. She missed the peacefulness of the woods when she was alone. The music of the forest settled her. Even though Bishop was scaring everything away she was enjoying being away from the camp.

When they finally came to a creek, Ace paused. She studied the ground, looked downstream, and then whistled Flint's tune. If Wolf was in the area he would come too, even though it wasn't his specific call. His personal whistle was more so that Ace could call him alone and needed the horse to stay away. It took a few minutes of waiting and one more complaint from Bishop, but the gelding finally trotted into view. His legs were wet, as Ace had suspected. The horse loved water almost more than Wolf.

She ran her hands over every inch of him. Bishop really complained at that point. In order for Ace to inspect her horse, Bishop's left hand had to follow her everywhere. Ace just rolled her eyes and ignored him. She was surprised at how the man's presence was starting to feel like a normal part of her life.

When she concluded that Flint was healthy and sound, she straightened herself and tapped the horse's chin. That was all she needed to signal Flint to follow her. Together, they all started the walk back towards the camp.

They had walked a fair distance from the camp, farther than Ace realized. On the way she periodically called Wolf, knowing he would show up eventually.

Bishop had stopped complaining near the beginning of the return trip when he realized Ace wasn't going to respond. He took this time to study her a little bit. For the first time she seemed completely relaxed and at ease, smiling when small rays of sunshine hit her face and listening to the birds. Every now and then she absent-mindedly reached a hand out to her horse and touched under his chin, and every few hundred yards she would whistle a specific tune.

The dog silently appeared out of the shadows, causing Bishop to jump, and trotted over to the woman and rubbed against her hip. When Ace glanced at Bishop, she frowned.

"What?"

"What what?" Bishop asked mischievously.

"Why are you looking at me like that?"

"I was just studying you when your guard was down, for a change."

She tensed. "My guard is never down."

Bishop raised his free hand in a show of surrender, "Okay, lowered. Your guard was lowered. I was just enjoying seeing you … peaceful I guess."

Ace shrugged. "It's a peaceful place. I love the forest. We didn't have woods like these in Skull Valley. I love it when I come north."

"Why don't you just stay north?"

"I travel south for the winters. Easier to survive that way. Winters are brutal when you don't have a roof over your head. I almost died because of the cold one year."

"Just because of the cold? Couldn't you get a fire going or something?" Bishop asked, honestly confused by the idea of dying simply because of weather.

"It's not that easy. I didn't have Flint or Wolf for the first few years you know. Travel was slow, and I had to do all of my own hunting. The wood was too damp to get a fire going. It was either raining or snowing and I couldn't get dry."

"How old were you?"

Ace scrunched her brows together as she tried to push away the bad memory. "Fourteen, I guess? Close to that, anyway."

"Was that the only close call?"

Ace laughed. "Goodness no. Haven't you been alive all of this time? Don't you know how hard it is to stay alive outside of your little camps?"

Bishop frowned. "I guess I was older. And I got in with the rebels pretty quick. With them, you have to worry about a soldier shooting you down, but other than that you are well taken care of."

Ace nodded but didn't say anything, so Bishop pressed further.

"What were some other close calls you had?"

She sighed. "Well, one year, before I decided to travel back south before the snows hit, I fell through some ice. I thought I would try ice fishing. I knew the ice was thick and I had stolen an axe. Turns out it wasn't *that* thick apparently, at least not in the spot I was at. Only a few hacks in the ice cracked between my feet. I could hear it going for a while in several directions. I just stood there frozen for a moment. When it all stopped, I stood up straight so I could leave. Big mistake. That's all it took. I plunged down faster than I could blink."

"How did you get out?"

"A little education and a lot of luck. I didn't plunge down very deep and came up in the broken ice. I remembered to breath calmly, not to gasp for air or hyperventilate even though that's all your lungs want to do. Kept my head above water, I knew I only had about five minutes before I would lose coordination. I found the edge of the solid ice, and basically swam onto it. I was able to get my upper body back on the ice and slowly worked my way out."

"There is no way you were functional enough to start a fire in the woods after that?"

Ace shook her head. "No, I could barely move. I ended up in abandoned town I knew was nearby and crawled into one of the buildings. I set an empty bookshelf on fire with oil from a lamp. It was enough to keep me alive through the night. And I started traveling south after I recovered."

Bishop looked at the ground. "I guess I forgot what it was like to survive on my own. It's been a while."

Ace just shrugged. "I'm not on my own anymore. I have these two," she motioned to Flint and Wolf. "They help a lot."

As they neared the edge of the camp Bishop pulled Ace to a stop.

"I want you to at least consider something over the next few days we are together. Just please think about it. Think about staying with me, with us. I promise if you ever need to get away we can send you out on a mission or you can just leave for a few weeks and come back whenever you want."

Ace pursed her lips in thought. It sounded nice but she just wasn't sure she could do it. She had been alone for so many years. She had never given any more thought to her future other than staying alive. "I could really leave whenever I want?"

"Yes, I promise. Maybe not right away. Jayce will want to do his thing and check into your past. Make sure your story checks out and all. But I promise once that's over you could come and go whenever. I will respect your desire for solitude and maybe try to understand it but I want to be with you."

Ace couldn't even imagine the stability of having a roof over her head, full pantry and wardrobe whenever she wanted. A boyfriend, or whatever you called in when you were in the middle of a war. It was such a foreign concept for her. But there were two big problems she needed to accept. If Jayce was any good at digging then he would find out some information about her that would instantly make her one of their prisoners. And there was the other problem.

"What about Chastity?" she asked, her tone a little bitter.

Bishop's brows pressed together. "What about her?"

Ace frowned. "She is all over you every time she sees you. If I am so important to you then why do you stick your tongue down her throat every time she leaps onto you like a hungry flea?" She was pretty proud of her word choices and at least he had the nerve to blush.

"There is nothing between us, if that is what you're asking." he said quietly.

"Really? Do you greet all of the females you come across in such a fashion?"

He frowned. "Wait, you are judging me? If I remember correctly you are the one who made a move on me at our second encounter."

"Oh please," she scoffed. "I was just distracting you to get away. I never intended on seeing you again."

"Is that your usual mode of distraction, then?" he accused.

"That was my first time ever kissing *anyone*, not that it's any of your business."

Bishop paused. He could not believe what she just confessed to him. "Really?"

"What you expected me to be professional or something? Because I seem like the kind of person who even has much social experience? I told you I hadn't spoken to anyone in years before you. When I said I have been alone, I meant A-L-O-N-E."

"I know, I-I just didn't think about it that way. Most women your age, you know-"

She frowned. "No, I don't know. That is what I am trying to get through to you!"

Bishop looked at her for a second before sighing. "Sometimes I forget just how much you don't know."

"Ok, before you changed the subject, were you trying to convince me that you haven't had sex with Chastity?" she asked bluntly.

Bishop physically flinched. "You know most people just say 'sleep with' or 'been with' or something instead of the actual word."

Ace rolled her eyes. "I'm not stupid. I know that, I just don't care. Again, I never had to worry about using socially acceptable words. Now, answer the question."

"No. I haven't slept with Chastity." he said, a little irritated. "Happy?"

"A little," she admitted.

"Now will you promise to think about staying with me?"

She was quiet for a few seconds, looking at the chain connecting her to him. She didn't have to decide now. She could use the next few days to see if she could sort out her feelings for him and how it would fit in with her life.

"Are you asking as the Rebel leader for me to join you and your people? Or are you asking just as a person for me to stay with you?"

He smiled a little, "You really don't understand how to be any other way than blunt, do you?"

She shrugged.

"I want you to stay with me, because I don't want to picture you not being around anymore."

"I'll think about it," she concluded. Bishop smiled as he leaned down and kissed her gently on the lips. "Come on, Jayce is probably wondering where we have been off to."

They stepped into the camp. Both of Ace's animals were still following her, though Flint was a little twitchy now that there were more people around.

Jayce impatiently stalked up to them within moments, just as Bishop had suspected.

"Where have you two been for so long?" he asked.

Ace didn't like the look he gave them, like he knew something about them that he wasn't supposed to but she didn't quite understand it. Did he really think they were doing something other than looking for her horse and dog?

Bishop frowned at him. "We had to find her animals. She lets them wander. The horse was a few miles from here."

"Well, let's get them back to the main base. We can head to the town at first light."

Ace threw her tack into the back of the ancient jeep they were using and hooked a long rope to Flint's halter. The rest of the camp would go ahead to the base and start getting supplies together while Jayce, Bishop, and Ace would drive slower so Flint could keep up. Wolf refused to get in the vehicle until Ace was in, then he reluctantly hopped into the back.

Chastity didn't look too happy when Bishop told her she was to go to the main camp and wait but she followed her orders and didn't throw too big of a tantrum about it.

Without the burden of tack, Flint was able to sustain a decent pace for five miles before Ace called for them to slow down so he could catch his breath.

It was a little over ten miles to the main base, which Bishop informed her was in Blanchard, Idaho. She had no idea where that was other than somewhere near the Washington state border. All she knew was that she loved the forests in the area. They were filled with stately pine trees and pristine bodies of water. She was concerned about leaving her animals behind. She had never trusted their care to anyone else. She had hoped Gwen would keep an eye on them while she was gone.

When they pulled into the camp Ace frowned. This wasn't where she had been before.

"Where are we?" She asked Bishop.

"Our main camp."

"I thought that was where you had locked me up?"

Bishop laughed. "No not at all, that camp is too small for our main base of operations."

"Is Gwen here?"

"No. But I promise your animals will be well taken care of."

Ace sighed. She wasn't sure she liked this place. It was huge, and there were way too many people around. It made her uncomfortable.

"Where is the place we are going to tomorrow?" she asked Bishop as she took off Flint's halter and watched him trot off towards the trees.

"Washington. It will take a bit longer to get there because we have to go around the Tri-Cities to get to it."

Ace had no idea why that was relevant. When she traveled through Washington, she went through the north part of it, skirting a main freeway for reference. "And that's bad?"

"That's where one of the largest government bases is," he said with a tone like "duh".

"Oh. I thought that would be in Olympia or something?" She knew she didn't have a lot of geographical knowledge of Washington but Bishop was making her feel like an idiot.

She must have had a blank look on her face because Bishop decided to explain a bit further.

"All of the obvious political places, like Olympia, Denver, and DC, were the first places of attack by the rebellion. There is nothing left there but giant holes in the ground. It was an effort to break the government quickly. It worked for a while and caused them to refocus while we went to ground. Now the head of all of the bases is in the Tri-Cities, in the southwest part of the State. We steer clear of it under all circumstances for safety reasons. It is well fortified. We take the back roads to avoid it. We will have to avoid what used to be Spokane and that area. Some of the roads aren't in the best shape so travel will be slow and we want to avoid traffic."

"Got it." Ace had no desire to go anywhere near that many soldiers nor people. The added travel time would be well worth it.

Unfortunately, still being stuck to Bishop and back at the base made sleeping arrangements a little more uncomfortable. It made everything a little uncomfortable. Nature calls were handled with some creativity. While Bishop didn't seem to have any issues with modesty, Ace wasn't about to share that activity with anyone! She had them string up a special curtain made out of a heavy blanket. It wasn't ideal and she still blushed to the point of death but it was the only acceptable solution. She offered to use a hacksaw to sever off Bishop's wrist but he didn't support that idea.

Sleeping arrangements were going to be difficult also. She wasn't going to be able to just sleep on the other side of the tent wall. Here in the base, he slept in his own quarters. In a bed. They had a whole room to themselves.

She learned it was actually in the same building as his office. He explained to her that originally it hadn't been, but he slept in his office so much that they just turned one of the back rooms into his regular bedroom.

No one else had quarters in this building, so they would be one hundred percent alone. Ace wasn't so sure she was okay with that. Sure she was considering staying because of him, with him, but that didn't mean she had to cross any of her physical comfort boundaries before she was ready. Still though, her options were limited.

Once Flint was settled in the back woods and the sun was setting there was no more avoiding it. Wolf insisted on staying with her. Normally she would send him to protect Flint but she wanted him in the room with her and Bishop, just as a comforting presence. Also, having a protective four foot tall wolfhound nearby should deter Bishop from taking advantage of their privacy.

"So either we are both sleeping on the floor or we are both sleeping in the bed." Bishop said as he opened a door and led her into the room. There wasn't much room on the floor for the two of them, not without reorganizing the entire room first.

"It gets pretty cold in here at night, so the floor might not be the ideal option." He said with a shrug. He was apparently oblivious to Ace's discomfort. Ace just stood in the doorway and looked at the bed. It was big enough that they could both lay down and not touch each other. She had slept next to him before, sort of. How horrible could it be?

"Well, I'm exhausted so I am going to get some sleep. I vote for the bed." He looked at her expectantly.

"Fine, bed it is. But you better stay on your side."

Bishop smirked, "I'll behave myself, don't worry."

At least she didn't have to worry about him taking his shirt off to sleep, it was pretty much impossible with the cuffs. She wished she had been wearing her leather jacket when the misfortune happened, but she was just in a tank top and there was no tent wall for privacy here. The handcuffs didn't prevent him from taking his pants off, however. As soon as he started undoing his belt Ace tensed and covered her eyes.

"What are you doing?" she gasped.

Bishop shrugged. "It's uncomfortable to sleep in jeans. I'm taking them off. Aren't you?"

"Of course not!" she almost squeaked, much to her disappointment.

The only time she ever took her jeans off was when she was bathing. She made sure the event happened at least once a week but no one was ever around, and she most certainly didn't *sleep* without them on. That was just inviting trouble. There had been many times that she woke up and had to flee for survival without time to spare. She would be dead by now if she had to stop and pull her pants on constantly.

Bishop laughed at her again. "Well suite yourself, but you don't know what you're missing. Especially since I'm guessing it's been awhile since you've been in a real bed. And I have cotton sheets. Might as well enjoy the full experience." He winked at her.

Wolf settled himself on the floor at the foot of the bed and went straight to sleep, not waiting for them to figure out what they were doing. With the dog on the floor it was obvious just how little room there was for them unless they slept on the bed.

Ace kicked off her shoes and took off her belts and all her various weapons, but kept her jeans on when she crawled into the bed and lay down on the far side.

Bishop was right behind her. He pulled the covers up from the foot of the bed and covered both of them. Ace settled in stiffly, but Bishop respected her space and she relaxed within a few minutes. She had to admit, the bed felt amazing. The last time she slept in a bed was years ago, and she didn't remember it being this comfortable. She sighed contentedly and fell quickly into a sound sleep.

***

Ace woke the next morning to Bishop's chuckling. She slowly opened one eye and saw him leaning over her, his black hair tousled from sleeping.

"What?" She mumbled, placing her free arm over her eyes.

"Sleep well?" he asked humorously.

Ace scooted up towards the head board and sat up. She had sunk down into the bed during the night and she could tell already that her hair was everywhere. Barely any of it was still in the braid she had left it in when she fell asleep.

"Do you want a mirror?" he teased.

Ace scowled at him. "No, I don't." She pulled the band out of her hair and put it around her wrist while she combed her fingers through her hair.

"We have showers here, you know," he mentioned while trying to move his left hand in motion with her right one to avoid hindering her work. He thought it was kind of nice watching her reorganizing her hair. It was such a normal, female behavior and seemed at odds with the person she tried so hard to be.

"I haven't had a shower since I was thirteen," she said dreamily.

"Well, that is something we will have to fix."

Ace stopped what she was doing long enough to give him an unamused look and shook the chain in his face. "I don't think so, at least not in the near future. But nice try."

He smirked. "Well then you are just going to have to deal with the steam, any maybe enjoy the view."

Her brows furrowed in question.

"I'm taking a shower before we leave. You can choose to stand on the other side of the screen, fully clothed and get wet, or you can take one yourself."

She paled. "Can't you wait? I'm not comfortable with this."

"Wait? Are you kidding me? I haven't gotten one the whole time I was out hunting for you. I've waited plenty. I'm not saying you have to do anything except stand there. Okay?" He got up without waiting for her to complain further and drug her along to the bath house.

They made their base on an old resort. The base had a large bathing room with multiple showers. There was a row of five showers and each individual stall was separated with curtains. Bishop went straight to the first one, putting his left hand up over the dividing curtain.

"There's a towel and soaps in there already for ya' if you decide to enjoy a hot shower. I know I will."

"How are you going to shower with your shirt on?" She scoffed.

"Simple." There was a pause, then suddenly his shirt was tossed onto the dividing curtain. "Problem solved." His shirt was wadded up, hanging at his wrist.

The water turned on, and for a few minutes Ace kept up her resolve. But as soon as the steam became visible she broke down and stripped off her clothes.

She took as quick a shower as she could, she was finished and re-clothed before Bishop even turned off his water. Even a shower at break neck speeds had felt heavenly.

She paid him back for taking such a long shower by making him stand while she French braided her hair. He had to figure out how to move his left arm along with her movements. That was just icing on the cake for her.

Once they were ready to go, Ace took Wolf out to Flint, who was hovering near the edge of the base. He seemed to like the woods as much as Ace did, but being so close to all of the people was making him nervous again.

Ace scratched Wolf behind his ears, then pointed at the horse and told him to guard.

Wolf knew the drill, protect the horse. Ace often left Flint. It was rare for her to leave Wolf somewhere but it happened enough for him to know his job.

Jayce was already impatiently waiting for them at the ancient jeep, so she kept the goodbye short. She would be seeing them again in a few days.

Chastity once again tried to weasel her way into going along but Bishop told her he needed her help at the base. Ace wasn't sure what exactly she brought to the table other than an ample supply of spandex. She thought that Bishop was still being too generous and friendly with the girl.

A few other men did come along. Bishop explained that it was for protection. Ever since his near death experience, Jayce had been a little over protective. It made for an uncomfortable ride as the seats were narrow and every one of them was full. On top of that was the supplies in the back.

Jayce was, of course, overly prepared. Bishop explained that he was always like this, which then made Jayce join the conversation saying he had to be over prepared to make up for Bishop being too care free. Ace was enjoying the relaxed banter between the two friends.

***

They traveled until an hour before dark, stopping with enough light to make camp and cook some food. Ace was happy to finally get out of the vehicle. Her legs were cramped from not moving and she couldn't stand to listen to the guys talk any longer.

They had some sort of stew for dinner. Ace thought it was the most amazing thing she had ever tasted.

"It's not that complicated of a stew, in fact it's very plain. The only thing in it, aside from the meat and veggies, is salt," Jayce said, not understanding her obsession with the food.

"Ohh," Ace's eyes closed as she took another bite. "I forgot about salt. I love salt."

"How could you forget about salt?" Jayce asked.

"The towns along my usual travel route are completely ransacked, nothing left in them but buildings usually. Last time I got my hands on some salt was five or more years ago."

"Oh, yeah. You were on your own. I keep forgetting that."

Bishop gave Jayce a look but Ace didn't understand why, it's not like she was upset that she traveled alone. She enjoyed her solitude, as long as she had her animals.

When it was time to get some sleep Ace surprised Bishop and herself when she settled down next to him instead of crawling under the wall of the tent. The night in his room back at the base had helped her overcome some of her personal discomforts. She had slept right next to him and didn't burst into flames nor did he transform into a man-shaped octopus trying to get his tentacles around her. She still wouldn't let his hands wander, but she was becoming more comfortable having him close to her. Bishop took advantage of every bit of the improvement, and stole kisses whenever he got the chance.

***

The next morning they got started in their travels fairly quickly. A little bread and dried meat for breakfast, then they piled back into the jeep and continued on their way.

"How far do we have to travel today?" Ace asked.

"Only about an hour or two," Bishop replied.

"Where is it exactly?"

"Toppenish. It was a diverse little town before the uprisings. Not a lot of wealth, just a typical farm town for the area."

Ace frowned. "What made people rebuild it?"

"I think it was more of a convenience thing. Only about half of the town has been salvaged at this point, but it's still one of the biggest citizen-run towns in the area."

"The Tri-Cities place doesn't interfere?" she asked.

"Well, they patrol it often and they have the town council terrified. There are guards everywhere. But I don't think they do much actual interfering with the people who live there. Visitors are free game, though."

That made her a little uncomfortable. "Then shouldn't we be worried?"

"Oh, we aren't going in through the front," he said with a tone like "duh".

"Why not?"

"Because we would have to talk to the guards, give them our names and such and let them search the jeep. A certain set of cuffs might tip 'em off that we might not be who we say we are. Not to mention that Scavengers hang out around the outside of the front gates. The guards will only protect you if you make it inside."

Ace had seen what Scavengers did to people they apprehended. She was never a victim herself and she never helped those who were being attacked, but she watched from a distance. A few years after the Retaliation she had been so desperate for human contact. She didn't have her animals yet and she was lonelier than she thought humanly possible. She had considered going into a small re-built town to live there near someone, anyone. But something in the back of her mind told her to wait and see what happened to the others who entered first.

She watched what she assumed to be sisters get attacked by the scavengers hiding alongside the road near the entrance to the town. The guards just stood there and watched, like Ace did. They all had guns in hand, but no one fired. She didn't understand how a group could prey on innocents like that. They were nothing more than common criminals.

"So how are we gonna get in?" she asked to change the subject.

"We have a way in through the back, don't worry." Jayce said.

A back way in was true enough. An hour later the jeep turned off the road and went straight through the fields. When she gave Bishop a questioning look, he seemed a little annoyed.

"There aren't a lot of trees around here if you didn't notice, so we have to be pretty extreme about sneaking up to our back entrance."

"This seems like a lot of trouble just for some oil," Ace muttered.

"Oh, aren't you cute. We aren't just getting oil. If that was the only thing on our shopping list we wouldn't have come. We are also in need of some supplies," Jayce said without emotion.

Ace decided not to reply to that. She was pretty sure Jayce didn't like her, and she didn't feel the need to encourage that opinion by irritating him any further.

Another thirty minutes later they came to a stop in an area that barely concealed the vehicle. They had to drive slow enough that they didn't raise up much dust. It felt like it was hours, driving at the impossibly slow speed. It must have been the same place they came to every time, because supplies were hidden in the dirt at the base of the few trees that existed. And they had a camouflage netting that was used to cover the jeep to help it blend in a little better.

Jayce handed her a semi-automatic pistol, "Use it on any of us, and I will shoot you myself."

She rolled her eyes at him, but nodded her understanding. Like she would shoot one of them when she was attached to Bishop.

"Alright. Ace, Bishop, and Carter are going to come with me into the town. I want the rest of you hidden at the edge of the perimeter in case something happens and we need your help. We should be in and out within an hour. Let's move," Jayce announced.

It was one of the few times Ace was glad she was attached to Bishop. She wouldn't have known how to approach the perimeter the way the rest of them did.

The sage brush was thick enough to hide them most of the way as they slunk up to the fence and pulled apart the chain link. Ace hadn't even noticed the fence was cut. She thought they were either going to have to go over or under it but instead they walked right through it. Then they ran into the building that was just across a small expanse of ground.

The first building was an apothecary. Ace could tell what it was the second she was inside by the smell of herbs. Jayce made a motion to Carter who snuck around gathering things that they needed and piling them into a bag he had slung over his shoulder.

The rest of them moved on. Apparently this strip of stores were all connected because instead of ending up back outside when they went through a door, they were in another store. And not just any store, but a clothing boutique much to Ace's happiness. She didn't even hesitate as she drug Bishop around the store and stuffed white tank tops, blue jeans, and bras into a duffle bag that she grabbed off a shelf.

Once she had the bag stuffed she turned to Bishop and Jayce with a huge smile.

"This has been a wonderful trip!" she exclaimed.

"You can't just take those." Jayce growled at her.

Ace frowned. "Why not? You guys are taking stuff. Besides, I always do this when I find myself somewhere that has plenty."

Just then Carter came through the door with his own bag of stolen goods.

"We don't steal them, Love," Bishop said. "We leave payment. This is how these people make their living. If they don't make enough at the end of every month and can't pay the guards, they are shot. If they pay the guards but can't buy food, they starve."

"And if I don't take stuff, I die. It's how the world works these days. It's called survival," Ace shot back.

Jayce glared at her so hard she thought his eyes would pop out of his head. She had never given much thought to how taking these things would affect other people. Until now, all she had to do was think of where she would hunt, where she would sleep, and where she was going next. It seemed like a perfectly normal way to live until she met these guys. With a dramatic sigh, she pulled a jeweled ring out of her pocket and placed in on the counter near the front.

"Happy now?" she demanded as she turned back to them. Jayce didn't smile, but he stopped glaring and nodded to the other door they had to go through. He decided not to ask where she got the ring from. Carter took Ace's bag of clothes from her as they continued on. The next store was of no use to them. Ace wasn't even sure what it was for because they didn't pause long enough for a look. The fourth store they came to was exactly what they needed. There must have been a few vehicles in this town because the automotive shop had plenty of supplies to keep several cars going with regular maintenance.

"Oil," Jayce said as he tossed a glass jar of it to Ace.

Ace happily opened it and dumped half the contents down her right arm.

Bishop jumped, but that only caused more oil to get on him. He made a disgusted sound and gave her a look, but she only smiled innocently at him. Once her arm was properly lubed, she sat down, dragging Bishop with her, and put the edge of her boots on each side of the cuff. When she was braced properly, she started slowly working the cuff towards her finger tips with her feet.

It started to get really painful at the base of her hand, but she didn't stop. She closed her eyes and clenched her jaw and kept pushing down with her feet until suddenly it popped completely off.

"Yes!" Ace celebrated. "I'm free!"

"Shh!" Jayce put his finger to his lips for emphasis.

"Sorry." She muttered as she flexed her hand and rotated her shoulders. "Now what?"

"We have to get-"

Bishop stopped as the sound of an alarm went off through the store. Panic flared in Ace's chest. "Did we trigger something?!"

Bishop held up his hand, telling her to be quiet as he moved towards the front of the store and peered out of the windows. Ace grabbed a rag off of a shelf to clean her arm, then followed Bishop and Jayce to the windows. Carter had already gone back to the fence with their things before they entered the automotive shop to drop off the bags and was then to return free handed for any additional assistance.

"We have to get out of here." Bishop said quietly while watching the streets.

"What is it?" Jayce asked, all of his muscles tense.

"Looks like a raid."

Alarms went off in Ace's head. "A raid? By the government? But why?"

"No, by the Scavengers. Every now and then a group of them gets big enough to raid towns like this."

Ace peaked out of a window and saw people running like mad in the streets. Some of them entered the same shop and ran to the back to hide, but none of them paid any attention to the three hovering by the front windows.

Ace saw the Scavengers. They were easy to tell from everyone else. They were unwashed, unshaven, and had an evil look of glee marring their features. Citizens and people fled down the street in front of them. It quickly became a setting of complete chaos.

"Come on, we're done here for now," Bishop said as he and Jayce started to back away from the window. He held a hand out to Ace. She was just about to take his hand and follow them when she saw a girl, no more than thirteen or fourteen years old, trying to get away from one of the Scavengers. She was scrambling across the ground on her hands and knees. Every time she tried to stand up, a ragged man kicked her back down. Tears were streaming down her face, collecting dirt.

This wasn't much different from things Ace had seen over the last nine years. And she had never felt the need to help before. The guilt had always sat heavily in her stomach while she safely hid away, but she quieted that guilt by telling herself that she couldn't do anything dead and tried to make that be enough to live with those feelings.

She was unsure why, but this time was different. Maybe it was because being with the Rebels opened her up to new possibilities and were helping her to see things from a different view. Whatever it was, it caused her to stand up and kick open the door.

With all of the chaos in the street, Ace was surprised at how calmly she walked out. She pulled the silver semi-automatic pistol out of her waist band, aimed, and shot the guy pinning the girl to the ground. He dropped to the street and was still.

That part of the plan-on-the-fly went very well. It was the following events that went bad.

The man hadn't been completely alone. While he had been alone in his attack of the young girl, he was not alone in his attack on the street. Several men turned with the gunshot and pinned their eyes on Ace. She hadn't really thought the next part through. She did the one thing that she was good at: shoot and run.

The girl she saved was nowhere to be seen, already hidden away somewhere. Ace shot at anyone who aimed a gun at her while backing up to the store she had come out of. She needed to get out of there before one of them caught her and before Jayce decided to leave without her.

As she reached the door, something bounced off the wall and landed at her feet. When Ace glanced down, it took a few seconds for her brain to register what she was seeing, mostly because it had been so long since she had seen a real one up close, and also because she had certainly never had one thrown at her. As soon as she recognized the hand grenade was missing its pin, she kicked it away, turned and ran for her life not even registering the bullets that were flying past her. Luckily the street was pretty empty by this time.

It felt like a microsecond before the explosion blew her off her feet, sending her into the wall of the building she was running next to. Right before she hit the wall, she had the thought that it would have been smarter to get inside the building instead of just running down the street. Everything slowed down as the reality of what happened hit her as hard as the explosion.

She connected with the wall and her vision went black. Pain burst through every part of her body as she felt herself slam into the ground and heard the echoing sounds of gunfire, but they sounded off, like she was in a bubble.

Ace managed to open one eye but her vision was blurred and the ground tilted sideways making her nauseous. She saw people running towards her, and she tried to pull herself to her feet to get away, but her limbs wouldn't obey the command. As one of the bodies neared her, shooting over the top of her, she tried again and managed to get her arm underneath herself to push up, but a shock of pain ran up her elbow to the base of her neck and she crumpled back to the ground.

She felt the edges of her vision going black and she recognized the feeling of unconsciousness trying to claim her but she fought it off. Voices were speaking around her, but she couldn't understand anything.

As Ace felt herself being lifted off the ground, she decided to let the blackness take her away. If they were going to kill her, she didn't want to be aware of it. And if they weren't, she definitely didn't want to be awake for what they wanted. Dying would be better.

Chapter 8

"Move now!" Bishop yelled to the men as they picked up Ace. She was covered in blood, but they were in too much of a hurry to figure out where it was all coming from. He had watched in horror as the blast from the grenade sent her sailing into the wall. The only upside to the explosion was that it took out half of the scavengers as well.

If Ace hadn't kicked it back towards them, they would have been safe and she would most likely be dead. As it was, she still might be. But he didn't have time to stop and think about that now. They still had to get away.

Carter and Billy were carrying Ace while Jayce, Bishop, and Ryan were holding off the guards that showed up with all of the commotion. The guards had overtaken the Scavengers right after the blast and were shooting at anyone who moved in the street. Their semi-automatic rifles managed to keep the guards hiding behind buildings and vehicles until they made it to the fence. Once there, the three men who were shooting stayed for half a minute longer to give Carter and Billy enough time to get through the fence and head to the jeep.

"Now!" Bishop yelled as he stopped shooting and dove through the fence. They were going to have to find a new way into this town if they ever came back. He doubted their little hole in the fence was going to be there much longer.

The three of them bolted for the jeep, occasionally shooting over their shoulder to deter any pursuers.

Ryan jumped in the driver seat as Carter and Billy laid Ace down in the back on top of their supplies. They jumped in with her to try and hold her steady during the initial getaway. Bishop and Jayce jumped in and stood up through the nonexistent roof and kept shooting. Ryan sped away to the closest cover they could safely stop at to stabilize Ace and determine how serious her injuries were.

"Can she make it to the base?" Ryan called over his shoulder while trying to avoid rocks and large sagebrush. Bishop glanced in the back. Carter was attempting to clean her off with a shirt he found so he could see where she was bleeding from.

"Carter, status!" Bishop yelled. All Bishop could see was blood everywhere. He felt the blood drain from his face when he saw how pale she was.

"Stop when you can!" he called back. "We should have enough medical supplies to stabilize her until we get to camp but she isn't gonna make it long like this. I think she took a bullet. Probably has a concussion at least. Best I can tell ya' right now."

Carter wasn't a formal doctor, but he shadowed one in the base whenever he wasn't out helping Bishop. He was their best field medic. He was good enough to fix most of the problems they encountered and to hold someone together long enough to get to real help.

"Ryan, step on it and head towards base. Stop when you find a place with enough decent cover to hide out at for an hour. Don't bother with roads for now," Bishop called forward.

Bishop and Jayce stood in the backseat watching for any signs of pursuit for a little over an hour before Ryan finally let off the accelerator and pulled into a small grouping of trees at the bank of a creek. Billy jumped out and laid out one of the tents on the ground so there would be something other than dirt to place the still unconscious Ace on.

Carter and Bishop moved her out of the jeep and Carter got to work right away. He cleaned her up as best as he could, noting all of her injuries. Aside from the head wound, she was mostly going to be covered in bruises and multiple abrasions. The main concern was her state of unconsciousness and the bullet that penetrated her leg. It came dangerously close to her femoral artery and he couldn't get the bleeding to stop.

He worked as quickly as he could, cleaning every wound down to the smallest scrape, and place a compression bandage around her leg which was still bleeding.

"Alright, that's all I can do for now. We need to get her to Shawn if she is gonna have any chance," Carter said tiredly as he wiped the sweat from his forehead. Bishop looked her over with concern. "Do you want a suture kit to sew up that leg? It's still bleeding!"

Carter looked up at his friend with understanding. "No, man. We don't want to trap anything in there. We need to get to an OR of some sort and clean it up proper. This is the best we can do in the field. We don't want to do anything to make it worse."

Bishop nodded in understanding. He knew to trust Carter. While he had seen plenty of people injured, it didn't usually affect him like this. He couldn't keep his concern and worry at bay.

"Alright. Everyone load up. I want someone in the back monitoring her at all times. Everyone else will rotate as needed between that and driving. I'll take first shift behind the wheel. We will take a direct route back and we don't stop for anything until we reach base."

***

Ace wanted to retreat back to the depths of darkness at the first feeling of pain she registered. Her head throbbed like something was trying to break open her skull. There was a sharp pain in her leg and a not so dull ache all over her body, and worst of all, an overall sense of weakness that made her start to panic. She tried to open her eyelids, but they wouldn't obey her so she moved to her hands. Her fingers felt slightly swollen and listened only sluggishly. She felt like all of her strength had been sapped away from her, no longer even in existence.

She let out a groan as she managed to convince her eyelids to open and looked at her surroundings. She was in a small, dark room. She was fairly certain she was naked beneath the blankets that covered her but a quick check told her she still had her bra and underwear on. The rest of her however, was in various wraps of linen.

Grudgingly, and with many curses, she managed to pull herself up into a sitting position and rotate so her legs were hanging over the side. She was able to touch the ground with her toes, luckily as she wasn't sure she would have stayed upright if the bed was any higher.

She glanced wistfully at her jeans draped across the back of a chair. They looked as though they had been cut off of her, completely unsalvageable.

She managed to pull herself off the bed and stood with a hand against the wall until a wave of dizziness subsided enough so she could look around. She found a t-shirt and some loose fitting shorts that were almost modest enough for her taste in a linen closet. It took all her scant strength to pull them on. She sat on the chair and caught her breath. A glance around told her she was in medical room of some sort. There were bandages on a counter and some basic supplies.

Once she gained a bit of strength back, she slowly limped her way to the door.

Ace had to hesitate upon opening it to let her eyes adjust from the darker room before continuing. The hallway was bathed in sunshine filtering in through a window. She wondered what day it was. She was now in the hallway and completely clueless on which way to go for freedom. She had no idea where she was or where she was going.

The last thing she could recall was getting to a town with Bishop. She had still been attached to him by the cuffs. Obviously her arm was free now. She had the sudden thought that they might have been captured. If that were the case, they would have most likely had her cuffed to her bed but maybe they weren't expecting her to wake up. Or she was supposed to have a guard and he got lazy or distracted. There was a number of possibilities.

Ace turned back into the room and grabbed a scalpel off the counter before continuing. She wasn't capable of a physical confrontation and it wasn't much of a weapon, but it was better than nothing and easy to conceal.

She slid down the walls of the hallway and finally came to a lobby-looking area where she found the doors that would take her outside. No one appeared to be in the room, not even a sound echoed through the halls. She made her way over to the heavy double doors that led outside. When she slowly opened the doors, people were milling around in a casual manner, not in any kind of uniform, and giving her odd looks as they passed by.

Ace looked around, confused and trying to fight off a wave of dizziness. Her head was throbbing even worse than before and her breathing was labored. She barely walked a few yards before she started to see spots in her vision and began to stumble. With the scalpel clutched in one hand she forced herself to make it across the clearing before having to stop and lean against a tree waiting to pass out again. She took slow deep breaths to try and stay upright.

"What in hells are you doing?"

Ace looked up and saw someone rushing towards her. A man that looked familiar but she couldn't recall a name. He was about her age, maybe a year or two older.

"You aren't supposed to be up yet," Billy said as he glanced around. "I can't believe no one stopped you before you made it this far."

Ace was still trying to catch her breath.

"You don't look so good. How did you make it this far?"

Ace tried to wave him off, but she ended up grabbing ahold of the front of his shirt until the world stopped tilting.

"I'm fine," she muttered.

"No, you're not. We barely saved you. You aren't even supposed to be out of the infirmary yet." He started to guide her back the way she had come from.

"What happened?" she asked.

Billy frowned. "You don't remember?"

She shook her head. That was a bad idea as it sent her world spinning all over again.

"Well, I guess that isn't too surprising. Carter said you hit your head pretty bad. And then you lost a lot of blood from the bullet wound in your leg."

"I was shot?" Ace's vision blurred and her stomach turned upside down. If she would have had anything in it, it would be all over the ground right now.

"Yeah, more like grazed, but still, yeah. Carter and Shawn spent hours patching you up and then for like a week they made sure at least one of them was monitoring your condition."

Another wave of dizziness hit her when a new voice yelled at them. She was going to have to get off her feet before her legs completely gave out from under her.

"Oh good, it's Carter." Billy waved him over as best as he could while holding Ace up.

"What the hell are you doing?" Carter exclaimed when he came up to her other side and helped Billy support her.

"I didn't know where I was," she managed to get out.

"So you wander about half dead instead of waiting for someone to come check on you?"

Ace didn't answer that one, it made her sound stupid when he put it like that. But she didn't know if she was in enemy territory or not. The last thing she was going to do was sit around and wait for someone to fill her in. They managed to get her back into her bed in her dimly lit room.

"Umm, what are you doing with that?" Carter asked when he noticed the scalpel in her hand.

"I thought we got captured," she mumbled.

Carter snorted and took the small knife from her. "And you were going to escape with that?"

"No. But I wasn't going to go down without a fight."

Being back on the stable bed helped steady her dizziness enough for her to open her eyes and look at Carter.

"Billy, go get Shawn. I want his opinion on her condition." Carter said as he checked her bandages to make sure she didn't rip out any of the stitches and start up bleeding again. They spent enough time getting everything put together in the operating room, he didn't want her damaging any of his work because she was too stubborn for her own good. Billy left without another word.

"You gave us a pretty good scare, you know."

Ace sighed. "It certainly feels like it."

"In a little bit of pain?"

"A little? Ace started to laugh but ended up cringing instead.

"Yeah, you're gonna feel it for a while," he said distractedly.

"What's the damage?"

"Concussion, nicked artery, and contusions all over the rest of you."

Ace racked her brain for the definition to that last word. She was certain she read it in a medical book at one point.

"Contusion? That means bruising, right?"

Carter smiled, "Good job. Interested in being a doctor?"

She winced. "No. Just interested in surviving."

The door opened then and someone that Ace had no rec-ollection of walked in.

"Ace, this is Shawn. Or Dr. Shawn. Whichever you want to call him."

The older man smiled. "Nice to officially meet you, Ace. I am going to check the stitches on your leg."

Ace was pretty sure the stitches were under the large bandage on her upper thigh. There was no way she was letting that happen.

"That's okay, I can look at them," she said as she shifted away from him.

Shawn's expression softened. "I promise it will be quick, and you can leave the shorts on."

He moved towards her, but Ace sat up, grabbed the scal-pel taken from her moments ago and held it out.

"I said I can check my wounds just fine by myself," she said as she pressed herself against the wall on the backside of her bed.

Carter stepped forward, "She has a little medical knowledge. If something goes wrong, she should be able to tell you." Then he looked at Ace and said in a direct tone, "Won't you?"

The doctor sighed. "If you aren't comfortable, that's fine. But if anything is questionable, I need you to let me know. It should be fine. The stitches will come out in a few days. We are just playing on the safe side since you were in pretty bad shape."

Ace nodded her agreement.

"Come on, Carter, she needs to rest."

As they stepped out and shut the door Carter turned to Shawn with a frown.

"I don't understand. Why is she so nervous?"

"She is a survivor, Carter, not a Rebel. She hasn't had the benefits all of us have with the Rebel support. She is used to being on her own. It's been just her for several years. We don't have a clue what she has been through to stay alive. And if that means she would prefer to check her own wounds, we will allow it."

"But what if something is wrong? I am sure that she won't tell you. She doesn't want you to touch her at all," Carter said, worry etched into his features.

"I want her to rest a little more for her head to heal. I think we should dose her for a week with some sleeping pills. Once she is under we can keep her there with an IV, but I doubt she will let us stick her with a needle while she is conscious. Even in her weakened state, I am not willing to wrestle her down. By the end of the week she should be well enough to start moving around without us worrying so much," Shawn explained quietly.

"Drug her? Are you sure that won't ruin her trust with us?" Carter asked.

Shawn ran a hand over his face. "It's our only option. I am not sure what else to do. If she starts moving around now it could worsen her condition. I would rather have her healthy and hating me than dying while trying to get away."

Carter looked back at the door to Ace's room.

"What do you think she has been through?" he asked quietly.

Shawn shook his head. "Things a girl her age should only hear stories about. But that is our world now. She is better off with us. Maybe she will realize it." He started to walk away but called over his shoulder, "I want you to check in on her regularly."

Carter turned to leave just in time to see Bishop coming towards him.

"Sir, what can I do for you?"

"Just stopping by." He looked at Ace's door.

Carter took the hint and left. Since their return, he had been buried in paperwork and intelligence reports. Bishop had been visiting Ace for the last several days whenever he had a spare moment or two. He learned his lesson about not visiting from when he held her in his office.

Bishop walked in without knocking, assuming her condition was the same as before. The last report he heard was from Shawn this morning and was that he wasn't sure if she would pull through or not. She was holding on but extremely weak from the extensive blood loss. So when he opened the door and saw Ace sitting in her bed with her back leaning against the wall, he was more than a little surprised.

"You're awake!"

Ace noticed something flash in his expression beneath the surprise and happiness. She wasn't sure what it was, but she would file it away and worry about it later.

She frowned, "Why wouldn't I be awake?"

"We... I thought... I was told you had a very slim chance of living through this. Shawn was afraid you lost too much blood, you've been unconscious for twelve days."

Bishop sat down in the chair beside the bed. "I can't believe you made it, and are sitting here talking to me."

Her frown deepened. "What happened? All I remember is that we went into some town."

"Well," he took a deep breath. "You ran out of the shop. We turned to leave and I thought you had followed. Jayce is actually the one who went after you. He said you ran out to save a girl being attacked in the street. I guess-"

"No," she interrupted. "I mean what happened while I was trying to decide to live or die. You're acting weird. Like you did something wrong or something bad happened that you don't want me to know about." She narrowed her eyes at him when he blushed. "Are Flint and Wolf okay?"

"They are fine. We only see glimpses of them every now and then, but they seem to be thriving well enough on their own."

"Good. So what the hell happened during my big nap?"

Bishop looked at the ground. "Nothing. I just wasn't expecting you to be doing so well. It took me off guard."

She gave him a curious look.

"Now that you are better, I wanted to talk to you about . . . you know. Staying."

She raised a brow. "I believe I have been unconscious for quite some time. I didn't have many spare thoughts about the whole staying or going thing."

Bishop grabbed her hand. "Ace, I want you to stay with me. I can protect you."

"If that is the reason you want me to stay, I will have to decline. I can protect myself."

He frowned. "But that's not the only reason. I want you by my side. I want to see you every day. I want to hear you keep me in line. And most of all, I want you to stay with me because I am falling for you and I don't remember what it is like when you aren't here."

She smiled at him shyly. "Sounds like something a cheesy romance novel would say."

He smirked, "Isn't that a good thing? Especially if I mean it? You make me cheesy."

"I suppose,-" she said with a sigh, "-that I would enjoy staying with you as well."

"Don't sound excited about it or anything," Bishop teased.

She frowned. "I am not very good at this. I don't know how to be with someone. You will have to help me." She thought about it for a few seconds, "And I don't like cheesy. It's weird."

He smiled, "Don't worry, it isn't that difficult. You just have to tell everyone how amazing I am and think about me constantly."

Ace smiled despite herself as she rolled her eyes. Just then the door opened and Carter came into the room. When he glanced up and saw Bishop still in the room he paused.

"Oh, sorry. I didn't know you were still in here." He walked forward and handed a few pills and a mug of something warm to Ace. "I need you to take these pills and drink every drop of liquid in this cup."

"What is it?" Ace asked as she hesitantly took the items.

Carter cleared his throat. "The, uh, the drink is an herbal tea that will help a little with the pain, not much but it should make you more comfortable. And the pills are to help your body replace all of the blood you lost."

She nodded and tossed the pills into her mouth, then chugged down the warm tea. It had just a bit of sweetener in it and tasted pretty good. Immediately she felt a little more relaxed. The pain in her leg subsided and the throbbing in her head eased. But as the seconds ticked by she noticed something else. Her thoughts started to become sluggish and the room spun slightly as she dropped the metal mug to the ground. She tipped to the side as Bishop jumped to his feet and Carter reached out to catch her, easing her down onto the bed.

"What, did you do to me, you bastards?" she asked as she felt her consciousness slipping away.

"You aren't well enough to be moving around yet. And you can be a little determined. Shawn wants you to rest a little longer."

"You drugged me!" She recognized the feeling now.

Carter didn't respond to the accusing look she gave him.

As Ace passed out, she had one more clear thought. The look on Carter's face was guilt and it was the same look that flashed across Bishop's features when he saw her alive.

"What the hell?" Bishop asked when Ace was unconscious.

"She isn't better yet. Her brain needs one more week of healing before she should be getting up and the wound on her leg will be closed by then. We won't have to worry about her getting an infection this way."

Bishop frowned but said nothing further. He made sure early on that he gave the doctors primary word on patients so he couldn't over rule their decision if he was too close to a patient. The rule came into effect when Jayce almost died three years ago and Bishop almost made it worse.

"Fine. But I want to be notified the moment she is awake."

Carter nodded as Bishop left the room and tried to swallow down his guilt.

"Keep your shoulders down so she can't sneak a hit in like that!" Bishop yelled. Ace smirked as Chastity picked herself up off the ground. Carter hadn't been happy when Ace started joining in on the training sessions, but she didn't really care. After the drugs wore off she was kept on lockdown for another week. That had been enough to make her want to go crazy.

Bishop wasn't too happy about it at first either, but when Ace and Chastity got in a brawl, he decided her energy could be put to better use than starting fights. It was Chastity who requested a formal match, thinking she could beat Ace when she was better prepared. She assumed that since Ace had no formal training that this would the perfect setting to humiliate her. But she underestimated Ace's abilities. The next time Ace put her on the ground, Chastity jumped up and lunged at her opponent.

"That's not fair! That was a cheap shot!"

Ace ducked under Chastity and flipped her over her shoulder so the brunette landed flat on her back.

"Have you never been off the farm? There is no such thing as a cheap shot out there. There is the people who live and the people who die. Get it through your head, no one out there is going to let an opportunity pass them by because it's not *fair*."

Chastity pulled herself up and looked at Bishop, waiting for him to say something. Bishop rubbed the back of his neck and avoided eye contact. The last thing he wanted was to get pulled into choosing sides between these two women.

"Look, Chastity, she's right. It's certainly not honorable," he said with a look at Ace, "but there are no rules out there. And, Ace, please stop calling this place the 'farm.' It's our main camp."

Chastity stormed off, leaving Ace alone with Bishop. Ever since she woke up, Bishop had been acting a little off. It wasn't much, and it wasn't always, but sometimes he seemed a little uncomfortable. She still wanted to know why he looked guilty the first time she saw him after her injury but she hadn't figured out a way to bring it up.

They had settled into a kind of routine. She still got tired but her strength was coming back quickly. She slept alone in her own room. She didn't want to have to deal with a lot of camp gossip and there was still some tension between her and Bishop that she hadn't quite figured out. Their relationship was more of nursemaid/patient than it was romance.

"I think we should avoid matches between you and Chastity from now on. Things are a little tense between you two already, and we don't need to add anything to that."

Ace rolled her eyes. If Chastity would show up in real clothes, she might be able to fight better. It must be hard to focus on self-defense when all she was wearing was a sports bra and shorts so small they could be mistaken for underwear.

"I'm not the one who requested or approved the match," she reminded him.

Bishop nodded. "I know. I was hoping it would help you two get along better."

"Made me feel better," Ace replied with a grin.

He gave her a look but didn't comment any further on the subject.

"I want you to check in with Carter before going out on your ride."

"Fine."

She learned several days ago that arguing with Bishop was pointless. And while she had agreed to stick around for the time being and get to know him, she admitted to him that he made her feel suffocated at times. He was always telling her what to do, where to go, and when he didn't approve of what she was doing. After nine years of surviving on her own, she didn't enjoy the sudden parental figure in her life.

"After your ride what are your plans for the day?" he asked.

"Riding."

Bishop frowned. "I thought we talked about this."

"We did. You told me you didn't like it when I don't follow the farm's strict check in times."

"It's not called the farm, Ace. How many times do I have to repeat that?" he said with irritation.

"Might as well be," she muttered. "But either way, I am going riding and I'm going for as long as I want."

"Ace, we have a very strict two hour check in time. Unless you are out on a mission you need to check in every two hours. Even patrollers have to. This isn't just an excuse for me to control you. Why can't you just come back, check-in, and leave again?"

"Because then I can't actually leave!" Ace retorted.

Bishop's reply died on his tongue. "You're leaving?" he asked quietly.

She rolled her eyes. "Not for good. Just for the day. After being alone for so long I get overwhelmed here. I need my space. And you promised me if I stayed, I'd have plenty of freedom."

"Yes, and you will, within the rules."

"That's ridiculous Bishop! Are you seriously telling me that no one leaves here for more than two hours at a time?"

"Other than the people out on missions, yes, everyone follows the rules."

Ace raised her chin a notch. "Fine, then. I want a mission."

Bishop laughed. "Glad to see your sense of humor wasn't damaged."

"I'm serious."

He stared at her for a minute, trying to read her. "Absolutely not."

Her brows furrowed. "What do you mean absolutely not? You told me I could when you first asked me to stay here with you."

"That was before you got hurt."

"Before I got hurt? Are you serious? I don't need you to protect me! I survived on my own for nine years before you came along, I don't. Need. A. Babysitter."

"I am well aware of that fact, it doesn't change my decision." He said with a finality to his tone.

Ace squared her shoulders. "Then I can just leave. It's that simple. I told you I refused to become a prisoner. Either I can go on any mission I please, or I leave."

"You leave, and I will make sure you are locked up with round the clock guards!" he threatened.

That was not how she wanted the conversation to go. She didn't understand why it was so hard for him to understand where she was coming from. She wasn't intentionally trying to be difficult. She hadn't been responsible to another human since this whole mess started all those years ago. She couldn't just change overnight. She knew he was just concerned for her and she wished she could control her mouth better. She wanted to find a way to help him understand. If she caved into him, he might as well make her a prisoner. It would feel the same way. Without another word Ace spun around and stalked off towards the medical building to speak with Carter.

She found him in the supply closet checking inventory. His company was one of the only things keeping her sanity together since her recovery. Though she hated him when she first woke up for drugging her, she got over it. He was honest about his reasons and a part of her even had to respect him for it. Carter looked up when she slammed the door.

"Bad day?" he asked warily. After observing a couple of her workouts, he decided that she was quite capable of kicking his ass and that gave him motivation to stay on her good side.

Ace sucked in a big breath to begin her rant when an idea hit her, and she slowly let it back out.

"No. Just working on my dramatic entrances. They seem to always make a big deal out of them in books. To change the subject, I have a question."

Carter raised a brow as he made a mark on his clip board. "What's up?"

"What kind of missions does the rebel group send people out on?"

Carter moved to the next shelf. "It all depends really. There is a large number of things we do."

"Well, what kind of stuff around here?"

"Not much at all. Bishop is trying to plan a mission for entering some headquarters for a special info grab but that won't be for a few weeks. The only other thing around here are the recruit camps. But we steer clear of those."

"What is a recruit camp?"

He stopped his counting and looked up in surprise. "You've never come across the recruit camps?"

She shrugged as she tried to pretend she was oblivious. "No. What is it?"

"It's where the government takes what they call "fresh meat" and brain-washes them. The one near here is where they take captives from ages fifteen to twenty, I think. It isn't pretty what happens there."

"What do they do to them? How do they get them to commit to their cause?"

"Well, it depends on how stubborn they are. There are a lot of methods they try. Drugs and torture are their favorite."

"But they aren't trying to kill them?" she clarified.

"Oh, some die. But they don't really care. They bring in truckloads of people every week so a few here and there aren't much of a loss. Besides, if they are using methods extreme enough to kill someone, it was probably someone who would always be a risk to them."

Ace studied him for a few seconds. "You look... I think 'haunted' is the right description."

Carter glanced up at her quickly before looking back at his clipboard.

"I know a few people who have been taken there."

"One of them was someone special?" she asked quietly.

"Yeah." He looked up at her again. "They took her about a week before I went on the expedition to help get you out of the handcuffs," he smiled sadly. "You remind me of her a little. The most dangerous thing she did was extraction assistance, so she wasn't a skilled survivor like you, but she had a similar personality. She was very strong and very out-spoken in her opinion."

"You talk about her like she is gone."

Carter looked away. "You either don't come out of that place alive, or you come out a different person. Either way, she will be gone. It's easier to think of her as already gone. I'm sure you understand."

Ace tried to picture it and thought that she probably could understand.

"What was her name?"

Carter smiled sadly again. "Tali. Her hair was honey brown, and she had the bluest eyes."

"She sounds very pretty. And a unique name, I've never heard of it before."

"It's a nickname. Her full name was Castalia, but she thought it was too weird for everyday use."

Ace smiled lightly. "I can relate to that."

He looked over at her, "I figured your real name wasn't Ace. What's it short for?"

She shook her head. "It's a well-kept secret. I could tell you but I would have to kill you. Where is this recruit place anyway?"

"It's directly south of here. Probably a day by foot. Why?"

"Curiosity. If she was so important to you, how come Bishop never sent anyone after her?"

He shook his head. "It's not that simple. And I'm not the first one to lose someone to the soldiers. That place is a fortress. The only way in is to be captured. And if you're captured, you aren't getting out."

Ace's mind was already swarming with ideas and partially-made plans. She wasn't sure where this sudden drive to help a complete stranger was coming from, but she knew she was going to do it.

Carter took a deep breath. "I think that's enough for depressing topics."

"Yeah, I need to get going anyway. I'm sure Bishop is about ready to give me another lecture about the rules. Got to be an outstanding citizen here, you know."

As she opened the door Carter spoke up, "You know he made those rules to protect us. I know it seems a little controlling, but he's just doing it because he cares about you."

"I appreciate you trying to help, but I'm not the kind of person you can lock in a cage and say it's because you care about me."

Ace went straight to the cooking area and stole a few loaves of bread and some dried jerky without anyone noticing. She knew the missing items would be noticed eventually since they kept a strict inventory of all of the food, but she hoped to be long gone by the dinner bell.

Her saddle bags were packed and hidden at the edge of the perimeter within the hour and Flint was tacked and ready to go. But before she left, she sought out Bishop.

He was in the middle of helping Chastity with her combat skills. When she saw his hands on the brunette's exposed waist, a flare of jealousy flamed up in her chest and all traces of guilt melted away immediately. She approached. scowling, and waited for Bishop to notice her. When he did, he looked a little surprised but didn't comment on why.

"Yes? You are interrupting us. Did you need something?" Chastity asked in irritation.

Ace ignored her and looked at Bishop. "I was just letting you know I'm heading out for my ride."

He furrowed his brows. "And you will be back for your two-hour check in?"

Ace's scowl deepened. "Yes. I will check in."

Chastity smirked, but wisely said nothing.

"Good," Bishop nodded. "I'll see you at dinner then."

"Why not until dinner?" She asked curiously since usually he was checking in on her almost every hour and it was still before noon.

"Chastity needs some extra help. I'm prepping her for a mission in a few weeks."

Chastity smirked again.

"To where? The spandex factory? Did she run out of inappropriate clothes to wear?" Ace asked in anger.

Bishop's look hardened. "I know you aren't used to being around people, but that isn't how you speak to friends."

Ace shrugged. "She isn't my friend."

Chastity smiled. "Oh, come on. I thought we were finally getting along."

"It doesn't matter, Ace. That isn't how you speak to *any* of the Rebels. Do you understand?"

Ace couldn't stand the look on Chastity's face any longer. "Oh, you have no idea how well I understand." She left without another word and didn't stop until she was on Flint headed south with Wolf in tow.

Chapter 9

Ace was surprised it took her so long to find the recruiting camp. The camp was huge. The twelve foot high electric fence ran around at least forty acres, with large concrete buildings taking up most of the space. Several of the buildings looked to be connected, but there were a few that stood off on their own. She had never seen this particular camp before, but she had certainly seen other recruit camps like it.

This was probably the largest she had ever seen, most likely because of its close proximity to the Tri-Cities base. It looked menacing and well-guarded. She wasn't surprised that no one had ever attempted to break in before. But Ace's mind was made up. If she couldn't figure out how to get in on her own, she would try to get captured.

Her options of entering were limited. The fence was elec-trified so she couldn't just climb it. The electromagnetic shock had knocked out the electricity right after the uprisings but that was nine years ago. Now the government had electricity to spare and a few of the larger towns that had been re-established even had electricity, if you didn't mind the occa-sional black outs. She could dig under it, but that would take days without a shovel and would be easily discovered during one of the perimeter patrols.

So far her only option was to go in through the front gate. Obviously she couldn't just walk in. Ace studied the front gates for almost three hours before an idea finally came along. As several large trucks stopped in front of the gates, they were waved in without so much as an ID card. If she could slip into the back of a truck headed in, she would make it inside without a hitch. She hoped.

***

By the next morning Ace had picked out what stretch of road she would wait on for one of the large trucks. Flint was secured for her to be away, and he seemed to want nothing to do with this area. She was nervous leaving his saddle on while she was away, but she would might need him ready to go in a hurry.

As soon as she released him, he took off deeper into the woods. Wolf was pacing and had a constant low growl in his throat, but Ace needed him to stay with her a little longer. If something went wrong when she tried to jump on a truck, she wanted a little backup.

It wasn't long until she heard the sounds of engines coming towards her but the first convoy was heading out, not in. Ace waited, very impatiently, throughout the day for the trucks to return. It was several hours after noon before she heard them approaching again.

Fortunately, they seemed to slow down for a sharp corner just as they neared the recruit camp. She waited in the brush at the side of the road. She watched as the first two trucks went by, then jumped out and sprinted directly behind the last one. The tall canopy kept her from being seen in the rearview mirror and she was able to jump in without causing too much noise.

Getting into the truck was pretty simple. She slipped under the cloth canopy and hoped it was enough to keep her concealed. As soon as she was inside that fence she couldn't allow herself to be spotted. Escape would be impossible. Of course getting out with Carter's girl would be difficult but she would find a solution to that problem when she came to it.

The vehicle she was in slowed, Ace heard someone talking but had no idea what they were saying, and then the truck slowly started moving forward again. It wasn't long before it stopped again and the engine turned off.

***

Bishop sat down at a table near the food tents to eat a late breakfast while checking on the new reports. Usually his morning routine was fairly simple and the only time of the day when he wasn't bothered by anyone in camp. The cooks made sure his coffee cup remained full and he got plenty to eat as he shuffled through the written reports from his men all over the northwest area.

"Bishop!"

He glanced over his shoulder to see Jason heading towards him.

"Shouldn't you be training right now?" Bishop asked as he turned back to his papers.

"Yes I should. That's why I'm here to see you," Jason said as he leaned against the table.

Bishop sipped at his coffee, "I'm not following."

"Ace didn't show up for training this morning. I was curious if there was a problem?"

Bishop looked up sharply. "What do you mean she didn't show up?"

"Well she never appeared at the training area. That is the only definition I can think of to explain to you her lack of presence."

"I don't appreciate your smart tone, Jason," Bishop said through gritted teeth as he stood up. "I can't think of any reason Ace wouldn't show up to train this morning unless you did something to upset her."

Jason shook his head. "No one has seen her since she went for her ride yesterday. I already checked with Carter. He said he last saw her when she checked in with him before she went for her ride. And Ryan didn't see her at the shooting range after dinner, which is out of her routine."

"That's impossible, she always checks in with someone after her ride."

"Well, that's why I came to speak with you. Don't you usually have dinner with her?"

Bishop frowned. "I was busy working with Chastity last night."

Jason raised a brow. "Well, maybe that's the problem."

"You would be wise to remember your place." Bishop growled as a thread of guilt started to worm its way through him. "If she didn't check in after her ride then she must not have come back. Who was the last to speak with her?"

Jason shrugged. "As far as I know it was Carter. But I already spoke to him and he doesn't know where she is either."

"I don't care, they spoke about something. Last time I spoke with Ace she was fine. If something happened that caused her to bolt maybe he knows where she might have gone."

Jason looked doubtful, but he motioned for Bishop to lead the way. The pair tracked Carter down at the north end of camp. He was just inside the tree line, looking off in the distance lost in thought. He had been so oblivious to his surroundings he didn't hear their approach, and jumped when Bishop put a hand on his shoulder.

"I know you come here to be alone," Bishop said with sympathy, "but I need to know what you and Ace spoke about yesterday."

Carter frowned. "Why? It was nothing very specific."

"She is missing. Bishop seems to think you know why," Jason said, his tone making it obvious that he didn't agree.

"Missing? She was fine when I spoke to her. She was a little annoyed, but nothing major."

"Annoyed about what?" Bishop demanded.

Carter rubbed the back of his neck uncomfortably. "Well... you, if I can speak freely. But nothing bad. She was just upset you wouldn't let her go on a mission. She was asking questions about what kind of missions we do and said she was upset you wouldn't let her leave camp. She just wanted some space is all."

Jason shrugged. "So we give it a day or two and see if she comes back. If not, then we do some more digging."

"I am *not* waiting days while she could be in trouble," Bishop said through gritted teeth.

"I don't think that is much of a problem. She is quite capable of surviving on her own. She did for almost ten years before you came along. Do you really think now that you are in her life, she suddenly can't tie her own shoes?"

Bishop glared at Jason. "How dare you-"

"You think she would have taken off if you hadn't been simultaneously suffocating and then ignoring her? She isn't a trophy you put in a case and leave at home! She is a person just like any other person in this camp. A talented one. You need to give her a reason to stay, give her a responsibility. Because sitting around the camp like your bimbo isn't going to-"

Bishop stepped forward just as Carter leapt between the two men and pushed them apart. "Both of you quit. Ace is gone, that is our priority. We can start a perimeter search and move on from there."

Bishop glared at Jason for a few more seconds before stalking off to find Jayce. His friend had been so busy lately that they barely saw one another, let alone had a conversation.

***

The man was studying some papers in his office with a grim expression when Bishop entered. Jayce motioned for

Bishop to wait, so he sat down in a chair and very impatiently waited for his friend to finish whatever he was doing. Normally people didn't tell Bishop what to do, not here, this was his camp. But Bishop and Jayce had a special relationship. Finally Jayce looked up.

"Ace is missing."

Jayce frowned. "Interesting."

"Interesting? Why is that interesting? It's bad."

"It's interesting that you came to see me before running off to find her," Jayce said drily.

The Rebel leader leaned onto the desk and rubbed his forehead. "She is unpredictable. I know that. I just wanted to know if you dug anything up on her before I left. In case . . . you know."

Jayce nodded and dug around the mess of papers on his desk until he found what he was looking for.

"I didn't dig anything up on her. It is really difficult without a surname. If she was ever involved with anything that was recorded since the Uprisings, she used a different name."

Bishop raised his brows hopefully. "She's clean?"

"She is clean more or less," Jayce uttered, almost disappointed he hadn't found anything. "But there is still something off about her. She is keeping something a secret, something big. Be careful what Rebel secrets you bestow upon her until she opens up to us more. She still seems a bit, unsettled here."

Bishop nodded. "She just doesn't know how to fit in with people yet, she isn't used to having others around her."

Jayce noticed his friend's brighter expression. "Now that may be so. But it doesn't mean I am going to allow you to use all of our resources to track her down. Again. You can take a non-fighting vehicle and two men and enough supplies for three days."

Bishop glared, but didn't argue as he left the room.

***

Ace could hear men talking as they climbed out of the vehicles. They sounded normal, spoke like the people in Bishop's camp. She tried to ignore their words, pretend they didn't sound like every day people because she would kill them if needed.

Quietly she crept forward and peeked through the canvas canopy. The men were gathered behind the truck that had been first in the convoy. It was different from the truck Ace was in. It looked more like an old furniture delivery truck. The five men were laughing and messing around. Their guns were holstered and their postures were relaxed.

For a few more minutes, Ace was very confused. They acted like they didn't have any new prisoners. But she knew those were the trucks used for bringing in fresh captives. She forgot how normal the people under government employ could seem as opposed to being monsters out of nightmares. It had been so long since she saw any of them while superiors weren't watching over their shoulder. But when they opened the back of the truck, she was reminded of what these people did when they weren't chatting amongst themselves.

Each man took one person that was bound and blindfolded, the last man took two. She couldn't tell how old they were, but none of them looked older than herself and one of them looked far too young to be there at all. One of them seemed to have a bullet wound in his leg. The rest were covered in various amounts of blood and dirt. The two men and four women were drug off through the nearest door.

Ace took several deep breaths to calm the flare of anger and waited a few more minutes to make sure the coast was clear.

Getting out of the truck was simple. Figuring out where to go afterwards, that was difficult. There was the door she had seen the captives taken through, but she knew for sure there were people that way so she wanted to avoid it if possible. That left three other doorways within reach. Going in any of them would be a risk but she couldn't just stand out in the open and wait to be discovered, so she chose one at random.

The door took her into a long hallway which left her several more door options or a direction of travel. The sound of voices drove her to dart through the nearest door. She left it cracked so she could still hear if someone was approaching and then got to work looking through the room. It was dark, but a quick check along the wall brought her to a light switch.

She looked around the empty room. It looked like it had been in use recently. She could smell the bleach used to clean it. But there was nothing in here that would help her much. Ace checked the hall to be sure it was clear, then snuck along the wall and checked nameplates on doors as she went. Finally she found one that might be useful.

The supply closet was full of uniforms for what she assumed to be the camp employees. Ace slipped one of the full coveralls on over her clothes and hoped her two handguns weren't obvious through the stiff fabric, then pulled on one of the small hats.

The hall was silent, and when she slowly peeked out, no one was in sight. Ace nervously stepped into the hall, constantly looking over her shoulder. Every noise made her flinch, every shadow made her stop in her tracks. This was definitely something she had never done before. Intentionally walking into enemy territory was basically a death sentence.

When the hallway rounded a corner and came to another long length of hall with nothing but doors, Ace decided to go inside of one. She chose at random, slowly easing the door open and peering in. The room was dark with a light shining onto one wall that kept flashing, with several chairs containing people. She almost closed the door to move on, but she noticed the people in the chairs were being restrained. With another glance down the hall, Ace entered the room and closed the door. She scanned the room for cameras or two-way mirrors but didn't see anything obvious.

The people looked like they were zombies. Each of their wrists were secured into large cuffs built into the chair, as were their ankles. There were seven total in the room, all females, and all in the same state of mind. Each had their own assortment of bruises and none of them seemed very capable of conscious thought.

As Ace stepped farther into the room, slowly, she turned to see the wall that the light shone onto. The light flashed between words and images onto the wall so fast Ace could barely comprehend what they were. And she knew she didn't want to. She knew what this was, and her stomach instantly clenched in fear. Immediately she headed back to the hallway and closed the door tightly.

Ace managed to sneak in and out of three more rooms before she finally stumbled upon someone matching Tali's description. The hair was duller than Carter described, but when Ace saw her eyes she stopped. They really were the bluest eyes she had ever seen.

"Tali?" Ace asked carefully. The room only had two other girls in it. They were all in better shape than anyone Ace had stumbled across so far. The girl's eyes flickered up at Ace, then down to the print on her uniform. She scowled and spit on Ace. Ace's first instinct was to react, but she managed to stomp down the feeling. So the girl really was a fighter. A smile crept up the corners of Ace's mouth.

"Tali, I was sent here by Carter."

The girl's eyes flew to Ace's face, her expression wary.

"Listen to me. I know you have been through hell, but I came here to get you out. Can you walk?"

The girl still looked uncertain. So Ace unzipped her coveralls to flash her hidden pistols.

"Carter really sent you? Is he here?" the girl asked, her voice scratchy.

"He's not here. He actually doesn't know I'm here, but he saved my life and I needed to return the favor."

Ace started pulling at the metal cuffs on the chairs, trying to find a week point that she could use to leverage them open, but with only her bare hands it was impossible.

"I need to go get something to get you out of that chair, I will be back as soon as I can."

Ace peeked into the hallway, when she was sure it was clear she bolted back the way she had come, back to the utility closet. There had to be something there that could get Tali out of the chair. She dug through every crevice she could find, went through every box. A few different keys she found went into her pocket, she had no idea what they went to but she would rather take them with her and not need them than the other way around.

After several minutes of frantic searching, Ace settled on a straight round metal bar that was flat on one end. Just before she headed back to the hallway though, something caught her eye. It was a box of weapons tucked in a space behind the door. She didn't have anywhere she could hide more hand guns, but she slung a rifle over her shoulder. There were also some hand grenades, and while she didn't like them at all because of her previous experience, it might be the answer to her getting out of here alive. Ace stuffed four into her pockets and then headed out.

She started jogging back to Tali, becoming anxious to get out, when she rounded a corner and saw two men in uniform walking towards her. They were escorting Tali and the other two women from her room. Ace ducked back around the corner and ran for her utility closet, but left the door cracked so she could see where the men took their captives.

She watched as the men rounded the corner, laughing and joking with one another like they weren't carting innocent people around to their deaths. The men stopped outside of the first door from the corner and roughly shoved the three women into the room. She couldn't see them once they followed their captives, but she could still hear their friendly chatter. She waited for what seemed like far too long before the men reappeared. Ace stood in the doorway until they were out of sight, just to be sure they wouldn't come back. As soon as the hallway was clear she bolted to the door leading to Tali and went inside.

She saw what had taken the men so long. The three women were re-secured to chairs and the projector was going through words and pictures too fast for proper comprehension. Ace rushed forward with keys in hand, fumbling through the selections until one finally opened the cuffs holding the girl. "They're gone for now, we have to go."

Immediately Tali straightened her posture and brushed her hair out of her face. Her eyes were still a little glassed over, but she didn't look nearly as helpless as she had a few seconds ago.

"Help me with these two, they were given a higher dose than I was," Tali said as she stumbled over to one of the other girls.

Ace frowned and didn't move.

"What's the plan anyway?" Tali asked as she took the keys to free her companions. Once free of the chairs she navigated both girls over to the door.

"The plan was only meant for two people," Ace said flatly.

Tali looked over at her with surprise and judgment. "Are you serious? You can see this and walk away?"

Ace glanced at the women, careful to avoid looking at flashing words. "I can see that the only way we are getting out of here alive, is if the soldiers don't know we are leaving until we are gone."

"I am helping them, all of them. And you are helping me. Understand?" Tali stated as her balance swayed to the side.

Ace's frown deepened. "We cannot save everyone. Have you seen them? A good portion of them cannot even sit up let alone run from soldiers with guns."

"I'm not leaving without them!" Tali yelled, the despair evident in her tone.

Ace cursed under her breath and started pacing. Tali was leaning up against the wall, sweat starting to break out on her forehead. Ace could tell she was getting worse, the men must have given them all a fresh dosage of some drug once they were settled into their new room.

"Fine. But I won't save them all. If they can't keep up, they get left. No matter what. Understand?" Tali started crying, but she nodded. "And some of them are going to die on our way out of here. You need to understand that, too. My only goal is to make sure you live."

Tali glared at Ace, "Why is my life more important than theirs?"

"Because I'm not the kind of person who cares about their lives. I'm the kind of person who cares about my life and I hate owing favors. I owe Carter for saving my life, so I'm saving yours. The rest of the people in here would probably thank me for killing them anyways, the ones who are still capable of a thought that is."

Tali was still glaring, but she nodded her consent to the plan.

"Glad we're on the same page. If you go after someone and I say leave them, you better leave them. I won't die for you because you decided to try and be a hero."

With that Ace grabbed the arm of one of the girls and opened the door. She peeked out slowly, then motioned to Tali to follow her.

"We will open the doors, undo the cuffs, and the ones who can get out will, we don't stay to give them any encouragement."

Luckily none of the doors presented the problem of being locked. The problem was getting the cuffs open. Tali was too shaky to even hold a key, let alone unlock something, so Ace had to find the right one again, then unlock everyone by herself. She decided to have Tali keep watch, and if anyone headed towards them she was going to drag Tali kicking and screaming out of there.

"How are we going to get all of these people out of here?"

Ace glanced at Tali, then back at their entourage. None of the people were in very good condition, but a surprising portion managed to get up and follow them when Tali said they were escaping.

"Not sure yet," Ace admitted.

"What? Are you just making this up as you go along?"

Ace glanced around the corner of the hall and noticed two men.

"Yep, pretty much."

She drew the rifle from her shoulder.

"We are all going to die because you didn't have an actual plan!" Tali exclaimed quietly.

"I had a plan. You decided you wanted to save the world instead of just ourselves, remember?"

The complaints didn't continue. Ace looked through the scope on the rifle to get a better look at the men on the other end of the hall. They were between her and the exit. She was hoping her grenades would come in handy to get them all

through the fence, but that was only if they didn't draw attention to themselves before they got outside.

"Are you going to shoot them?"

Ace glanced back at Tali, her face was flushed and she
was leaning on the wall for support.

"No. We don't want to draw any attention until the last
possible moment."

"Well, can that moment hurry up? I don't know much
longer these guys can hold up."

Ace lined up the cross hairs on her scope with the temple
of one of the guards. She exhaled slowly, and just as her finger
was about to squeeze the trigger someone burst through the
door right next to the guards.

Ace immediately ducked behind the corner of the wall
again, out of sight. She could hear the men talking, but she
couldn't hear what they were saying. Several agonizing
minutes passed by before the sound of a door closing had Ace
peeking around the corner again. From what she could tell,
the hall was clear. She motioned to Tali to stay as she crept
around the corner and started sneaking along the wall. Now
that she was stuck with these rescues, she wanted to give
them the best possible chance of not dying.

When Ace reached the door she double checked every
nook and cranny, then slowly peeked outside through the
smallest crack in the door she could manage. Only one guard
was in view.

Ace motioned back to Tali, it was several seconds before
the group of people clumsily came around the corner. The
more lucid ones were trying to help along those that couldn't
move on their own. Ace had to admit she felt a small tug of
sadness for them. Because of their selflessness, they would
lose their lives. But it didn't change that she wasn't helping
anyone other than Tali. It just seemed such a waste. As soon

as the thin girl was close enough Ace reached out and grabbed her arm.

"I am going to blow up the fence, everyone is going to make a run for it. Including you. I need you to run straight. Straight into the trees on the other side of the road and keep running straight. You will come to a stream at some point. When you get there I want you to find a place to hide and wait for me to come find you. If I'm not there by morning, find your way back to Blanchard. Okay? Can you do that?"

Tali nodded her head as quickly as she could without getting too dizzy. Ace cracked open the door again. Two guards were now in sight but they were facing the other direction. Carefully, she pulled two grenades from her pocket. She thought about removing the pins with her teeth, but the thought of the metal on her teeth sent an odd tingle down her spine. It was just so cliché from old movies she remembered watching.

Ace motioned to Tali, who shakily pulled the pins out and dropped them to the concrete floor. Ace paused and took a deep breath. She cleared her mind, removed all thought so her instincts would take over and then swung open the door.

Ace had to throw the grenades one at a time so they made it to the base of the fence, then she pulled her rifle off her shoulder and shot one of the guards right as the grenades went off to cover the sound of the gunshot. The explosion would certainly attract attention but she didn't want them to think they were under an attack by gunfire as well.

The explosion worked and completely destroyed a section of the fence. The noise from the explosion made Ace's ears ring and the blast made her fight for balance momentarily. Thankfully it didn't take long for Tali and the others to start their mad dash for the fence. With a quick glance around Ace started sprinting for the fence herself. The explosion took care of the second guard, but the commotion would bring more people to the scene. Ace hadn't made it to the fence yet when reinforcements started showing up and shooting at anything that moved.

Ace stopped running and started shooting while walking backwards towards her freedom. She had lost sight of Tali in the mob that was running for their lives. Several bodies already littered the ground, but she couldn't tell if any of them were Tali and she wasn't taking the time to look.

Ace shot guards as quickly as she could manage, taking them out one at a time, wishing she still had her semi-automatic rifle so she didn't have to frequently work the bolt which took up precious seconds. A bullet whizzed by so close it nicked her overalls and she had the sickening thought that if a bullet hit one of the two remaining grenades in her pockets, she was screwed in a bad way. Taking a bullet was one thing. There was a possibility of her surviving. But being blown into a thousand pieces was a little difficult to come back from.

The mental image was enough to make her regret this suicide mission for Tali in the first place, but it also reminded her she had two extra grenades which might make the difference between her getting out alive or dying in this ridiculous escape attempt. Ace pulled out one of the remaining grenades, pulled the pin, and then chucked it as far as she could towards the line of soldiers shooting at her. She turned to sprint to safety but she stopped in her tracks when she saw Tali trying to carry two people as she slowly trudged towards the fence. The explosion made her flinch as Ace cursed. She ran to Tali.

She grabbed the girl's arm and yanked one of the half conscious bodies away, noticing a bullet wound in the woman's stomach.

"Leave them! We have to get out of here now!" Ace yelled over the gunfire.

"No!" Tali said through tears. "We have to save them, we can save them."

Ace noticed the two women were the ones that had been held in the same room as Tali but she didn't have time for sentimental rescues. Ace grabbed the other woman and set her down as gently as she could in a rush. She turned back to Tali and grasped both of her shoulders.

"Listen to me, you can't save them. One is already dead, the other is going to be. We are leaving now even if I have to knock you out. I will but it would be a hell of a lot easier if you would cooperate!"

Tali shook away. "No!"

Just then a bullet whizzed past Tali's face but it didn't cause her to run for the fence. It did make her frantically try to pick up one of the women again. Ace cursed, drug Tali back to her feet, and punched her hard enough for her to slump back to the ground. Pulling out her last grenade, Ace hoped this got her enough time to carry the stubborn girl to safety.

She threw it towards the ragged line of soldiers then hauled Tali over her shoulder and ran. When the grenade went off Ace stumbled but she managed to keep her feet underneath her. She was glad for all of the war movies she had watched with her dad when she was a kid, because it was the only way she knew how to sufficiently carry a limp body while running.

Ace made it to the trees, but she kept running. She set a pace, blanked her mind, and pushed herself forward.

Her shoulders were cramped and her thigh and calf muscles were on fire by the time she came to the creek and collapsed. She laid on the ground next to Tali gasping for breath for almost an hour. When her heart rate finally came down, all she wanted to do was pass out but she managed to convince herself to get back to her feet. She drank some water and periodically whistled into the night. It was almost three hours before Flint finally came walking into view from the other side of the creek.

Ace was thankful she wouldn't be carrying Tali any further. Standing up, she called Flint through the creek so she didn't have to get wet then got started on the task of getting Tali onto the horse.

She considered tying the girl behind the saddle, sort of how she would a dead deer, but she quickly pushed the thought aside and slung her over Flint's neck in front of the saddle.

When Ace mounted, she arranged Tali so she was sitting astride Flint just in front of the saddle and leaning back into Ace. It seemed to work well enough for the time being. She wouldn't be traveling fast but it was faster than if she had to carry the girl.

The trio headed north. Ace didn't want to give the soldiers time to find them so she rode all night. Every few minutes she would whistle for Wolf, but by the first light of morning there was still no sign of him. A few hours after sunrise, Ace's stomach was just beginning to complain about a lack of food when Tali started to slowly wake up. It didn't happen quickly and Ace didn't stop Flint. Every now and then the girl would groan or shift to get more comfortable.

Ace finally decided she had gone far enough for a little rest when she heard an engine starting up and come roaring towards her. Ace just managed to get Flint off the road as they came into view and a few more strides had her safely in the trees. If the driver wasn't looking for anything, he might not notice her. But if he was paying attention to the road ahead of him, she could have easily been seen. She urged Flint fifty yards into the woods before pulling him up while attempting to make as little noise as possible.

The truck slowed, then came to a stop right where Ace had just been. She closed her eyes and tried to control the fear that started creeping up in her chest as she drew a handgun. She took several deep breaths and focused on her escape routes when a familiar voice called out.

"Ace? Get yer ass over here now!"

Despite how angry he sounded, Ace smiled. She signaled Flint forward and headed back to the road. Bishop was standing there waiting, looking extremely pissed off, with three other people. She knew he was going to be mad but she was still relieved to see his face. Her smile widened when she saw Carter, who was busy doing something in the bed of the old truck.

"I will give you two minutes to explain why I shouldn't beat you for causing such a mess," Bishop growled as she pulled Flint up a few feet away.

Ace looked at Carter, "I don't need to explain anything, and I'll just show you." She answered loud enough to get the young man's attention. It wasn't much. He just glanced up for a second, then went back to what he was doing but it didn't take long for the situation to register. He straightened and just stood there, frozen, staring at Ace and her companion. Bishop waited impatiently for a few minutes and he wasn't happy about no one explaining anything to him.

"What?" he yelled when no one spoke up.

Ace hopped to the ground and started to pull Tali off, jolting Carter out of his daze. He leapt out of the bed of the truck and ran over, helping lower Tali to the ground. He cradled her face and choked on a sob as he knelt with her in his lap. Tali groaned and her face scrunched up, but she remained unconscious. Carter looked up at Ace, "I can't believe it. You went in after her. How did you – I can't believe you aren't dead. How did you do it?"

"Someone explain this to me right now!" Bishop yelled with a shake of his fist.

"Calm down, Hulk. That's Tali, I got her out of the recruits camp yesterday."

"What's wrong with her?" Carter asked. "Why is she unconscious?"

Ace made a vague motion with her hand. "They drug out the people they take there. She was pretty out of it when I found her and during the escape attempt she took a hit to the head. It wasn't too bad, just enough to knock her out. She has been coming in and out for the last hour or so."

Bishop was just standing quietly in the background. He looked even madder than before, if that was even possible, but Ace ignored him. He looked like he was just about to speak when a bark from the woods caught Ace's attention and she spun around. Wolf trotted out of the trees, his tongue hanging out of the side of his mouth as he panted.

"There you are!" Ace hugged her dog and scratched him behind the ears as he licked her face.

"Ace."

She rolled her eyes and looked up at Bishop. "Yes?"

"You want to explain a little further?"

She sighed and stood up. "I told you, I got Tali out of the recruit camps."

"I heard that part. I would like to focus a little more on the how and why? I didn't authorize you to go on a death mission. And you didn't tell anyone, which means the whole camp has been out looking for you. Lives were at risk. Because of you!"

"You really thought I was injured or captured instead of just ran away or something? Flint and Wolf were gone, too. I took all of my essentials."

"Oh, he thought you ran away. That's why he was trying so hard to find you," Jayce said in his usual monotone.

Ace looked around Bishop and smiled, "Jayce. Haven't seen you in a few days. I missed your sparkling personality. Still hate me. I see."

He glanced at her and she noticed the barest of smirks for almost half a second before his serious expression took over again.

"Still causing me trouble I don't need, I see," he said blandly.

Bishop threw a hand in the air to quiet them, "Enough, both of you. Ace, how the hell did you get out of the recruit camps?"

"Grenades. Blew up the fence," she said with a shrug.

Bishop cursed, Jayce frowned. "You couldn't think of anything more noticeable?" Bishop asked through gritted teeth. "A spectacle like that will have the soldiers on our asses, they WILL retaliate."

Ace stepped back so Carter could carry Tali to the truck as she replied, "Look, I didn't want to do it that way. I had a great sneaky little in and out plan. Tali, there, ruined it all with her 'save every life possible' rebel brain. She tried to free everyone in there and the only way to get out was to blow up the fence and half the guards."

"How many made it out?" Jayce asked.

She shrugged. "How am I supposed to know? I was too busy trying not to get my own ass shot off."

Bishop crossed his arms and shook his head. "I don't want to deal with this right now. Get in the truck. We will discuss this later."

Everyone turned to get in the truck as Ace jumped back into her saddle. Bishop noticed when he got to the truck door and scowled.

"What do you think you are doing?!"

Ace looked up in confusion. "Heading back to camp?"

"No. Get off the horse and get in the truck. You have proven I can't trust you."

She rolled her eyes, "I'm not leaving Flint here. I will ride back to Blanchard camp and you will have to deal with it."

Before he could get close enough to grab her reins, or do something else that would piss her off, she cantered into the trees and out of sight.

***

Ace rode in to Blanchard Camp a full day later. Bishop and his group were back already, they had pulled in around noon the previous day but Ace didn't see any of them anywhere in the near vicinity. She took her time taking care of Flint before heading to the cook area in search of food. A few people waved to her as she walked through the camp. Some she recognized some she didn't, but either way she didn't wave back. As she came to the food tents, she wandered around for a few minutes before finding some fruit. She selected an apple and was just about to take a bite when a stick flew past her face, narrowly missing her by less than an inch.

Ace slowly turned around to see a fuming Tali glaring at her. Her left eye was swollen almost closed and a bruise was starting to show up quite nicely. Ace set her apple back on the table and raised a brow.

"Can I help you?" she asked calmly, aware that every person in the vicinity was staring at them. Just then Carter came running up. "Tali! What has gotten into you, she saved your life."

"She knocked me out!"

Carter looked around Tali at Ace. "What? Why would you-"

"How dare you!" Tali screamed at Ace. "I could have saved them!"

Ace rolled her eyes. "Is that really what this is all about?"

"You left them there to die!" Tali picked up a rock and threw it but Ace easily dodged and started walking towards the angry girl.

"Yes I did," she said calmly. Ace knew she wasn't very good at talking to people, especially emotional ones, so she tried her hardest to be understanding. "I know you are probably upset right now-"

"What kind of evil person are you?"

As Ace got close enough Tali swung out with her fist. Ace blocked it then raised her hands to show she didn't want to fight.

"Listen to me for just a moment-"

Tali swung again, but this time when Ace deflected it she swung again and again and again. Ace put up with it for a few swings, but then she got tired of it. She stepped in quickly, hit Tali in the chest and used her leg as leverage to pin Tali to the ground.

"Yes! I left them there to die! I left a lot of people there to die and I killed a lot of people so that your little friends had at least a slim chance of making it out! You know what they were doing with everyone in there! Drugging you up and numbing you out so they could do Lord only knows what with you? Death was far better than staying there." Ace leaned down over Tali, "I'm not a savior, I'm not a hero and I don't try to be. You got a problem with the way I do things, let me know and I'll make sure to leave you for drugs and torture next time. Got it?"

She didn't wait for a response, she didn't want one. This was why she was always alone. People thought you were evil if you didn't do everything their way and Ace just didn't care enough to try to appear as though she did. She straightened, glanced at a pale Carter and then walked away, her appetite forgotten. Half of the camp had been witness to the scene, which meant everyone probably thought she was some black hearted monster now. She had no desire to stand around to be judged.

***

"Ace? You in here?" Carter asked as he stepped into Ace's room.

Ace was stuffing her clothes into her saddle bags as she glanced up. "If you've come to tell me to get lost, don't bother. I'm leaving."

Carter crossed his arms and leaned against the door frame.

"Where ya' goin'?"

"Away. Back to my old life."

"Why?"

She glanced over at him. "You were there. Why do you think?" She stood up straight and turned to face him. "What are you doing here anyway? You should be leading the angry mob to chase me off the farm."

"Ace, you saved the girl I love. Why would I want to chase you out of camp?"

"Because of the way I just spoke to her? Because everything she accused me of is true? I let people die so that I didn't." She turned back to her packs, "Isn't that like against the Rebel code or something?"

"Probably," Carter said casually with a shrug. "But I don't care."

She glanced up at him again. "Why not?"

"Look, Ace, most people here think the same way you do. They just refuse to admit it or say it out loud. You make them uncomfortable because you say exactly what you think. Most people aren't like that."

"Yeah I know. I'm not good at being around people."

"True," he teased. "But that isn't what I meant. You saved Tali, and no matter what, I am thankful for that. No one is going to chase you out of camp. They might give you weird looks and talk about you when you walk away, but they have always done that."

She rolled her eyes at his teasing look, then glanced around her room at all of her bags as Carter stepped into the room.

"I know leaving seems like the easier thing to do, and it probably is. But the truth is, we could really use your help."

"Why would you need my help, you have plenty of volunteers who actually believe in the no-one gets left behind motto."

"Exactly, we have no one who doesn't. We have no one to look at us and tell us we are being stupid. We may not listen to your opinion every time, but sometimes it would come in handy. We could also use someone with stones like yours when no one is willing to give something a try, like breaking into one of the recruit camps." He winked at her.

Ace sighed. "I was terrified out of my mind in there."

"If you weren't, then I would be worried."

"How many lectures from Bishop do you think I'm going to have to listen to for this? He hasn't even come by to yell at me yet," she asked with a sardonic smile.

Carter groaned. "We are *all* going to have to listen to those lectures, he doesn't want to encourage others to start disobeying orders and running off to do their own missions whenever they want."

"I didn't think about it like that," Ace muttered.

"Doesn't matter, what you did saved a lot of people."

"What I did killed a lot of people."

Carter looked at her curiously. "You don't really care though, do you?"

"No. Because the guards I killed have done horrible things to people and the innocents I killed were saved from whatever torture was in store for them. I never claimed to be a saint." She watched him warily, waited for him to accuse her of being a horrible person. But he didn't.

"And what if the innocents were being treated fairly? What if they weren't being drugged and they weren't being tortured, simply being kept by the guards. Would you have still let them die?"

"Yes."

"Why?"

Ace squared her shoulders. "Because I am a survivor, not a hero, and I don't try to be anything else. I have worked too hard to keep my own hide over the years to get sentimental over a stranger. I have no reason to risk my life for them."

Carter nodded slowly, "I understand where you are coming from with that thought process. But have you tried to think of it differently?"

She shrugged. "There is no other way to think about it."

"Yes there is, you just haven't tried. Or you don't want to admit that you have tried. Helping doesn't mean you are weak. How are you so good at surviving?"

She frowned. "What do you mean?"

"Bishop says you are an amazing shot with a gun. That doesn't just happen. And you were what nine or ten when the uprisings happened? I'm guessing any family you had was killed in the Retaliation. So how did a ten-year-old know how to live on her own?"

Ace tried to push down her nerves as she made a vague motion with her hand, "I don't know, my dad I guess. He was former military. He taught me survival skills, how to shoot. Stuff like that."

"How to fight? I also heard you can wrestle pretty well."

"Yeah, so he taught me some stuff. He predicted something bad happening and made sure I was prepared. What does that have to do with anything?"

"My point is, not everyone was that lucky. Some people were living in group homes because they didn't have any parents, or on the streets. Not everyone had the advantage of knowing how to live through a war like you did. Those are the ones who get captured, who get tortured, and who are taken advantage of by the government. That is why I help the rebellion. To help those who weren't as lucky as me."

Ace stuffed the flare of pain back down. "So because you just happened to be lucky, not by choice but by chance, you feel guilty and try to alleviate that by helping strangers who might have been unlucky or maybe were just stupid."

"That's the part you don't understand, Ace. It's not about guilt. It's about helping fellow people. We were *all* wronged by the government. We were all affected and we should stick together and help each other if we want to come out of this alive. I know you are just thinking in the now. But what about in thirty or forty years? Don't you want to have something left inside when all this is over? Don't you want to try to end this?"

Ace snorted, "I don't even know if I will be alive in *one* year, let alone thirty."

"Which is exactly my point. Why should we have to think like that? That isn't living. We shouldn't have to expect to be dead next year more than we expect to be alive. That's what we are fighting for. You can fight for yourself if you want to, fight for your own life, fight for the possibility of *your* life if you don't want to fight for the others. Don't you think your family would have wanted at least that?"

Ace had to remind herself to breathe as memories of her brother's last words came flooding back to her. It was so long ago and she had put all those memories in a vault in her heart and now they were seeping out. When the words faded away she was left with guilt sitting heavily in her stomach.

"Fine," she said without looking up at him. "I'll help you and your ridiculous cause."

Carter smiled, "That's more like it."

"But I'm only doing it for myself," she called after him as he closed her door. She glanced around her small room and sat down on the wooden chest heavily. If she was going to stay and help, she was going to have to get used to people staring at her like she was a circus freak. Especially after her encounter with Tali.

Chapter 10

The training sessions the next morning were interrupted by Jayce and Bishop calling over several specific people from their routine and sent them to the garage. Obviously they were going somewhere. Even though things had been strained between them, Ace expected Bishop to come say goodbye before he left. He hadn't allowed her off of the farm since she snuck off to the recruiting camps, even for a leisurely ride. So she was surprised when he grudgingly motioned for her to follow him.

Ace jogged to catch up with him. "What are we doing?"

"Carter mentioned that you almost left the other day," he said quietly.

Ace scowled. "I'm going to kill him."

He gave her a look. "Coming from you that is not a threat I take lightly. So I feel I have to tell you to leave Carter alone."

She rolled her eyes, like she would ever actually kill Carter for something like that. She was getting a little tired of Bishop's grudge and wished he would just get over it.

"So, it's true? You almost left just because Tali verbally attacked you?"

"It wasn't just that. There was other stuff." Ace made a vague gesture with her hand.

"Like what?"

She caught Bishop's pained expression before he managed to hide it.

"It wasn't because of you," she looked at the ground.

"But I wasn't enough to make you stay. Was I?"

She frowned. "That's not it. I wasn't thinking about you.-"

He laughed sadly, "Is that supposed to make me feel better?"

"That's not what I mean," she rolled her eyes. "I don't know what is going on between us but it didn't have anything to do with me leaving. I had tunnel vision. I just felt like I needed to leave. I don't fight the government or their soldiers. I avoid them. I kill them if I have to but I don't fight the system for freedom or for other people or for the good of the cause. I have no reason to do anything other than run away. I feel like a fraud around here most of the time."

"That's what Carter told me he thought was the problem."

"Then what's the point of this conversation? Where are we going?"

Bishop motioned to the group of vehicles in front of them. "We are taking a short trip. I do it every now and then with the newbies. It helps reinforce their loyalty, remind them of why we are here. I thought you might like to come along."

Ace stopped and watched him warily. "Where to?"

"You aren't allowed to know before we get there." He held his hand out and for the first time since she came back he looked at her with a softness in his eyes. "Just trust me. It won't kill you, I promise." As much as she wanted to tell him no, her curiosity won out. But she didn't take his hand. She didn't want to give him any wrong ideas. They had a lot they needed to talk about.

Bishop made sure she was in his vehicle, the third one in the convoy, as they pulled out of camp. None of the other "newbies" knew where they were going either, but that didn't stop Ace from prying for any guesses they had.

Bishop ignored her pleas to tell her, but her persistence made the two-hour drive seem much longer. It had been a while since he took the newbies to the old bomb shelter, but he felt it was time.

When they finally arrived, everyone slowly got out of their vehicle, stretching and passing around water. Ace studied the small area they had pulled the four vehicles into for several minutes before turning to Bishop with her hands on her hips.

"You said you brought us here to help us commit to what we are fighting for."

"Yes, I did."

"I don't get t."

Bishop smiled, "Well, if you would chill for half of a second and let me show you, you *would* get it."

Impatiently, Ace waited for Jayce to finish his conversations and join Bishop. After the pair shared a quick private conversation, Jayce lifted up a part of the ground. At least that was what it looked like at first.

Upon further examination Ace could see that it was a steel door, only the top of it was overgrown with grass so it blended into the surrounding meadow. The group filed into the underground room, but Ace hesitated at the top step.

"I promise there is nothing down there that will harm you." Jayce said blandly, without looking at her.

He was still holding the door. They were the last two remaining above ground.

"I don't like going underground," she said quietly with a glance into the dimly lit stairwell.

"It is an old bomb shelter.-"

"It isn't what the room might be that I don't like," she snapped.

When he raised his brow at her she sighed.

"I don't like being underground because there is only one way in or out. Once down there, I'm trapped."

Jayce studied her for a few seconds before looking down the stairs. "Something bad happen to you when you were in a room like this?"

She glared at him.

"Fine, don't tell me. I don't want to know. I don't like you, remember?"

Despite herself, she smiled at him. She was pretty sure they had the weirdest friendship in the world, if you could even call what they had a friendship.

"I don't like you, too."

Jayce gave her the barest of smirks.

"Tell you what, you can stand between everyone and the door so you know for sure you won't get trapped. I really think you are going to want to see what is down there."

It didn't make her happy, but it was the best option she had. Bishop had better have a good reason for taking her down there. She and Jayce descended the stair case, which was much too dark once the door was closed, and the two stopped at the base of the last step. Ace had no want to go any further and Jayce didn't seem too eager to get into the middle of the group of young energetic recruits.

"You are all here because within the last few months you have dedicated yourselves to the Rebel cause. But before we go any further, I have a video I want you all to watch. We had to drive two hours to watch it because this is the only TV in Rebel possession and we have to keep it well guarded. This video . . . it is going to be difficult to watch. And before I start it, I want you to know it is an unaltered video. We, the Rebels, did not make it. We took it from the soldiers. Several people died to get this to Rebel hands. It is the backbone of why we do what we do. The government soldiers document every-thing. Even during the blackout period they took detailed notes on everything they did. This is documentation they filmed. Not to get at us in any way, it is only for their own per-sonal records. These aren't even rebel people, but their own. This video shows you why we fight."

He rolled an old TV on a wheeled table out of the corner of the large open room and turned it on. Ace distantly wondered how they managed to get electricity down here, but she was more concerned with what was on the video to do too much investigating.

She knew the soldiers had to document everything they did but she had no idea the Rebels had that kind of access. And if it wasn't documentation on tortured rebels from the past, what did Bishop think would be moving enough to commit the loyalty of so many people in just one sitting?

The TV slowly came to life showing a fuzzy screen until Bishop put in a large black video tape. The screen flickered to a small concrete room. In the middle of the room, a chair was bolted to the floor and on the chair was a young boy. He was maybe fourteen years old and he looked terrified. A man came into the screen, dressed in camo cargo pants and a plain beige shirt.

"Soldier trainee four five seven," the man stated to the camera.

His heavy tread boots scuffed along the floor as the man walked a circle around the little boy. He stopped when he was facing the kid.

"State your title, boy," the man said.

"Soldier trainee four five seven, sir!"

The man back-handed the boy.

"You are here for training, to learn what torture is. You will learn this so if you are ever caught by the Rebels, they cannot torture information out of you!"

The boy unsuccessfully tried to contain his whimper. "Y-yes, sir."

"You do not relinquish even the smallest bit of information. Do you understand me, soldier trainee four five seven?"

"Yes, sir."

The scene went on. The man tortured the young boy, asking him questions which the boy desperately tried not to answer. The scene continued for over ten minutes and before the man was even finished, it switched off.

"We cut that tape short," Bishop said quietly. "You don't want to see the ending. That one . . . he didn't make it."

For the next hour they watched different people of different ages get tortured. Sometimes the scene cut out before it was over, other times it went until the very end. Ace watched the whole thing. While the other "newbies" looked away or cringed or made soft sounds of horror, she couldn't seem to drag her gaze away no matter how much she tried. She managed to keep herself from reacting, until they showed a little girl of about eleven years old. It was the youngest of everyone they had seen so far, even younger than very first boy shown.

"Soldier trainee three one two four." The man announced to the camera as he entered the scene. The little girl looked dwarfed by the chair restraining her. She struggled against the ropes keeping her where she was and whimpered as the man came closer.

Ace choked down a gasp as she tore her eyes away and looked at the floor. She felt like all the air had been removed from the room. She felt the walls pressing in on her. She wanted to run away, run up the stairs and out into the sunny meadow and pretend none of this ever happened. She wanted Bishop to turn it off and say it was all a fake. She wanted those images to leave her mind.

But she couldn't run away from it. She couldn't be the only one not strong enough to stay. For some morbid reason, she lost the ability to move. She didn't watch, she didn't need to. But she couldn't do anything about the sounds. They imprinted themselves in her mind and inflamed every feeling of anger in her body. This wasn't one of the scenes that was cut short.

It went all of the way to the end, lasting a total of eighteen minutes. It was the longest session on the whole tape.

When it finally ended, the screen went black and Bishop turned off the TV. He waited a few minutes for the group to settle. Several of the women had started crying and many of the men looked like they were trying not to. Every one of them looked haunted.

"I know this is difficult to absorb. I have seen this exact video more times than I would like to recall and it never gets easier. As you heard, these were not Rebel captives. They were not children of Rebels being tortured for their parent's actions even. These were their very own trainees."

"Why do they do that to their own people?" one of the younger of the guys asked.

"They get their loyalty through fear. And these aren't *their* people when they go through this. The trainees are *our* people. Anyone who has suffered at the hands of the government are our people. These are children taken off the streets of 'safe' cities and towns, drug away from their families and livelihood to be tortured and brain washed into soldiers. Only when they succeed in doing so do these children turn into *their* people."

One of the sobbing women spoke up. "The last girl was so young. Why do they do that to them so young?"

Bishop shrugged sadly. "We don't know. Although, from all our intel, it seems like that little girl was a bit of a rare case. None of the videos I have seen on this process show anyone else that young. But it doesn't mean it is any better a few years older. It is barbaric. This is why we are fighting, why we continue to fight and sacrifice."

Everyone nodded and verbally agreed it was worth it. Ace didn't wait for the inspirational moment to overcome them all. She turned and bound up the stairs two at a time until she made it back to the outside. She took several deep breaths of fresh air and cleared her thoughts, willing the screams of that little girl from her mind.

When she was relatively back under control, she heard everyone moving around in the bunker and starting to follow her out. She didn't want to face anyone so she decided to wait in her vehicle. No one really spoke to her. They were all too distracted with their own thoughts to even notice she fled the shelter ahead of them. The only one who gave her a concerned look was Jayce.

Even Bishop didn't notice. He just looked grim. When he climbed into the driver's seat, he didn't even look at her at he quietly said, "I told you."

Ace glared out her window. "I never said they were good."

"But now you know just how bad."

"I already knew. I didn't need to be reminded."

He shook his head. "I wanted you to see what I was fighting for. I didn't mean to upset you."

She remained silent. It wasn't long before the group was once again on the road. This time Ace's vehicle was in the very back, getting thoroughly dusted out every time they moved off of the ancient pavement. Ace watched the scenery go by, lost in her thoughts. Those thoughts are what distracted her. Suddenly she looked around, noting that the scenery was different from the drive down.

"Where are we going?" she asked Bishop.

"Back to camp," Bishop said with a confused look.

"Why are we taking a different route?"

He glanced at her, "Were you not listening?" She shook her head.

"There were some sightings of a patrol squad on that route, so we changed course to come in the back way. It will add about an hour to our drive but better to avoid trouble, to not have a run in with them."

Ace frowned. Why would there be a patrol squad way out here? They were in a very remote area. The government didn't usually patrol abandoned roads. They patrolled roads in between and around their own bases, but the road they originally took didn't lead anywhere. She looked around, trying to figure out why this made her so uncomfortable. She tried to remember everything she knew about the soldiers' tricks, but nothing was coming to mind.

The group cruised down the down the dirt road at a speed that made Ace nervous. Maybe it was because she still wasn't used to riding in cars, but she blamed it on the uneasy feeling that had settled into her stomach.

Bishop glanced over at her. "Are you okay? You seem-"

An explosion erupted in front of them, taking out the first two vehicles and causing the last two to crash into the southern ditch. Ace thanked her paranoia about cars and seatbelts as the man who was sitting behind her was launched over her head and out of the jeep. Another explosion went off, sending the recruits running for cover.

"No! Stay here and regroup!" Bishop tried to call, but no one could hear him. Gun shots rang out as soldiers stepped out of the trees on the other side of the road and fired at anyone who came into view. Ace unbuckled her seat belt and dove over the driver's seat and into the ditch.

"Bishop! Give me a gun!" she called.

But Bishop was too busy trying to gather his recruits. Ace cursed and dug around in the jeep, but she couldn't find weapons.

"Here," Jayce handed her a gun as he ducked behind her jeep. "Don't shoot me."

Ace rolled her eyes. "Seriously?"

"I meant accidently," he said in annoyance.

She scowled. "How about on purpose, because now I'm really tempted."

He smiled, like an actual full on smile for the first time since she had met him. But the moment was short lived. Bullets pelted the side of the jeep causing them to hit the ground.

"Anyone aside from us still alive?" she asked him.

"Don't know. Why? You got a plan?"

"Well, if it's just us, I say we bolt."

Jayce gave her a look of disapproval. Ace groaned. "Or we can stay here and die for no apparent reason but be remembered as heroes. Yeah, you guys make total sense!"

She stood and started firing the assault rifle at anyone in uniform. She could see Bishop on the other side of the road hiding behind a tree while soldiers kept shooting to keep him where he was.

"Got a plan yet?" she called to Jayce.

"Yeah, don't come so unprepared next time!"

She would have given him a look, but she was too busy shooting people.

"I said a plan! Not common sense!"

Jayce glanced around. "Maybe."

Ace ducked back down and looked at him, "Maybe is an improvement. What do you have?"

"A really bad idea."

Ace smiled, "I happen to be a fan of really bad ideas."

He grinned, "Oh good. Because I will need your help."

He snuck off while Ace kept shooting, but the soldiers pinned down her location and stopped giving her easy targets. Jayce returned almost as quickly as he departed, full of curses.

"Our really bad idea just became really bad and desperate."

Ace smiled bitterly, "Oh joy. What's my part? The bad or the desperate."

Jayce smirked. "Bad. It's most suiting, I think."

"Flattery at a time like this?" She glanced at him. "I like it."

He quickly explained what he needed her to do. When he finished, she stared at him like he had grown a third eye.

"Are you insane? That's not bad, that's suicide!"

"No it's not. Besides, don't you think it would help your rep at camp if you saved the day?"

She scowled at him. "For the record, I don't care about my rep at camp. But Bishop does need his ass saved. Again."

Jayce actually laughed that time. But Ace didn't have time to bask in her victory. She had to do something stupid.

"I'll cover you while you bolt out of cover."

"Sure take the easy part," she muttered as she positioned herself.

When Jayce stood and started firing, Ace sprinted like her life depended on it, which was easy since her life really *did* depend on it.

When she safely made it around the next corner in the road she allowed herself one second to celebrate the fact that she was alive. Then she continued on to one of the soldiers vehicles. She hopped into the driver's seat of the first military grade hummer. It was missing all of its windows including the windshield, but that didn't matter. The key was in the ignition like she figured it would be.

Ace turned the key until the engine roared to life, then she nervously put it in drive. She remembered driving a vehicle once before when she was eight and was sitting on her brother's lap. It hadn't gone very well. Her window of opportunity was going to be limited, so she pushed the accelerator to the floor and desperately tried to steer as the vehicle shot forward.

As she came around the corner she aimed for the cluster of soldiers, still firing from their ditch. The hummer flew off the road and landed roughly on the uneven terrain as she began plowing over men in uniform. Two made it to the safety of the trees before she managed to hit them, but the rest weren't so lucky.

However, neither was Ace.

She had no idea how she was supposed to regain control. Her foot stubbornly remained heavy on the gas pedal, her adrenaline making it impossible to move. As she drove, Bishop came out of hiding just in time to have to scramble out of her way.

Ace swerved back onto the road, narrowly missing him, when she saw Jayce and the jeep in front of her. She yanked on the steering wheel causing it to make a hard left just as she drove part way into the ditch. Her sharp turn and the slope on the edge of the road made the perfect formula for unbalancing the hummer and it flipped over.

Ace wrapped her arms around her head as the vehicle slammed into the ground and continued to roll into the field on the south side of the road.

When everything finally came to a halt, she slowly extended her limbs and looked around. The hummer had come to a stop on the driver's side which pinned the door. Amazingly enough, she was pretty much unharmed. She had a small cut on her left arm, but that appeared to be all. She shakily unbuckled her seat belt, glad for the second time that day that she used it, and climbed out the passenger window. As she drug herself out Jayce, Bishop, and the few surviving recruits were running towards her.

"That was *NOT* the plan!" Jayce yelled. "How are you even alive?!"

Ace slid to the ground, a little out of breath. "Seat belt," she muttered.

"You were supposed to spook them up onto the road so I could shoot them while you saved Bishop! Not mow them all down and almost run over him and me in the process!"

Ace shrugged. "I don't know how to drive."

"No kidding!"

"I told you I was good at bad plans." She smiled up at him, and he gave her one of his barely smiles even though he was still trying to be mad at her.

"Come on, we have to do a body count," Bishop said quietly, effectively killing the playful mood she and Jayce had going.

"Wait, two of them made it into the woods. Keep an eye out," she said as she dusted herself off. Out of the seventeen recruits that left the camp that morning, only six made it through the ambush. Jayce probably had a mild concussion from crashing his vehicle, which he claimed was the only reason he smiled at Ace. Everyone had minor bumps and bruises, but nothing that would be fatal. The most important emergency they faced was the fact that Jayce's jeep wouldn't start.

With two of the government soldiers still unaccounted for, it was possible that more troops could arrive at any moment. Bishop and Jayce worked on the jeep for almost an hour before finally giving up.

Ace felt useless, knowing nothing about mechanics. But she wasn't the only one that just sat around waiting. When they gave up, they decided the nine of them were just going to have to squeeze into the five seat jeep that was remaining. Bishop drove, with Jayce in the passenger seat and Ace uncomfortably stuck in the narrow space between them. The other six people had to squish together in the back seat, half standing and half sitting. It made for a very uncomfortable drive home, with still an hour and a half to go but at least they didn't encounter any additional problems.

Returning to camp minus three vehicles certainly had an effect on the atmosphere. As they drove in, people's expressions fell without even having to be told what happened. The whole camp became quiet and sullen for the rest of the evening.

The next morning, a memorial service was held for the ones who didn't return. Ace had never been to one before, so she felt very uncomfortable. All around her people were crying and saying kind things about the people they knew.

She stood off to the side and observed, unsure of how to react. She didn't know the name of even one person who died. She didn't have any special moments or experiences with them that she felt needed to be shared. But even people who didn't know them seemed sad and sorrowful during the ceremony. Ace watched the service with mild fascination as people stood up and spoke words about what each individual had been like and told a short story here and there as signs of respect were given to those that left families behind.

She also noticed that everyone was wearing black some-where on themselves. Some were fully clothed in black while others wore just a black band around their arm. A small part in the back of her mind told her it was a sign of grief to wear black when someone was lost, but even those who had no relation or friendship seemed to wear black.

In fact, as the days came and went for one whole week, Ace was the only person in the entire camp who *didn't* wear black. She noticed most of the people giving her dirty looks, but she didn't understand why. She wasn't in mourning. It seemed more disrespectful to pretend she was mourning than to go on like it was just another day.

She wasn't happy that the people had been killed, nor that they had all been ambushed. But she didn't feel any grief at their passing either. She wondered why they didn't cele-brate that nine of them survived. Death was too common to mourn every time it happened. If she mourned every time someone in close proximity to her died, she would never get out of black clothes again in her lifetime. So she ignored the looks, and kept to herself until the one week mourning period was over and things returned almost back to normal.

Chapter 11

Ace wiped sweat from her brow as she paused to catch her breath. "How ya' doin' with the new regimen?" Jason asked as he sat down and handed her a bottle of water.

Ace took a long drink before responding. "Great. It feels good to be doing something semi-productive finally."

"You are progressing really fast. I can't believe how quickly you pick up new techniques."

She smiled. "My dad didn't support the 'learn at your own pace' motto. It was now or nothing. Having two older brothers taught me to keep up or get left behind."

Jason leaned forward on his knees. "So, if you don't mind my asking, why isn't Bishop training you? I mean I just assumed he would since you two are, you know, together or whatever."

Ace took another sip of water. "*Together?*"

"Like a couple or whatever."

"Oh, yeah, it's just weird to hear people talk about it to my face."

He laughed, "I don't know if they are more scared of Bishop, or you, but they won't talk about their leader's relationship to the person he is in a relationship with."

She rolled her eyes, "Bishop is a bit controlling. And a bit protective. He won't push me the way you do. I need that if I am ever going to get out of here and do a mission. Which I will need your help for since he will never send me out on my own."

Jason smirked. "Yeah, downside to dating a macho man." Ace gave him a questioning look. "Basically means he's got a lot of testosterone. Anyway, I doubt he will send you out on your own for quite some time. You'd have better luck pushing for a group or pair mission."

"He won't ever let me do anything I push for. What I need is you to recommend me in front of witnesses with good reasons I should go so he can't show any favoritism."

Jason ran his hand over his jaw. "I see. You want me to manipulate my leader."

"Yes, but only to do something he should do in the first place."

"Now, Bishop and I rarely agree. Like almost never agree. But you don't understand how hard it is to be in his position. He has to send people on missions with the knowledge that they might die. And since he cares about you that makes it difficult."

Ace set her jaw. "No, it means he shows a weakness. One that could easily get us both killed. And it's one I refuse to condone."

Jason laughed as she stood up. "I have a hard time seeing you condone *any* weakness, no matter what the excuse."

She rolled her eyes. "Yeah, because you know me so well after two weeks of training."

"Well, one example proving my point is standing about ten feet behind you."

Ace turned around to see Tali hovering nearby with her arms crossed and an unpleasant expression on her face.

"If you're here to throw stuff at me again, I hope you have been working on improving your aim," she said flatly.

Tali pursed her lips for a few seconds before taking a deep breath and walking a few slow steps closer. "I'm not here to attack you. I'm here to apologize."

Ace frowned. "What for?"

"For throwing things at you and the things I said to you in front of everyone."

"I don't see why that requires an apology to me. You are the one who made a fool of yourself."

Tali glared at her. "Look, are you going to let me get this over with or not?"

Ace shrugged. She knew she was making this difficult but it was slightly entertaining. "I don't see why you have to apologize for acting like a child when you were upset. I believe it is a fairly common reaction."

Tali stepped forward, "I was not acting like a child! And I was upset because you let countless people die!"

Ace raised a brow. "Yes. But like I told you before, *I* didn't want to die. But I don't see why you should apologize for being upset about the fact that strangers died for reasons you had no control of."

All of a sudden Tali stopped, her posture relaxed, and she actually smiled as she looked at the ground and shook her head.

"You're right. I had no control over anything, not only did you knock me unconscious but I was drugged. I couldn't have done anything other than die with them." She looked up at Ace. "And that would accomplish nothing. So, in a weird way I guess, thank you."

Ace stared blankly at Tali for several seconds before shrugging with one shoulder. "Okay."

Tali rolled her eyes, waved at Jason, and walked away.

"You are really bad at talking to people," Jason said as he stood up and stretched.

Ace shrugged. "Is that a problem?"

Jason laughed. "Only if you talk to them on a regular basis. Tali is pretty tough and she has a lot of influence here. You might wanna get on her good side."

She rolled her eyes. "I don't need to be on anyone's good side. I'm not trying to make friends here."

"Oh, don't worry I know. Everyone knows. But your life here might be a little easier if you just tried to be a little less abrasive."

Ace rolled her eyes again. "I should change, so they accept me, which they haven't because I make them uncomfortable. Why don't they change for making me uncomfortable?"

"It doesn't work like that Ace. *You* are the strange one here, not them. It's easier for you to change a little than for all of them to change a lot."

"Become one of them?" she laughed. "No. Because then I would be like a sheep. Cowering and hiding, following all of the other sheep around until I am eaten by a wolf. I would rather stay indifferent and friendless."

Jason smiled, "But you're not friendless."

She frowned, "You just said I was."

"No, I said you weren't *making* any friends. Not that you didn't have any. I am a friend. Carter is a friend. Bishop is a . . . well, he is more than a friend," Jason finished lamely. "But you get my point."

Ace blushed, suddenly uncomfortable with the conversation. She didn't like it when people spoke about her and Bishop. She wasn't really sure how to define their relationship. When things settled after the ambush, Bishop reiterated his feelings for Ace. They were both trying to figure the whole thing out as they went along but it was understood throughout the camp that they were together.

The pair tried to put aside time for each other and take little walks and have private conversations but it seemed like someone was always interrupting and in need. They stole kisses in the shadows and often held hands under the table but there was still something holding them apart and Ace wasn't sure what it was. The few times she tried to bring it up, Bishop brushed it off as him just being stressed from the demands of running the camp. She decided not press the issues and give him the space he apparently needed. She liked him. He made her stomach feel weird. He made her smile. She liked it when he kissed her, but he also infuriated her to no end, even scared her a little. And she didn't like that.

Jason put his hands up in surrender, "Sorry I forgot. No talking about he-who-shall-not-be-mentioned."

Ace ignored him and got back into her fighting stance.

* * *

She spent most of her days like that: practicing with Jason, arguing with Bishop, kissing Bishop, and taking Flint and Wolf out for daily rides. On occasion she went to the shooting range and did some target practice but she was the best shooter on the place so the instructors couldn't do much to help her. She just liked to clear her mind once in a while.

That's where she was during her next Tali encounter. She had just hit the three hundred yard bull's-eye with a 7mm Tikka rifle when someone whistled behind her. Ace glanced over her shoulder and saw Tali leaning against the ammo counter with her arms crossed.

"You have a talent."

Ace looked down the shooting range at her target. "I have a skill, attained from countless hours of practice and coaching."

Tali gave her a bitter smile. "You don't make anything easy, do you? Not even complimenting you is easy."

Ace's eyes narrowed, not sure if she was being taunted or not.

Tali sighed as she pushed herself away from the counter, and slowly took a few steps towards Ace.

"I didn't come here to bother you. And I didn't come here to apologize needlessly again, either. I just came to say I appreciate your honesty." She glanced at Ace, "No matter how brash and insensitive you are about it." She picked up the

Tikka and shouldered it, testing the scope. "That is a rare thing to get around here."

Ace eyed the young woman warily. "I'm not sure what to say here. Other than acknowledge you for pointing out an obvious trait in my character."

Tali pursed her lips as she lowered the rifle. "You are going to be good for me, I think. Teach me to think before I react. Since you tend to get on my nerves almost immediately anytime you open your mouth."

Ace shrugged. "Reacting before thinking can be a good thing. That is your first instinctual response. It will save your life several times." She stepped forward and took the gun back to begin cleaning it.

Tali laughed. "I think I will like you once I get used to you. And Carter seems to think very highly of you, which says a lot. Almost made me jealous, the way he talks about you."

Ace didn't look up as she began the cleaning process. "I don't understand."

"Oh, Carter and I are together. I assumed you knew that since you came to save me and all."

"Yes, I know that. I just don't know why you would be jealous of him being my friend."

Tali laughed. "Are you telling me you don't get jealous when Bishop is surrounded by other women?"

Ace paused in her work and thought of Spandex Barbie. "I guess I understand more than I thought. But I don't touch Carter, so I didn't see the relation at first. But I guess I do now."

"Touching doesn't have to be involved for there to be jealousy. He spoke so highly of your talents and bravery that I didn't need to see you even near him. That's probably part of why I was so angry with you at first."

"He saved my life. I owed him," Ace said as she put the gun down on the table.

"Yes, so you've told me. Speaking of which, how did you get the idea to come after me? Carter would never have asked you to and it's against the rules to carry out a mission without an order."

Ace stared down at the rough wooden table. "He was talking to me about you one day, nothing in particular, just about you in general. When I asked where you were he told me. I could tell by the way he sounded when he mentioned you that you were more important to him than his own life. The way he took care to describe his favorite of your features and personality." She looked up at Tali. "I didn't have to think twice about the best way to repay him. Nothing else would ever measure up to getting you back to him. You are very lucky to have him."

Tali sniffed and looked away. "Thanks, for telling me all of that. It's nice to hear."

Ace squinted as she looked at the sky. "I suppose I should get going if I am to take Flint out for a decent stretch before curfew. I am not allowed to break it again, I suppose."

"No, I suppose breaking the rules too many times might get you in trouble," Tali said with a smile. The young woman turned and walked away without another word, leaving Ace slightly confused. But she had to admit to herself that she had enjoyed the conversation in an odd way.

***

Ace squinted up at the angry dark clouds a few weeks later as she headed toward Bishop's office. She walked into the small building just as the clouds let loose and rain came pouring down.

"Wow, someone has good timing," Jayce muttered as he brushed past Ace and trekked out into the rain.

"Better than yours!" She called after him.

The weather was actually a nice break from the dry dusty days they had been experiencing. But it was turning the camp into a muddy mess. Ace continued on to Bishop's office. He was leaning back in his chair reading a report when she stepped in.

"You wanted to see me?"

He nodded, but didn't answer for several seconds as he finished reading.

"Yes. I wanted to let you know I decided to bring Gwen to this camp."

Ace raised a brow. "And?"

He frowned. "And I thought you liked her."

She shrugged. "Sure."

"I brought her here to make you more comfortable."

"Why?"

Bishop sat up in his chair. "Because you said you liked her."

"So? I liked her when I was being held captive and she was the only person who visited me. That is like saying you like the guard dog that is too timid to attack you." He raised a brow in question to her example.

"Oh, please don't tell me you didn't send her in there hoping I would open up to the doe-eyed little girl who was all sweet and innocent."

At least he had the courtesy to blush. "Either way. I wanted you to know she was coming here. I planned on having her here to check on your animals in case you were to leave on a mission or anything."

Ace rolled her eyes. "If you ever give me one, that'll be fine. She shouldn't have a problem with them. But what is the real reason you brought her here?"

"What do you mean?"

"Oh, please you didn't bring her here out of the blue to take care of my animals while I'm away on a mission I don't even have yet."

Bishop rubbed his face. "Fine. She was driving everyone at the other camp crazy with requests for a transfer to here. I finally decided to just get her here to get them off my case."

Ace frowned. "That's weird."

Bishop made a frustrated gesture with his hand. "And why is that weird? I get reports all day, every day. The last thing I need is to be pestered by an annoying request that has no impact on our cause what so-"

"Not that. I mean Gwen being that assertive about something. She was so timid and passive. She didn't even express an individual thought or opinion. Why would she be so persistent all of a sudden?"

"I don't know. I don't care. She wanted a change of scenery. Look, you only knew her for two weeks when she brought you food. This isn't that unusual of a thing."

Whether or not it was unusual in the general aspect, Ace knew that didn't sound like the Gwen she had known.

"Okay, if you say so. When does she get here?"

"Any day by now I'm sure," he said distractedly as he picked up another report and started reading. Ace waited for a few seconds.

"So are we done then?"

"Huh?" Bishop glanced up. "Oh yeah. Yeah, we're done. I have to plan a high grade mission anyways. Just keep an eye out for Gwen please?"

Ace nodded as she left the room. She would be keeping an eye out for Gwen, alright. There was something odd in that entire situation.

***

Ace and Tali went off to discuss theorized strategies. The summer storms had been hitting off and on all that week, making training a difficult muddy mess. But Ace had found other ways to occupy her time. Tali was made the camp strategist. She was solely responsible for coming up with the strategies for every mission that was issued out of their camp. According to Bishop, she was a genius. After a few conversations without any confrontation between Ace and Tali, Tali asked Ace to look over some of her theorized strategies for an outside opinion.

"I want to see what you think of my pre-planned strategies because you seem to pick out flaws really well. You have a strategist's mind paired with a soldier's experience."

Ace shrugged as she looked down at the papers. "Comes with the territory, I guess."

"What territory is that?"

"Saving my own ass every day," Ace muttered.

Tali studied Ace. Carter told her what he knew about her but it was vague explanations more than actual details.

"So, you have never been with any sort of group before?" Tali asked.

Ace glanced up at Tali warily. "No. Why?"

"You just seem to have a really disciplined mind. I was just curious where it came from."

"I wouldn't be alive today if I didn't have a disciplined mind. I can't tell you how many times I had to hide somewhere uncomfortable while soldiers or scavengers tore through the area attacking people and taking whatever they wanted. You have to discipline your mind to get through that."

"They were attacking people around you? And you did nothing?"

Ace scowled. "I survived. That's what I did. You try surviving for as many years as I have and keep your righteous attitude." The conversation ended there. Tali didn't bring up Ace's past ever again.

***

The weather slowly cleared up, and as the mud began to dry, the training resumed. Ace started going to the weekly war council meetings, much to Bishop's dislike. She sat in her own corner and managed to listen without speaking out, even when stupid ideas were brought up. For three weeks she listened to the mission ideas and updates from other Rebel territories.

She learned that Bishop wasn't the leader of the whole Rebellion, just this specific territory. There were several territories across the nation and each one had their own person in charge.

Ace kept to herself in the corner as people piled into the small room for the next weekly meeting. She wondered why they didn't find a better place to meet when this many people were in residence at the farm. She hid away in her little corner trying not to draw attention to herself. She had only been allowed to start attending meetings because Jason announced that she was mission ready in front of a group of others while they were eating dinner. It gave Bishop no choice but to grant her a seat and include her. He still wasn't happy about it but he at least made a show of granting her request to be involved. Not that there were enough seats available. She stood pressed in the corner with her arms crossed and an unfriendly expression so people didn't crowd too close.

Jason winked at her from across the room, making her roll her eyes. She didn't know everyone here. Not even half of the people could she say she had ever spoken to. But she was surprised when she saw Spandex Barbie enter the room.

Ace had understood why Tali was present since she needed to explain and develop the missions. Tali was a genius when it came to thinking of the unthinkable. But why would Spandex Barbie have to be here? She didn't have the greatest combat skills. She wasn't much of a strategist. All Ace had ever seen her do successfully was wear less clothes.

"Everyone, please find a spot and quiet down so we can get started," one of Bishop's sidekicks tried to shout over the noise of the room. It had very little effect. The people nearest him glanced in his direction but no one stopped talking.

"QUIET!"

Jayce's stern voice easily made it to all corners of the room, creating instant silence. As much as Ace didn't get always along with the man, she had to admit he had respect from every resident at the farm. Bishop stood up, "Let's get started before we suffocate in here. We have a new mission." He glanced at Jayce, "One that I'm not too happy about, but one that needs to be done. I want to make sure everyone understands the level of danger there is going to be on this mission. It will be going inside the Tri-Cities Nest." There were a few audible gasps from the room and several murmurs.

"Sir, no one has ever gone near there. We don't even try to survey from outside the perimeter fence. Why the sudden need to take such a risk?"

"We have recently received word that it is the least dangerous facility that contains detailed information on their plans of attack, their movements, and their numbers. Everything we need to get the upper hand and turn things around is in the Tri-Cities Nest. A most recent update was just delivered to the Nest, and we need it."

Jason cleared his throat, "This is going to take a skill set that you don't have, sir. You need someone cunning, willing to take lives without a blink. Someone who isn't going to think twice about what they have to do to get in and out. And it needs to be someone smart enough to not get caught once inside so they can get out."

"I know that. That is why I am looking to my trainers to tell me who they think is suitable for the job. You know our recruits better than anyone. You know their skills, their strengths, and their weaknesses. I will need a very specific group. There has to be a strength to fill in every weakness and, most important, they have to be able to work together." Everyone was silent.

"Just how deep into the headquarters do we need our people to get in?"

"Deeper than we would like, Sam. Almost to the center domain," Jayce said quietly. Sam nodded. Ace recognized him as one of the trainers, but she had never personally worked with him.

Jason stood, "I would like to put in Ace for consideration for this mission."

Everyone, Ace included, stared at him in disbelief. She had asked Jason to volunteer her for a mission in front of enough people so Bishop couldn't turn down the suggestion without a real reason. But she hadn't even considered he would put her up for a mission of this magnitude especially for her very first.

She briefly wondered if this was his way to get rid of her for good.

"Why?" Bishop asked through gritted teeth.

Before Jason could answer, Bishop's sidekick spoke up, "She has never even been on a simple mission before. This is too important for a rookie."

"Yes, she has. She got in and out of the recruits camp by herself, without even an extraction team. She helped with the ambush. She has the exact skill set needed to get in and out of this base alive. She is not a soldier, she isn't someone who is used to following rules. She is a survivor. She doesn't blink when taking a government life. She is the best shot on the place and she is smart enough that can assume just about any identity in that place without raising suspicion."

Bishop was still clenching his jaw and staring Jason down with a look that could maim. So Jayce answered, "That is an excellent point. The question is, can she work with a team?" He looked at Ace.

She snapped her jaw shut and as it all sank in, she met Jayce's gaze with a calm face. "I'm in." In truth she was petrified. She avoided soldier camps like they were the plague, not to mention the main headquarters. But she couldn't refuse without looking weak, and it would prove to everyone that she wasn't some sort of fraud. Besides, even though this sounded like a suicide mission, she needed to prove something to herself.

Jayce nodded, "It's done then. Ace is going. She will be one of the two going deepest into the base."

She nodded.

"We need someone else to go deep with her and a few people to be waiting for extraction at the perimeter."

It was several seconds before Spandex Barbie stood up. "I'll go."

There were a few raised brows, but no one seemed nearly as surprised as when Ace had been volunteered. Jayce looked to Sam, her trainer, and then to Bishop, who also oversaw her training. "What do you think?"

"She would be a valuable asset to the mission," Sam answered.

"That settles it. Ace and Chastity will go into the core of the compound to attain any and all information they can about government movements. Carter will put together a team to aid in the extraction and Tali will work with you two on strategy. We have some blueprints of the base before they added onto it. It won't be completely accurate but it will at least give an idea of what kind of set-up you will be dealing with."

Ace tried not to scowl. She refused to even look in Chastity's direction. They both knew they didn't get along, so why would she volunteer to go on a mission with Ace? She was suddenly less nervous and a lot angrier about her upcoming mission. She could not imagine what Chastity could bring to this mission unless it was her own agenda.

Bishop went over several more topics needing discussion and votes, but Ace didn't pay any attention. All of her focus was directed to how Chastity could plan on sabotaging Ace. She had to have something planned or she wouldn't have volunteered. Ace knew the Spandex Barbie did missions, but she also knew they were small information gathering missions, and she was pretty sure she knew how the information was attained.

When the meeting adjourned, Ace wanted to be the first out the door. But she didn't want anyone to think she was scared, so she waited for a few other people to leave before she got up and made for her escape. She didn't want to have to talk to Chastity yet and she knew they would be spending a lot of time together planning.

Wolf was waiting for her at the edge of the farm when she stepped into the trees. He was still uncomfortable with the amount of people so he stayed in the forest most of the time. But he was always around when Ace needed to find him. She confided him everything that had happened, including her worries about whether or not she could trust Chastity, and her fears of the mission itself. Wolf sat patiently while she spoke and ran her hands through his fur with a sigh of content.

"I'm not sure about this, Wolf. We don't belong here, they don't know what I am."

The large dog yawned and rolled over to expose his belly, demanding more attention. Ace absent mindedly rubbed him along his rib cage.

"I can't just walk away. I tried. Every time I do, something stops me," she sighed. "And then I hear Quinten's voice. I had almost forgotten those words until Carter was talking to me about helping people. But if they knew what I was, they would shoot me in a heartbeat." Wolf flopped onto his side and whined when she stopped scratching him. Ace let out a big breath and stood up as she wiped her hands on her jeans.

"Well, enough of the pity party. Time to go risk my life for people I've never met before. The ghosts of my past would be proud." She barely made it fifty yards from the tree line before Bishop was angrily stalking over to her. She rolled her eyes and stopped to wait for him, better to have the confrontation as far away from witnesses as possible. It didn't look like it was going to be a heartfelt declaration of love.

"Damn right you're going to stop there and let me talk to you. Where have you been?"

"I was checking on Wolf."

"You should have waited outside of the meeting room until I was finished so I could talk to you." She rolled her eyes again. She really had a hard time when he was so controlling and over bearing. At first she told herself he was like this out of fear of her being hurt, but lately she wondered if it was just the way he was. She really liked the snuggly and kissing Bishop better. Maybe he was bi-polar or multiple personality or something.

"What do you want to talk about? You already approved me to go on the mission. Nothing you say will get me to withdraw my involvement. We have nothing to talk about until you calm down."

He stepped forward so she had to crane her neck to look up at him. "We have plenty to talk about. Do you even understand what you are getting yourself into?"

"Jason thinks I am one of the best people for the job, and you are the one preaching to me about helping people all of the time."

"Yes, helping people when it isn't a death mission," he exclaimed.

"I already accepted. Besides, it would be dangerous for anyone. Does my life have more value than anyone else here? If I back out now I will look like a coward."

"So what? You will be alive!"

Ace shook her head and tried to walk around him. But Bishop grabbed her wrist and spun her around so she was facing him again.

"Stop walking away when I am talking to you. I need you to understand-"

"Let my arm go. That hurts," Ace said quietly.

"No! Not until you listen to me-"

Ace swung out with her right fist. When Bishop blocked it she tried to bring up her knee to hit him in the groin. He twisted so her knee just contacted his hip, then he pulled her forward and flipped her to the ground so hard and fast the air whooshed out of her lungs. Before she could regain her breath he was pinning her wrists together under her back and using his weight to prevent her from getting up. Ace had never seen him so angry, she was more than just a little frightened of his temper.

"I don't like it when people disrespect me. Stop interrupting me. Stop walking away before I am finished talking to you. Stop disobeying me at every turn!" he said through gritted teeth.

"Get off of me," Ace gasped.

"No! Not until I am finished!" Bishop yelled.

"You are hurting me. Let go now!"

"What do I have to do to get this through to you?" He jerked her arms to emphasize his point, not caring what she said until she cried out in pain. Bishop froze at her scream just as he heard a snarl and was tackled off of her. He rolled to his feet to see Wolf standing between him and Ace, snarling. Ace rolled and sat up slowly, clutching her left arm.

"Are you okay?" he asked. He tried to take a step towards her but Wolf's growl deepened. When he looked back up at Ace for help, he noticed the odd angle of her shoulder.

"Shit. Ace I am so sorry. Let me help you-"

Wolf snapped in Bishop's direction when he tried to walk towards her again. Ace finally got to her feet, still cradling her left arm, and glared at Bishop.

"*This* is why I avoided you after the meeting. *This* is why Wolf won't let you near me. You think you are the first man he has had to pull off of me? You hurt me when you get angry. It's happened before and it will happen again. Of course I walk away from you when you start to lose your temper. It's called self-preservation."

She left him and his pained expression as she went off to find Carter. A dislocated shoulder wasn't too big of a deal for her. It was extremely painful, but she had had one before. At least this time she wouldn't have to put it back into place on her own.

***

Ace had to admit by the time she got to the medical building she wasn't feeling very good. And judging by the look on Carter and Tali's faces when she flung open his office door, she didn't look too good either.

"What the hell happened to you?" Tali asked as she jumped up from her chair. Carter was already by Ace's side examining her arm. "You know you aren't supposed to get hurt until *after* you leave for your mission right?"

"Just fix it so Tali and I can go meet with Spandex Barbie and get this all over with."

Carter laughed.

"Are you talking about Chastity?" Tali asked as she looked around Carter at Ace's shoulder.

"Yeah, that's what Ace refers to her as. The two despise each other. But don't worry," he said with a smile at Tali. "I'm sure the three of you will have a great time arguing and painting your nails and such."

"Carter," Ace said in annoyance.

"Right. Let's get you to a treatment room. Tali, come with us I will need your help."

They walked down the hall to an empty room and Ace laid down on the treatment table. Carter took a towel and put it under Ace's back, then wrapped it under her left arm and over her ribs. Then he handed the two ends to Tali.

"Hold those two ends steady. I'm going to pull on her arm and you need to pull on the towel against me so she doesn't move when I pull on her. Okay?"

Tali nodded, a little uncertainly.

Carter slowly straightened out Ace's arm, then pulled on it and rotated it slowly from her side working his way up while Ace grimaced until it suddenly popped back into place. Ace took a big breath.

Tali looked like she was about to turn green, but she stood steady while Carter palpated Ace's shoulder.

"You okay?" Ace asked, a little short of breath.

Tali nodded. "I, uh, I don't usually do this medical stuff."

Ace chuckled. "I can tell. Another side effect from luxury life on the farm."

Tali's brows furrowed together. "What's the farm?"

Carter shook his head, "That's what she refers to this camp as."

"Oh." Tali let go of the towel she had still been clinging to as Ace sat up. She rotated her arms and stretched around-

"Stop that!" Carter chastised as she went through her range of motions.

Ace paused. "Stop what?"

"You shouldn't do that so soon after a relocation. The joint is a little traumatized at the moment."

She waved him off, "It'll be fine. It's happened once before."

"That isn't a good thing. That's worse actually. How did this even happen? I know you weren't training with Jason because he was just here a few minutes before you came up."

"It was an accident," Ace replied nonchalantly. She wasn't sure if Bishop's followers knew of his anger issues. And she didn't want to cause him any extra trouble.

"If someone is responsible for this you have to tell me. I have to report all medical stuff back to Bishop. He's going to want to know who did it."

Ace smiled tightly, "Oh, no he's not."

"Ace, I'm reporting this to him no matter what. It will be easier on all of us if you just tell me." She got up and walked away without answering any of Carter's questions. Tali seemed to agree that it wasn't any of their business and she followed Ace out of the building without a single mention of the incident.

"So, we have to meet with Chastity and the other members of the mission and formulate our plan. The two of you will have to prove that you can put aside your issues. We will study the blueprints we have, even though they are ancient, but it's better than nothing."

"Who is going to be our extraction team?"

Tali pressed her lips together in thought. "Carter will be there, in case someone is injured. Jason wanted to go but Bishop turned him down,-"

"Why?" Ace interrupted.

"You really have to ask that?"

Ace tried to think of a reason, but none came to mind. As far as she knew Jason and Bishop got along just fine. Tali rolled her eyes. "Bishop is getting jealous of you and Jason spending so much time together. And the close contact through all the hand-to-hand training."

"He's the one who assigned me to train with Jason," Ace thought out loud.

"Yes, but now Jason has stood up for you in front of everyone."

Now it was Ace's turn to roll her eyes. "Well, fine. Who is actually going then?"

"Carter, Luke, Sam, and me."

Ace nodded. "At least you and Carter will be there."

"You don't like Luke and Sam?" Tali asked.

"I don't know them is all," Ace said with a shrug.

"Ahh," Tali said with a nod. "Therefore, you instantly don't trust them."

Ace frowned. "You say that like it's a bad thing."

"It must be so annoying, instantly not trusting anyone."

"Why would I trust someone I don't know? I am not saying anything bad about them. I just don't instantly trust them nor anybody. That's just stupid."

Tali shook her head, "Never mind. Let's just get to the meeting."

Sam, Luke, and Chastity were already waiting in the file room when Tali and Ace arrived. Carter arrived just a few seconds before Tali found the proper blueprints in one of the files. The filing system made no sense to Ace but she had no intentions of going through all the old blueprints so she decided it wasn't a necessary piece of knowledge for herself.

When Tali spread out the blueprints on a dusty table that was drug out of some corner, everyone gathered around and listened as she explained the interior design of the building. Ace had to admit Tali had valuable knowledge. She had an educated guess on what almost every room would be used as based on the placement of the few rooms they had intelligence on.

"The problem is the add-ons," Tali said in frustration. "We have no way of knowing if they kept to the same design or if they changed it up." Ace listened quietly to the conversation as people suggested different possibilities. But they were all speculation and no idea was ideal yet. They were still trying to all agree on an optimal entrance point.

Ace looked around and quietly offered, "I think they might have just updated the rooms, maybe combine some or size one down regardless of what those particular blueprints show. But really it will probably be similar so those who frequent the halls wouldn't get confused." Everyone stopped and looked at Ace for several seconds.

"And why should we listen to you? I mean, seriously, you don't even know how to have a conversation with anyone let alone guess what architectural minds thought about when they built this almost five years ago," Chastity replied bitterly. Ace glared but kept her snide comments to herself.

"Look, if *I* was worried about my blueprints being stolen which detailed building an extra outer layer of buildings for added layers of security that's what I would do. Make it look confusing to your enemies but keep it similar enough that it doesn't have a negative effect on workers within."

"How would you know their reason for the extensions?" Luke asked curiously.

Ace felt her nerves start to flutter in her stomach. "You think I've never been inside a soldier camp before? They talk like idiots when they drink no matter how many captives are nearby. You hear stuff if you are smart enough to listen."

He held his hands up in surrender, "No need to go on the defensive. I was just curious if you had a source on the inside. That would be helpful."

"Ha," Chastity burst out. "In order to have a source she would have talk to someone."

"At least I don't walk around in nothing but two sizes too small underwear just to make me feel like people actually like me," Ace bit out.

"Enough!" Tali yelled while banging her fist into the table. "This bickering between you two is not productive and it will get you killed on this mission. You realize you have to go into the Nest right? No Rebel has *ever* been into the Nest and lived to tell about it. You want to be the first you need to get over your personal issues and work together on this." Ace and Chastity glared at one another for several more minutes before Chastity finally looked away.

"I can put my issues aside for the good of the cause," Chastity said quietly. Ace didn't say anything until she realized everyone was staying silent and staring at her waiting for her to agree.

She rolled her eyes, "Oh, please! Like I would risk getting myself killed because of her. I'll play nice."

Carter looked pleased with the response, so Tali ignored her instinct to press for a better commitment and moved forward.

They discussed strategies and entrance points until the blueprints became blurry and no one could see straight. Carter finally gave up after he thought he heard Tali say something about cheeseburgers. She looked at him like he was crazy.

"What?" Carter shrugged and mumbled something about being hungry. "I think we need a change of scenery,"

Tali conceded. "We are done for the day. But I want to reconvene back here after breakfast tomorrow. We will be going over this plan until we are talking about it in our sleep and it's rock solid. And we have to know all of that in one week."

The group dispersed. Ace decided it was time to go find a cold creek for a bath and to soak her tender shoulder. She knew the farm had an area designated for bathing where you could have heated water in a shower or bathtub, but she never felt comfortable there. And the warm water was not worth the risk of someone walking in on her.

So she got on Flint, called Wolf, and rode out into the woods. There were little streams of mountain snow runoff all over the place but she knew of a big creek that would suit her needs just a short ride away. The solitude was even better therapy than the cold water would be. Ace didn't have to worry about what she was saying or pretend she didn't notice the weird stares people gave her. The water was indeed freezing, but it cleared her mind and eased the ache in her arm. After she quickly scrubbed herself clean, she remained submerged until she was numb then she climbed out and dug through her saddle bags for clean clothes.

Ace had to admit the farm did at least one thing right: they kept her in clean clothes and, after only some minor arguing, she didn't have to share her clothes with anyone else. Once in clean clothes she quickly pulled her hair back into a French-braid and returned to the farm.

By the time she wandered back, it was almost dark. Ace didn't feel like sitting down for the community dinner so she snuck into the cooking area and stole some food, then headed to her room. Unfortunately, it appeared that she wasn't going to be able to continue her solitude as she had hoped. She opened the door to see Bishop waiting for her in her room. Ace frowned as she entered. "What do you want?"

"I wanted to see how you were doing. And apologize for earlier," he replied without looking up. "Carter came to report to me that you came to him with a dislocated shoulder. Why didn't you tell him I did it?"

He was sitting on the edge of her bed, elbows rested on knees and head bowed. She ignored his question. "You're interrupting my alone time so can you please make the apology quick?" She set her food down on the chest she kept her clothes in and crossed her arms.

Bishop glanced up, "Don't look at me like that."

"Why not? You dislocated my shoulder after throwing me to the ground because I didn't obey you."

He flinched. "I didn't mean to. You're just so infuriating. You don't listen to me, and I'm used to people listening to me. I don't know how to let you do something dangerous. I am afraid to have something happen to you and I don't know how I could handle that. So I guess I handle it by getting angry or by completely ignoring you so I don't say something. This relationship stuff is new to me, also. But if you tried just a little bit, I wouldn't get so mad. "

She rolled her eyes. "Your anger issues are not my fault."

He nodded. "I know. That isn't what I meant. And I am sorry they affect you. I never wanted to hurt you."

Ace sighed and rubbed her eyes. "I'm too tired for this. I don't think relationships are supposed to be this much work. Maybe we are just too different. I want to just be able to walk away and I don't understand why I can't. I wish that I didn't care anymore."

Bishop stood up and slowly walked over to her, "Am I allowed to touch you?"

He was standing so close she thought it was impossible not to be touching, but his hands remained at his sides.

"I haven't decided yet," she replied tauntingly.

Bishop smiled, "Is that so?"

"Yes, it is."

"And what happens if I touch you anyway?"

"I might hit you."

"Might?"

"Yep. You're just going to have to decide if that's a risk you're willing to take."

Bishop waited a few seconds before wrapping his arms around her and holding her to his chest.

"I wish you wouldn't argue with me," he whispered.

"I wish you wouldn't order me around like a subordinate," she replied softly.

"Okay," he said. "How about this: until morning, I won't give you a single order."

She smiled into him. "I think I can go that long without arguing."

He was quiet for a few minutes before asking tentatively, "Can I stay with you tonight?" She stiffened against him, but he didn't let go. "Clothes on, I promise. I just need to hold you and know that you are still here," he said as he kissed the top of her head. She relaxed slightly, but was still a little suspicious.

"Okay, but don't expect this to become a regular thing," she replied nervously. He smiled and pulled far enough away so he could look down at her face. "I would never do such a thing." He leaned down and kissed her lightly on the lips before pulling her to the bed.

Chapter 12

Ace woke up with Bishop's arm draped over her chest. She slowly scooted out from under him and grabbed her boots on the way out. She had been getting up early to train with Jason for two weeks now. While everyone else on the farm slept, she was putting in extra hours. And now that she was going into the Nest she was going to train even harder.

"You're out here early," Jason said as he started stretching. Ace had already stretched and warmed up. She paused her drills and looked at him. "I want the largest possible chance of surviving the Nest."

He nodded. "Did it finally sink in?"

"That you volunteered me for the most dangerous mission proposed on the farm since this place was started? Yeah, you can say it sunk in."

"Look, Ace, I know it's a bit of a shock that I put you up for that, but I wouldn't have done it if I didn't think you had a better chance of coming back than not."

"Oh, yeah? Did you predict my chances before or after Chastity was put up to be my partner?"

"Now, now. I know you two don't get along but you don't seriously think she would spoil this entire mission just to get at you do you? She has been with the Rebels for years. She's here because her family was slaughtered during a government raid a few years ago and she wanted to do something to avenge them."

Ace brushed some stray hairs out of her face. "I guess I didn't know that."

"I know you didn't. You never asked. You never do. But trust me, she isn't going to do anything to spoil this. It could change the direction of the war."

Ace felt something heavy settle in her stomach. "I guess I didn't think about the big picture."

"Give her a chance. She wants this to go successfully just as much, if not more, than you do. So she doesn't like you and she doesn't have to. But you two have a common goal in this. Besides, if she throws the mission her life is at risk, too."

She sighed. "Fine, I'll stop expecting her to sabotage me."

Jason smiled. "That's better. It must be exhausting to be you."

Ace rolled her eyes. "Would you stop talking and attack me already?"

***

They only drilled together for an hour before being interrupted. The rest of the camp was beginning to wake up and go about their routines. Ace was surprised when she look up and saw Tali was standing nearby with her hands on her hips.

"What are you doing?"

Ace wiped the sweat out of her face and motioned to Jason to stop.

"I *was* training. Why?"

"We need you to come work with Chastity," Tali said in irritation.

"Why? And how was I supposed to know? Was I imparted with some telepathic abilities that I didn't know about? Wait, is that an oxymoron?"

Tali just looked at her in disbelief. "Now you're a comedian? Look, Chastity said she spoke to you about it last night. And now we are all sitting around waiting and you don't even bother to show up."

Ace pressed her lips together in an attempt to stomp down her flair of anger. She put two and two together about what was going on. "Hmm? It must have slipped her mind or maybe she got sidetracked," her tone wasn't pleasant, but she didn't care. "I'll go with you now since you asked so nicely and all."

Tali frowned but nodded as she turned and started walking to the other side of the camp. Ace decided she wasn't going to say anything about this to Chastity. It was obvious that Spandex Barbie was making things difficult for her but there was a difference between a minor stab and total sabotage.

While Ace didn't think that Chastity had as much to lose if they were caught on their mission, she still didn't think the girl would give her own life just to get Ace caught. As she and Tali approached the group gathered in the private practice room, Chastity looked up and snickered.

"Forget about our meeting?"

Ace ignored the sugary sweet bait and addressed Tali.

"So, what are we doing here?"

"We need you and Chastity to drill together so you two know everything possible about each other's fighting techniques. It will help in case there is a physical confrontation when you are in the Nest. We also need to be able to assess what areas need improvement or adjusting before the mission."

"Do we need to okay this through your boyfriend, Ace? We know how upset he gets when you don't get his permission first," Chastity smirked. Ace bit the inside of her cheek in order to keep her words to herself.

"Quit it, Chastity. Did you already forget that you promised to get along?" Carter scolded as he walked through the door. Chastity pouted, but Ace felt better about keeping her own mouth shut.

"Let's get started with some unarmed combat," Sam said as he got to his feet.

For the next several hours, Ace and Chastity went through drill after drill until they were so exhausted they could barely stand. Tali was studying maps and blueprints the whole time while Carter and Sam tried to help Chastity and Ace improve their fighting style and support each other's weaknesses as they went along.

"Okay, I know every gap in her defenses. Can we take a break now?" Ace asked while panting.

Sam and Carter glanced up from their papers. "I don't think you will have too much trouble. It is nice that you two aren't afraid of hurting each other because it helps us analyze you as if you were really attacking someone else. The problem is we are concerned how that will affect you in the field," Sam said.

Chastity rolled her eyes. "Oh, please. I won't be concerned with leaving her to die if that is the sacrifice that is needed to complete the mission."

Carter frowned. "That is not what he meant."

"We called a truce," Ace said as she straightened. "I won't leave her unless she's already dead."

Carter and Sam frowned at her until she threw up her hands. "I didn't mean it like that. I mean I will not leave her in there. But I'm not going waste my energy to drag a dead body out. All that will do is get me killed. However, if she still has a pulse I will do whatever I have to do to get her out."

Chastity narrowed her eyes. "What are you playing at?"

"I'm not playing at anything. When will you get it through your head that I want this mission to succeed? In order to give us the best shot, I have to stop expecting you to stab me in the back and stop plotting when I can get at you. Whether I like you or not doesn't mean we can't work together."

Chastity was quiet for several minutes. "You mean that? You aren't setting me up for something?"

Ace rolled her eyes. "I'm not setting you up for anything. Did you not notice that I didn't tell anyone you really didn't tell me about the meeting this morning to make me look bad? Or when you insult me every time we turn around I keep my mouth shut? Get it through your thick skull. Besides if that is how I felt about you, I would have removed you by now. It would make my life a lot easier to have one less irritation."

Chastity pursed her lips in thought. "Fine. But when we get back I'm not going to have some sudden realization that you are my long lost friend. I will still hate you and you will still be the dumb bitch getting in my way."

Ace smiled. "And you will still be the trashy slut who tries to steal boyfriends."

Sam, Carter, and Tali were staring at them with gaping mouths. But Ace and Chastity shook hands and relaxed, no longer waiting for the other one to attack them without notice.

"That's it?" Carter asked.

Ace looked over. "What's it?"

"That's it? Now we won't have to listen to you guys bickering constantly?"

"We just made a real truce. I thought that would make you happy," Ace said.

"Yeah but you admitted you still hate each other," Sam mentioned.

"So?" The two said in unison.

Tali shook her head. "Never mind, as long as you two can work together on this I don't care what you do to one another when you get back."

"Did you find any good entrance points?" Carter asked to change the subject.

Tali looked back down to the map in front of her. "I think so. The southern entrance looks like the best bet. We are going to try to get our hands on some uniforms so you two won't look quite so out of place."

Ace nodded in agreement. "We will need to know what kind of work our uniforms are for. How close is the southern entrance to the office we have to get into?"

"It's about the same as the rest of the entrances. The office is smack dab in the middle of the whole complex. Unfortunately they were pretty smart in their design of this place. And there is a reason no one has tried to penetrate it yet."

"You aren't instilling a whole lot of confidence here," Ace muttered.

Tali shook her head. "I know, but I don't want you going in there thinking I have made it so you guys can just waltz in and out without a problem."

"Okay, so what are we going to have to go through to get in and out?" Chastity asked.

Tali frowned. "A lot. But if Sam and Luke are ready to cover you on the way out, I think it will be doable."

"Let's get started with this then," Luke said as he got out of his chair to view the map. They went over details of the Nest until they were memorized, created a strategy, and ran through every possible flaw they could find then they went over what Chastity and Ace would need to work on over the next few days.

And they worked hard.

Ace and Chastity were training or memorizing strategy every waking hour. But, as the day they were supposed to leave approached, the group still didn't feel rock solid with their plan. So they decided to do a practice run.

Their camp wasn't as formidable as the Nest was but at least they would be able to put their thoughts into action before having to jump into an enemy infested building. They got every trained fighter involved to play the "government soldiers" for the run through and armed everyone with rubber bullets.

Ace and Chastity staged out with Tali, Carter, Luke, and Sam one mile from the entrance to the building, the same distance they would start from the Nest.

When the two started making their way to the building, they had to avoid patrolling guards and once they entered they had to make their way to the center most room and retrieve a file. It wasn't completely realistic because they knew their way around this building but they didn't know the guard routes and the pain the rubber bullets would cause was very real if they got shot.

Ace and Chastity made it in and out in only four hours, much quicker than the real thing would take but they managed to get through it without getting caught and they stuck to the discussed strategy.

"I like it," Tali said when they met up after the file was retrieved.

"How did you two feel about it?" Sam asked.

"Well, I feel as good about it as we can at this point. I can't think of anything I would change," Chastity said. She glanced at Ace. "What about you?"

Ace shook her head. "No, I agree with Chastity and Tali. It won't be that easy but it's as good as we can make it." The group nodded.

"Everyone remember what to do if Ace and Chastity make it outside and get discovered?" Tali asked.

"Shoot like crazy so they think they're under attack and get distracted from our girls," Luke said with a smile. Tali didn't look impressed but everyone else smiled and nodded.

"That pretty much sums it up," she muttered. "I can't think of anything else for us to go over. So I guess go get a good night sleep. We take off at four tomorrow morning."

The group dispersed, Ace included. But she didn't go to her bed like she was told to, not yet. Bishop would be waiting for her. He would want to stay the night with her before she left. But that wasn't what she needed. She needed to spend a quiet hour with her animals.

Unfortunately, she just wasn't that lucky. On her way to the woods, she ran into Billy with a quiet Gwen in tow.

"Hey, I have been looking for you. Gwen got here this morning and I think she is supposed to do something with your animals while you are away? Anyway, since you are leaving so early I thought it would be best if you showed her what she was supposed to do while you were gone."

Ace was too tired to smile politely or do anything overly friendly. "Sure. Come on," she motioned for Gwen to follow her and continued her travel to the woods. Gwen was quiet and seemed a little on the nervous side during their walk, but Ace was too tired to care. When she got to the meeting place near the creek she whistled for her animals and waited.

"So what made you so desperate to come here?" she asked bluntly, making Gwen flinch.

"What do you mean?"

"Bishop said you were begging so incessantly that he let you transfer just to get you off his case."

Gwen nervously started rubbing her hands together. "Oh, that. I just really wanted a change of scenery is all."

Ace narrowed her eyes. "Okay. But why did you want to come here specifically? It's the most active camp, most dangerous one in the area. Why would you want to be here right now?"

"Is there something special about right now?" Gwen asked. "I just wanted to be able to help more and, since this is where most of the stuff happens, I thought I would be most useful here."

Ace wanted to press the matter further but Flint trotted into view. She walked over to him and ran her hands over his body, making sure he was uninjured.

"I want you to check him over a few times a week just like this. Doesn't need to happen every day, just make sure not too many days pass between checks."

Gwen nodded. "Where are you going?"

"On a mission."

"Oh. Where to? They made it sound like you wouldn't be gone long."

"I won't be gone long if it goes well," she muttered.

"So, it is dangerous. I thought you wanted to escape the Rebels."

"Bishop and I have grown close. I decided I didn't want to leave."

Gwen's eyes widened. "Oh. Wow, I didn't know you two were together."

Ace shrugged. "Why would you?"

Gwen shifted awkwardly and shrugged.

"So where is your mission?"

Ace rolled her eyes. All she had wanted was some quiet time with her animals. "The Nest."

Gwen visibly jumped. "THE Nest? Isn't that the main base in the Tri-Cities? What are you getting from there?"

Ace frowned at the girl's reaction.

"What does it matter to you?"

Gwen flinched. "Oh, it doesn't obviously. I was just taken off guard." She was quiet for a few seconds. "You are leaving in the morning?"

"Yes. Early. Why?"

Gwen shook her head but wouldn't look at Ace anymore. Ace narrowed her eyes and took a step towards Glen, but before she could do anything a low growl from the darkness brought them all to a halt.

Gwen squeaked and stepped closer to Ace. "Is that your wolf?"

Ace rolled her eyes. "He is a dog named Wolf, not an actual wolf."

"W-Well, is that h-him?"

Ace stepped forward and whistled to Wolf, curious what it was that upset him. He came out of the shadows with his hackles raised and head low. But he walked right past Ace and circled Gwen.

"What is wrong with him?" Gwen squeaked as she jumped away from him.

"He doesn't like you," Ace said as she watched with interest. "My question is, why doesn't he like you? You have been around him before and he was fine. What's changed?"

Gwen backed into Flint, who could care less about the girl but was getting nervous from Wolf's behavior. "N-nothing! I s-swear! Call him off!"

Ace raised a brow as she watched, curious how far Wolf would actually go. Whatever Gwen did to piss off her dog, it couldn't have been anything direct. Gwen was far too timid for that. If she hurt anyone it would have been indirectly.

"Ace, please! I swear I haven't done anything. I don't know why he is upset but I p-promise it isn't because of anything I did."

She thought about it for a moment before sighing. "Wolf, back off."

Whatever was going on with Gwen, it would have to wait until Ace got back from her mission. There was nothing the girl could do in that short span of time.

"Forget about checking on them. If everything goes well I will be back soon enough. If not, they will move on."

She waited for Gwen to nod and rush off, then turned back to Wolf with a curious look.

"Sometimes I really wish you could talk."

Wolf opened his mouth in a yawn before sitting down and wagging his tail at her. Ace took a deep breath and said goodnight to her animals before deciding enough excitement had happened for one night. She needed to be well rested for tomorrow's mission. And the night wasn't over. She would bet her pistol that Bishop was waiting for her in her room and he was going to want to talk about their relationship before she left.

But procrastinating wasn't going to make it go away. So she trekked off to her room. She wanted to roll her eyes, but the sight of him actually brought her relief. She was secretly looking forward to snuggling up to him knowing that it would calm her nerves.

Ace pulled off her boots and jeans, then quickly pulled on some shorts while watching Bishop to make sure he didn't wake up. Then she crawled under the covers and snuggled up to him. She had just taken a deep breath and closed her eyes, when Bishop snaked an arm around her. At first, Ace smiled. But when his hands started to roam farther than she was comfortable with and his lips found her neck, she pushed away from him.

"What on earth are you doing?" she asked as she jumped out of bed. Bishop sat up slowly and rubbed his eyes.

"What do you think I was doing? You are leaving in the morning for a mission you might not come back from.'"

"So your first thought is to get my clothes off?"

She turned to leave, but he jumped out of bed and grabbed her arm to stop her. That's when she realized he had already taken his own clothes off. Ace yanked her arm out of his grip and spun away while closing her eyes, thoroughly trapped now that he was between her and the door. And with him being naked, she wasn't about to wrestle her way to freedom.

"Put your clothes back on!" she yelled.

"Would you keep your voice down?" Bishop asked. "Yes, I might have jumped to conclusions but you snuggled up to me, remember?"

"I didn't know you were naked! After everything we have been through, what about your knowledge of me made you think I would actually go through with something like this just because I might die tomorrow? We promised we would talk about doing anything else before we decided to do it! You know that I am not ready to just have sex with you or anyone. And you want me to give it up so I don't die a virgin? That is a classic line."

Bishop took a deep breath to try and calm his rising anger.

"I asked you to keep it down. You don't want to wake anyone up. And I thought maybe you would want to have a special night with the one person in this world who cares about you before you go off and might not come back."

Ace balled her hands into fists. There were so many reasons she was angry with him right now and his last statement just made it in the top two of her list.

"Get away from my door so I can leave."

"Ace-"

"Now!"

She could tell he was trying his best not to get angry with her but she didn't care. She was so insulted that he thought she would sleep with him just because her life was at risk. Her life was at risk every day. She never let that fact make decisions for her. And definitely not decisions like this.

Slowly he stepped away from her door. Without looking at him, Ace left the room and ran through the camp. She had no idea where she was going to stay for the night. She needed sleep, but there was no way she was going to be able to sleep right now.

Without even trying Ace, ended up at the garage. All of her stuff for the mission was waiting inside in the back of an old jeep; waiting for their departure. It sounded better than facing Bishop. Ace went inside and crawled into the backseat of the vehicle where she curled up into a ball and tried her hardest not to think about anything.

Chapter 13

"What are you doing?"

Ace slowly opened her eyes against the glare of a flash-light but before her could eyes could adjust someone flipped on the overhead garage lights, blinding her further. Tali was looking down at her with her brows furrowed into concern.

"Nothing," Ace muttered as she sat up. "Just never made it back to my room I guess."

Tali didn't buy that excuse it but she didn't say anything further on the matter.

"Hey, Ace. Bishop brought you a change of clothes," Luke said as he tossed them into the backseat. Then he leaned on the edge of the vehicle staring at her intently. Ace stared back at him in confusion until Tali hit him.

"Look away loser! She isn't going to change with you watching her." Tali looked at Ace, "Don't worry. I'll keep watch, you get dressed."

Ace changed as quickly as she could, then slipped on her boots without lacing them and hopped out of the jeep. Bishop and Jayce were standing with her group waiting to see them off. As much as she really wanted to still be mad at him, she just wasn't. She did understand that Bishop cared for her. The guilt-ridden expression he wore as he looked at her told her how sincerely sorry he was. He just needed to understand that she wasn't ready to take her clothes off for him. For her, inti-macy was a big deal and not just some recreational activity.

"Okay, this is it for now. I don't think there is anything left for us to go over," Jayce said as he patted Carter on the back. Ace and Bishop locked eyes as people started loading into the jeep around them. She was about to break the contact and get in herself, when Bishop marched over to her and pulled her to him as he kissed her like his life depended on it.

Ace was as taken by surprise as everyone else was. True the entire camp knew they were together but Bishop never showed any extra affection or emotion towards her when people were around. It was one of his own rules and one that Ace respected. But she had to admit, it felt kind of good to know Chastity was watching. As he pulled away he still had his eyes closed and shook his head. "Sorry, I couldn't let you leave without doing that."

She smirked, "Now that would be on the list of acceptable things you can do before I go off on a life or death mission."

Bishop smiled slightly as he opened his eyes and looked at her. "Be careful."

"Be careful, yourself. I don't want to have to come back just to save you again."

"Okay, love birds, break it up. You're making Luke jealous" Carter joked.

Ace smiled as she pulled completely away and hopped into the passenger seat. She looked back at Bishop and winked at him but said nothing else as the large door was pulled open and the jeep slowly started to back out. She had left a note telling him to keep an eye on Gwen and that something was going on with her so she didn't have to worry about things if she never came back.

As the long road ahead of them came into view with the rising sun, Ace took the time to tie her boots on properly. They had several hours of driving ahead of them before they would ditch the car and sneak in to the edge of the Nest on foot. Once she was settled, she realized just how tired she was after her late night. A big yawn interrupted her thoughts. With a glance around at her fellow passengers, she decided there was no harm in a nap and then she wouldn't have to be bored the entire drive. Chastity seemed to have the same thought. She was already passed out with her head leaning on Sam's shoulder. So Ace sunk down into her seat, closed her eyes, and was asleep in no time.

***

Ace woke up as the jeep went over a large pot hole and nearly jolted her out of her seat. She pushed her hair back out of her face and looked around. There was nothing but sage brush and a few scattered trees along a river.

"Where are we?" she asked Carter who was now in the driver's seat.

"We are almost to the drop off point for the jeep."

She looked around again. "I can't see anything, though."

"As you shouldn't. If we can see them, they can see us. We have to walk the rest of the way."

Ace sighed. She was wishing for Flint at that moment. She pushed herself up in her seat and put a rubber band in her teeth so she could French-braid her hair. As her brain woke up she recalled the details of the plan.

***

They pulled the jeep into a gully and camouflaged it with Sage brush and Russian Olive branches. They had to walk for about two hours before they would reach the Nest from the drop off point. The hardest part about leaving the jeep was that they had to carry all of their supplies and equipment. They got everything tied onto packs, put them on their backs, and headed out. The sun was hot, even next to the water, and with minimal tree coverage, it made for a very warm walk.

"It's not this hot in Blanchard," Chastity whined as they trudged along the shore of a river.

"Blanchard has more trees and is several hours north. Of course, it isn't this hot," Tali snapped.

"Hey, hey! Everyone just take a breath. Let's stop and drink some water, eat some food. That way we are prepared when we get there," Carter said as he let his pack drop to the ground.

Luke shielded his eyes and looked downstream. "We can see the city, let's just get there."

"It's not that easy," Carter said as he opened his backpack and took out a water bottle. "The city is right there, yeah, but the Base is still a half hour away. We can't do anything until dark, which is still a few hours away, and we are currently out of sight from danger. If we are going to relax at all, this is the time to do it."

"I'm definitely game for some relaxation," Chastity said. She dropped her duffle bag and took off her already too revealing shirt to expose an even more revealing bra, then ran into the river. Luke wasn't far behind her, then Sam. Even Carter and Tali joined them after a few minutes.

Everyone was stripped down to their bras and underwear, swimming around and splashing one another.

Ace set her bag down, dug out some water and dried meat, and then sat in the shade of a small tree cluster. Luke was the first one to get properly pruned and bail on the swimming and received several splashes for doing so. He came over and sat to the side of Ace in the sun so he would dry off.

"Scared of water?" he asked.

Ace rolled her eyes. "Being scared of water makes absolutely no sense since you need it to survive."

He laughed. "My bad, I forgot how practical your fears were. So you can't swim then?"

"Not being able to swim is impractical for survival. Of course I know how to swim."

Luke shook his head. "Okay, I don't get it then. Why not go swim with everyone?"

Ace squinted as she looked out at the water. "I didn't feel like it."

He glanced over at her, then smiled. "I get it. You, my friend, are a prude."

She gave him a look of confusion. "You didn't want to take your clothes off in front of anyone," he teased.

"So?"

Luke sat up. "Seriously, it isn't that big of a deal. You don't have anything all of us haven't seen before."

"That isn't the point," Ace muttered, getting irritated with the conversation.

"What? It's not like you've never been naked in front of anyone."

Ace looked away from him, off towards the city.

"Wait, are you serious?"

She didn't answer.

"That is ridiculous. You're what, nineteen? Maybe twenty? That's rare these days." He laid back down. "Especially being with Bishop for as long as you have I just assumed . . . I mean, the man likes his between-the-sheets time."

Ace looked over at him. "What do you mean by that? What is sheet time?"

Luke stuttered over his words as he looked away. "I just, you know, I figured you knew and all. Everyone else does. Like everyone. I figured Tali or Carter or someone told you."

Ace sat up and turned to face Luke. "Luke, what is *sheet time*?"

He sighed and sat up while shaking his head. "It is a reference to the time a man spends in bed with a woman without clothes on. I would be blunter but I don't want to make you uncomfortable."

She looked away. "Does everyone really know? Do they think that's why he's with me?"

Luke started to look really uncomfortable. "Not exactly."

"What do you mean?"

"Look, you don't want to know some of this stuff. I know you're badass and all, but you don't need or want to go down that road."

Ace met his gaze, "Luke, tell me."

He sighed. "Fine. Everyone knows how Bishop is. Everyone knows how you are. So, they kind of think he is with you because you are a challenge. Because you're different and you challenge his authority. Like, the big conquest, you know?"

She stared out at the water. "Everyone knows about this?"

"If you are asking whether or not Carter and Tali knew, yes."

Ace nodded. "They didn't tell me."

"That doesn't mean they aren't your friends," Luke said as he sat up. "If anything it shows how much they really *are* your friends. They didn't want you to get hurt, and they knew Bishop must be with you for different reasons."

She rolled her eyes. "Don't console me. You aren't good at it and I don't like it."

"Oh, good," Luke said with a sigh of relief. "I don't usually handle emotional women well."

"You show it," she said with a nod as she picked at the weeds around her. They were quiet for a few minutes before Ace spoke up again. "Do you remember much? From before the war?"

Luke snorted. "Which one? It seemed like we were always at war with someone. This war is just the first one with ourselves."

"I mean before the Uprisings. What was your life like?"

He shrugged. "Pretty normal I guess. I had a big family, seven siblings. My parents were happy. We were all really close."

"How old were you when it happened?"

"Little older than you were."

Ace twirled a weed between her fingers. "Your family now?"

"I have a sister and two brothers left. They help out with the rebellion too, just in different areas."

Ace stared out at the water in silence. For a few minutes, she got an idea of what the Rebellion was fighting for. She almost felt like there was nothing to fear, like this was a moment from before the Uprisings.

"It's kind of amazing isn't it?"

Luke glanced over at her. "What is?"

"That our lives are like this. We made all of this happen because of one changed law."

He studied her for several seconds before shaking his head. "It wasn't that simple. They didn't *just* change a law. They took away one of our rights and punished us for not liking it. And it wasn't just the law. They were taking control of everything we did. We had to do everything their way. Besides, the world was messed up before the Uprisings."

"What do you mean?"

"People were selfish, greedy, entitled. Traditional values were seen as outdated. Little kids had cell phones and attitude problems. They didn't respect adults and it was suddenly okay to have kids before graduating high school simply because it had become common. Modern culture practically encouraged underage sex. And everyone was so busy looking down at their cellphones and living their lives virtually we started to lose contact with each other."

Ace raised her brows in thought. "I never had a cell phone."

Luke laughed. "Then your parents would have been considered outdated."

"They didn't let me watch much TV either. Just classic VHS movies. I don't even know if we had a DVD player."

"Then they were *really* outdated. And you were lucky. Kid's shows right before the Uprisings were horrible. All about drama and spoiled rotten people getting what they want. Teaching boys to be entitled jerks and girls to be stupid and slutty because it's cute. The kind of makeup and clothing some young girls would wear used to only be acceptable in a night club."

Ace smirked. "So if I would have watched TV when I was a kid I might have turned out like Chastity?"

Luke tried not to smile. "That's not what I meant."

She shrugged. "I'm just saying she fits your description."

Luke gave her a look then changed the subject, "But besides society needing a wakeup call, it wasn't just a law that the government took away from us."

"Okay, so explain what you mean by that."

"They took away our rights, they tried to control the opinions we were allowed to have. Having guns wasn't a law, it was a right. The right to bear arms. The second amendment didn't give us that right, it protected that right. And the government took it away, like it was nothing. Then they just expected us all to take it laying down."

"Were you surprised when people stood up to them?"

"No, but I was a young hot head. So I was hoping for everyone to put the government in its place. I didn't expect a full out war though."

"I was too young to expect or hope for anything. I didn't even really have an opinion on the whole thing until the Retaliation."

"I think the Uprisings would have stopped if they had just given us back our rights. The Retaliation was what really set everything into motion."

Ace sighed. "Seems strange that everyone was so willing to fight back like that."

Luke rested his forearms on his knees. "I heard a something once, just before the Retaliation. *Live free or die trying, death is not the worst of evils.* It's amazing how true it is when you are faced with that actual choice."

"Who told you that?"

Luke smiled, "My oldest brother. He told all of us that and said our choice was coming sooner than we realized."

"Did he know about the Retaliation?"

"He was involved in the Uprisings. I didn't know it at the time, but a lot of my older siblings were. Most of them died during the Retaliation because they refused to swear in. They were only caught because they were creating a diversion so we younger kids could get away."

"Wow. Sounds like your family was really close. I know a lot of people who wouldn't have done that."

He smiled again, "They are pretty awesome now that you make me think of it. But that is all just in an attempt to be as cool as I am."

She couldn't help but laugh at him as she got to her feet.

"Where are you going?"

"Calling them in. We need to get a move on. And swimming is more exhausting than people realize until they get out of the water. I don't want overtired people watching my back."

It took a little longer than Ace would have liked to get Chastity and Sam out of the water, but thankfully everyone else was on her side and the peer pressure won out in the end. Everyone was re-clothed and headed the last few miles to the city before they had a chance to dry off. They were all pretty quiet as reality started to set in.

Once they were in the city, things got a little more complicated. They knew the Nest was on the southern edge of the city and they wanted to approach from the city side so that they had the cover from the buildings, but now they couldn't see the Nest. They navigated their way through the streets until they came within several hundred yards of the outer fence. Then they found a decent place for the extraction team to set up.

"The fence is electrified and topped with razor wire. That will be the first task."

"Did we confirm that the dead spot we had intel on is really there?" Sam asked.

Tali nodded. "Yes. There is one spot the electricity shorts out on. It's only about a foot square though. Give or take."

Ace snorted. "Oh, great."

"Once you guys get through the fence you will need to move quickly without being seen until you are in the building. There should be signs on the doors saying what they are," Carter looked at both women. "Remember. Stick to the plan. Once you are inside we can't do anything for you. If you get into trouble you have to make it at least outside on the eastern side for us to help you. If you can't make it outside, try to hide somewhere until things calm down and you can make another attempt."

Chastity and Ace nodded.

"As soon as it's dusk I want you two at that dead point in the fence and trying to crawl through it. That will be the best opportunity for you to get in without being seen. There is about a seven minute period where it is too dark to see much before the flood lights come on. That is the time span you have to get through the fence and into the building," Tali reminded them.

"And if all goes according to plan, we should see you running your asses off in the morning," Luke said with a big smile. Ace nodded and checked the time on the wrist watch she had been given for the mission. As soon as they found a good spot to hide out they were supposed to wait until four-thirty in the morning, then they would grab the file and run for safety.

Ace and Chastity were stationed at a nearby building with Sam. It was the closest point to the dead spot in the fence that would keep them concealed.

"Remember the plan?" Sam asked for the tenth time.

Ace wanted to roll her eyes, but she was too nervous. It wasn't long before the sun was going down and the three of them were sneaking up to the fence. Sam had some sort of meter that could determine where electricity was. According to Bishop it was worth more than Sam's life so he had to make sure it didn't get lost or damaged.

Once they found the area that was dead, they just had to figure out how to use it to their advantage. The fence was sturdy and tall, much too tall to go over even if there wasn't razor wire at the top. And the electricity usually prevented anyone from going under. The safety area turned out to be fairly high up on the fence. They had hoped it was down near the bottom. Now they had to come up with a contingency plan for getting through.

"Can we cut a hole in the wire right here or something?" Chastity asked.

"No, they check the perimeter every day for tampering. Besides, you really want to touch an electrified fence with metal wire clippers?"

"How high is the voltage here?" Ace asked.

Sam frowned. "Too high to touch without doing any serious damage."

"Okay, mark the edge of the safe zone very clearly," Ace said as she pulled on her jacket.

Sam did as he was told.

"Wait, you aren't going under, it are you?" Chastity exclaimed.

Ace laid flat on her stomach right in between the safety zones. "Okay, I need a rope or something."

Sam handed her a thin rope, about twice the thickness of a shoelace. Ace carefully snaked the rope through the holes. She used a stick to snag the free and pull it back under the fence. Then she tied it to the bottom of the chain link fence and looped it up through the top of the safety area. When she pulled on the thin rope it bowed the fence slightly away from them.

"Here." Ace handed it off to Sam. "Pull on that as hard as you can until I'm through."

He did as told, making a small opening at the bottom of the fence. It wasn't much for a person to fit through, but she was hoping it was enough for her to drag herself through. It was a slower process than she would have liked it to be and she bumped the fence outside of the safety zone twice, which earned her a zap so painful it left burn marks. When she finally pulled herself through to the other side she turned back to Chastity.

"Your turn."

Chastity looked at the fence. "Are you freaking kidding me? Some of us actually have a shape, you're unattractive bones may have fit through there but there is no way I will."

Ace smirked. "You telling me I'm thinner than you?"

Chastity scowled as she pulled on her jacket. She turned to Sam and kissed him, and kept kissing him.

Ace got uncomfortable and turned around to keep an eye on the enemy territory until her coconspirators were finished.

Chastity got stuck once at her hips, and Ace had to help pull her through the rest of the way. When they were both through, Sam slid their weapons underneath then took off the rope and put it back in his pocket.

"I will be waiting here when you return to help you back through. The other three will either be here or stationed along the fence, depending on what kind of ruckus you cause on your departure." With that he left.

***

Ace and Chastity started slinking their way towards the destination building. They had to enter through the south-ernmost door on the east side of the outer building and then find a good hiding place for the night.

Going in and staying there for a whole night was risky, but they decided that they wanted plenty of time to go slow and easy. Rushing things would just lead to mistakes. That way they had the best chance for escape. They also had to sched-ule everything around when the floodlights would be turned on and off.

When they arrived at the proper door Ace's heart was beating so loud she was surprised the guards couldn't hear it. She and Chastity positioned themselves on opposite sides of the door as they each pulled out a hand gun. Ace reached for-ward and gripped the door handle, she nodded to Chastity, then slowly pulled it open. With a peek inside she confirmed the hallway was empty and slid into the room, then knelt in the corner until Chastity was inside.

"Let's find some cover and hunker down for the night," she whispered.

Chastity put up her hand in a signal to stop. "I think we should find the proper room first, then we can get a hiding spot as close to it as possible."

"You want to go wandering through this place before it shuts down for the night? Are you kidding me?"

"I think it will make our move in the morning easier."

Ace paused before she said the nasty things to Chastity that she wanted to and took a deep breath.

"That isn't a part of the plan. We discussed that option, remember?"

Chastity pressed her lips together. "I want to find that room so I know exactly where I am going tomorrow. Are you coming or not."

Ace was getting nervous sitting in an open hallway like they were, she just wanted to get somewhere dark and comforting. She looked at Chastity. If they split or started arguing, it was a direct route to failure and getting captured.

"Fine, at least listen to my counter proposal. We find a place to hide for at least a few hours until everyone settles for the night, then we can discuss looking for the room early."

Chastity scowled but nodded. "Fine."

They crept down the hall, checking the signs on every door. They were looking for a room that would most likely not be entered at night and ended up going into a room that had no name tag on the door. With a quick check inside it appeared that it was used for storing extra furniture. There were desks and chairs, a few couches, and everything was coated in a layer of dust thick enough to prove no one had been in that room in quite some time.

"I think this is as good a place as any for now," Ace said as she found the farthest corner from the door and hid her stuff there. A desk hid her from view if someone came into the room but she would be able to look under it for a partial view. Chastity didn't say anything. She just scowled and stood in the middle of the room.

"Look, I know this isn't what you wanted to do but we have to stick to the plan. That is the only way we are making it out of here alive." Chastity stayed in the middle of the room.

"Would you at least find a spot to hunker down? If you get your head blown off I have to complete this thing on my own," Ace snapped.

Chastity rolled her eyes but she moved to the far wall and curled up behind a couch. Ace got herself as comfortable as she could leaned up against the inside of the desk. She glanced at her watch. She set the alarm to vibrate and double checked the time to make sure it was set to go off when they were supposed to head to the other room then closed her eyes.

Chapter 14

Ace's head snapped up as she heard the door being opened and light poured into their room from the hall. She was about to start cursing at Chastity, when she peered under the desk to the couch Chastity was supposed to be hiding behind. It was dark, so she could just barely make out part of the woman, but it confirmed she was there.

A pair of giggling people came into the room wrapped around each other and kissing. Ace couldn't tell if Chastity was awake or not so she just prayed that she was smart enough to stay quiet.

"We are going to get in so much trouble," a female voice whispered.

"You will just have to make it worth my time then," a male voice replied.

Ace rolled her eyes. She couldn't believe they might get caught by two people trying to have a tryst in an abandoned storage room. She could hear furniture sliding across the ground as they bumped into things, all giggles and kissing, and stumbling. The two were anything but stealthy.

"Let's go to one of the couches," the female voice whispered.

As they fell onto a couch a cloud of dust puffed into the air and Ace realized they were on the couch Chastity was hiding behind. She was surprised at how difficult she found it not to start laughing hysterically at the chances.

Chastity wasn't nearly as entertained. She readjusted her position so Ace could see her face. She was scowling the whole time, especially when things got heated between the couple and Chastity was pinned between the moving couch and the wall. It didn't last as long as Ace thought it would, she was surprised at how quickly it went once all of the clothes were finally off. She was also a million shades of red at having to sit through all of the sound effects. She was just thankful they hadn't decided to turn on any lights. The couple was still all giggles as they started putting clothes back on.

"We need to get back. It's almost time for the walkthrough," the female voice said as she stood up.

"Come on, they won't do a check for at least twenty minutes," the male whined. They spoke about the best route back to their rooms as they left. When the door finally clicked closed Chastity roughly shoved the couch away from her and stood up, making gagging sounds.

"I'm going to have bruises from that stupid fumbling couple," she muttered.

Ace stood as well and checked her watch. "Not everyone can be as skilled as you when sleeping with people they aren't supposed to," she muttered back. Chastity scowled back at her.

"Those two were soldier trainees. If the walkthrough is about to happen then we should wait here another forty minutes or so until after it's completed. Then I say we get the files and get out. It will be a little earlier than we planned but I think it will work out."

Chastity frowned. "How do you know they were trainees? And what is a walkthrough?"

"They are trainees because they had to be in their rooms for the walkthrough. They bring upcoming soldiers here after they get out of the training camps to get them some field time and test out their skills. The walkthrough is a check on all of the trainees to make sure everyone is where they are supposed to be."

"How do you know all of this?" Chastity asked with her hands on her hips.

Ace rolled her eyes. "I have been living on my own since I was ten. You think I didn't have to learn about all of this stuff in order to survive? Besides, it was in some of the intel that Tali and I went over."

Chastity smiled, an evil smile that made Ace uncomfortable.

"What?"

Chastity sobered and shook her head, "Oh, nothing. Let's stick to your plan. I think it is our best shot."

Ace nodded and sat back down, not wanting to talk to Chastity any further. She reminded herself that Chastity wasn't worth the risk of getting herself killed due to their dislike of each other.

***

They waited in uncomfortable silence for almost an hour. The light from the hallway was enough to see each other if they were standing up but if they stayed in their hiding places it was almost impossible to make out any detail.

As soon as it was four o'clock, Ace stood up and gathered her things. "Okay, things should settle down until it's time for everyone to wake up around five-thirty. I don't think they will make another walkthrough in that time span. Let's get the file and get the hell out of here."

Chastity nodded as she strapped on her backpack and pulled out her pistol.

"Before we go, I want you to promise me something," Ace said with her hand on the door handle.

"What do you want now?"

Ace met Chastity's gaze. "If I get caught, and you have a chance to escape - shoot me."

Shock registered on Chastity's face.

"I don't want to be helpless to whatever torture those bastards have in store for me. So if they get me, I want you to shoot me. Deal?"

Chastity was quiet for several seconds before nodding quickly. "Yeah, okay, I guess. If they get you for sure, I will."

They quietly entered the hallway and started working their way towards the center of the building. From outside, the building looked like a confusing labyrinth of hallways being connected to the next inner ring of another building. But from the inside it was fairly simple just as Ace had guessed it would be. The two followed along the straight halls instead of the curved ones so they headed deeper into the building instead of around it. Once they neared the center ring Ace motioned for Chastity to stop.

"We don't want to go into that center room, looks like a hang out spot. The room should be in this ring right here. You go one way I will go the other. If you find it wait outside of the door until I get to you and I will do the same. Deal?"

Chastity nodded and started down the left hall as Ace headed down the right. Ace checked every door sign in the hall and looked into every room that seemed like it might be a possibility. Luckily they were all empty at this hour. Her only concern was random guards that might be passing by in the halls. When she made half of a loop and she still hadn't found the room, she carefully crossed the intersecting hallway and started looking on Chastity's side. She was almost done when she finally came across Chastity waiting in the hall.

"About time" Chastity whispered harshly.

Ace rolled her eyes and went into the room Chastity was guarding. There was a large number of filing cabinets in the office with a hefty desk in the middle that was also piled high with papers.

"Oh great," Chastity muttered as she looked around.

They couldn't see much in the dimly lit room just stacks of papers and rows of cabinets.

"Don't turn on your flashlight. The file we are looking for should be plain, but slightly different color than the rest. It won't be obvious, just different enough that you can tell if you are looking for it."

"Will it have a "confidential" stamp on it?"

Ace bit back an insult. "No, it won't have any definitive markings. That would make it too obvious to a spy."

They started going through file after file after file. Thankfully they weren't looking for a specific piece of paper, just an entire file. It made things a little easier. When Ace glanced at her watch it was four forty-five and she felt herself starting to panic.

"We're running out of time," she whispered to Chastity.

Chastity glanced at her own watch. "We can't leave without this file. No one has ever gotten this far in here before. We need to get this."

Ace glanced into the hallway quickly. "People will start getting up at five-thirty. We need to be sure we are near an exit before that time."

Chastity nodded and the two got back to work, sorting through files even quicker than before. At four-fifty-nine Ace finally pulled a file out of the bottom desk drawer. She had to break a lock to get into it and smiled in relief. "I think I found it!"

Chastity rushed over. "We need a little light to confirm. I'll grab another file we will make sure it isn't the same color."

She turned on her flashlight and held another file up to the one in Ace's hands.

"Finally," she said when they confirmed it was different from the rest.

"Let's get out of here while we still can."

They rushed through the halls much faster than they had been doing before and taking a lot more risks. They still checked around corners for guards, but they didn't double check and take it slow. Ace still checked over her shoulder every ten seconds to make sure no one had appeared behind them but they were still traveling in record time.

They were in the second to last hall when both of them froze at the sound of people approaching. Ace quickly scanned the rooms around them trying to find something that they could hide in.

"This way," Chastity said as she bolted through a door. Ace blindly followed her into the room and closed the door as softly as she could. They listened through the door as three people slowly walked down the hall they had just been in. Ace could hear them talking in a casual tone, but the words were too muffled to make out. They waited until it was silent again. Ace opened the door and peered out, confirmed the hall was clear, and stepped back into the hallway with Chastity following.

"Looks like they are starting to move around already. I wish we had some sort of distraction to up our chances at getting out," Ace whispered as she watched the hall leading deeper into the buildings.

Chastity slowly stepped several yards away and looked like she was pondering a thought.

"I think I might know of one."

As Ace turned to look at Chastity and wait for an explanation she heard a gunshot. Then pain exploded throughout her body. Chastity shot her five times before turning and sprinting for the exit leaving Ace on the ground.

Ace gasped for breaths as she rolled on the ground, but her lungs didn't want to respond. She tried to stifle down the panic and did a quick inventory of her injuries. She was pretty sure she been hit twice in the chest, once in her arm, and twice in her leg. Her mind was a buzz of pain and confusion. Chastity had sacrificed her. That much was obvious. She was bleeding, but not in the amount one would expect from gun-shot wounds.

Her hand moved over something on the floor and she grabbed it as hard as she could, making sure she wouldn't drop it. She could hear shouts of people running towards her to find out what the gunshots were about. Ace looked down and saw that she was holding a rubber bullet.

She cursed Chastity. The wench didn't even have the courage to kill her, she left her alive. Ace had made her prom-ise not to leave her in this place alive and yet Chastity made sure it would happen. The voices were getting closer and alarms went off washing the halls in red flashing lights as a siren blared. Ace pulled herself to her feet as quickly as she could.

Rubber bullets were usually used for practice battles but they weren't painless. They still broke skin, broke bones some-times even, but most of all they still hurt like hell. Especially from mere feet away. Ace couldn't see all of her wounds but the one on her arm was bleeding and already had a bruising welt. The bullets that hit her leg left the muscles in spasm, making it difficult for her to use the leg at all. Her arm still had pain shooting down into her finger tips any time she moved and her chest felt like it was in a vice grip so she couldn't take a full breath of air.

Ace used the wall to support herself as she ran for the ex-it. She knew she wasn't going very fast, but luckily the alarm system was flawed. The red flashing color created no con-sistent lighting and made it difficult to see, the alarm made it impossible to hear, and they had no idea where exactly the shot had come from. Her lungs finally started working a little better as she reached the door that would take her outside.

Ace took three seconds to breathe, then she pushed open the door and sprinted for all she was worth.

It was short lived.

There was already a group of people out there. Chastity either didn't make it or barely made it because there was a team of guards at the section of fencing Ace needed to go through and another team of guards had her surrounded in seconds. Ace picked the smallest guard and ran for him, shooting those on either side as she did. She tackled the person to the ground and came up shooting as she staggered to get back to her feet and keep running.

She felt a bullet graze her arm and another hit solid in her stomach but she still fought. She almost broke free, but the guards at the fence decided Ace was more of a danger and came to help restrain her.

As she felt herself losing the upper hand, Ace caught the gaze of Tali. Luke, Carter, and Chastity were all standing there with her but it was Tali's gaze that Ace kept because she knew Tali would understand what she was about to do. She knew Tali would be able to explain it best when they got back to camp.

Ace fought the guards off of her one more time, held Tali's gaze, and put her pistol to the side of her head. A strange calm fell over her and all of her fear vanished as she thought about her family and hoped her dad could be proud of this last act of defiance. She was a little sad about all the things she hadn't done yet but felt at peace with her decision.

She squeezed the trigger just as one of the guards grabbed at the gun and deflected it so that it just grazed her forehead. Ace screamed in anguish as she realized they wanted her alive and they weren't going to let her die if they could help it. She fought again, fought harder, but they had her hands cuffed in seconds. She called out to Tali to shoot her, to end it for her.

Ace watched her friend pull a rifle to her shoulder and aim, but she didn't shoot. Several agonizing seconds ticked by while Luke and Carter shot at the guards to try and give Ace a chance, but Tali's gun never went off.

The guards formed a wall around Ace and started dragging her back towards the building as others began shooting at the extraction team. Ace still struggled and fought, making the people around her curse several times over. One of them got fed up and brought the butt of his gun down into her face knocking her unconscious.

Tali tried to stop the tears from falling as she lost sight of Ace through the scope of her rifle. She understood perfectly well why Ace would rather die than be taken captive. She remembered Ace telling her that she would never want to be a captive of the government. When Ace saved Tali, she killed a lot of the other captives, and told Tali it is what she would have wanted if she had been in their situation and that was why she didn't feel any guilt over it. Tali understood perfectly and yet she still wasn't able to bring herself to pull the trigger on her friend. She knew exactly what Ace would face in captivity but it hadn't mattered in the moment she had her barrel trained on her friend's heart. She knew she had let Ace down and saw the forgiveness in Ace's eyes when Ace realized that Tali wasn't going to do it. She just couldn't pull trigger and felt like a coward for it.

"They're going to send a party after us any second, we have to go," Carter said quietly as he tugged on Tali's arm. Tali nodded and turned away from the fence. They grabbed their bags and sprinted. Sam had gone to retrieve the jeep several hours earlier and he should be almost to them so they could make a quick escape. Everything had gone according to plan, except for the loss of Ace. They ran for half a mile before Sam finally pulled up and they jumped into the vehicle.

"They're in pursuit, get us out of here!" Chastity yelled as she jumped in.

"Ace?" he called.

Tali jumped into the passenger seat and shook her head. Sam nodded and floored it, taking the most direct route possible to safety. They only had one distant sighting of followers and after driving like a maniac for almost an hour, Sam finally slowed to a more fuel efficient pace. When they were going slow enough to talk to one another, Tali turned around in her seat so she could see Chastity.

"What the hell happened in there?"

Chastity shook her head with an overwhelmed expression. "I don't know. We got the file. She had me take it and we were almost to the exit when we heard people coming. We ducked into an office to hide for a few minutes and then, when we thought the coast was clear, we made another run for it. Ace fell behind a little bit but she shouted to keep going so I thought she was right there with me. I didn't realize she didn't make it out of the building until those guards almost got me coming through the fence."

Tali studied her expression for several minutes before turning back around and refocused on not crying. She and Ace had become fairly good friends over the weeks. As much of friends as Ace would allow anyone to be. Going into this mission Tali hadn't even thought of Ace not making it. She was such a fighter everyone just assumed Ace would be okay.

"Let's just get home for now. We will get the details later," Sam said as he turned onto a dirt road.

The group traveled in silence the rest of the way to the camp. They were only an hour behind schedule when they pulled in. Everyone they drove by clapped and cheered all the way to the garage.

As soon as the large door was closed Chastity grabbed her stuff and left. Sam wasn't far behind her. It was Luke, Tali, and Carter that were moving slowly, still in a daze from the mornings events.

"She risked her life to save me before she even knew me. And all I had to do to repay her for that was pull the trigger," Tali said quietly from the passenger seat. Carter and Luke were still in the back seat, not finding any reason to rush off.

"I didn't even worry about her getting out," Carter said. "I thought if we had any loss it would be Chastity because Ace left her behind. Not the other way around."

"You think she got shot? And that's why she fell behind?" Luke asked.

"She was shot once she was outside, but I didn't see any obvious injuries before that," Tali said numbly.

"She was moving like she was injured though," Carter responded.

Luke nodded. "Yeah, but if she wasn't shot how did they get her?"

"Maybe they were expecting us and had rubber bullets or sand bags loaded up? I saw them using them when they held me." Tali suggested.

Luke looked down at his hands. "What do you think they're gonna do to her?" he whispered. No one answered for several minutes. Tali finally spoke up as she looked out at the other vehicles with a vacant look on her face. "They will do whatever they can to get answers."

"Even though she doesn't know much?" Luke asked.

Tali shrugged. "They don't know that. And they won't believe her if she tells them that. I know what they did to me and they didn't even know I was a Rebel. I was just a random person they took to the recruit camps. I can't imagine what they do to a Rebel they catch inside their own Nest. That alone will tell them she knows something."

Just then the small walk door opened and Bishop came striding in with Jayce. He looked up at them and smiled for half of a second before he realized they were sitting in the jeep not moving.

"Did you get the file?" he asked cautiously.

Tali nodded, but didn't say anything. Carter climbed out and turned to his leader.

"There's no easy way to say this. Ace didn't make it, Sir."

Bishop's face became expressionless. "Was she killed?"

"I'm afraid not, Sir. She was captured between the building and the fence. We think they were using rubber bullets or something similar. She was injured but we didn't see much blood."

Jayce came forward and put a hand on his friend's shoulder.

"They got her alive?" Bishop muttered. He suddenly felt his strength drain and a cold numbness start to set in.

"She tried to kill herself when it was obvious she wasn't going to make it to the fence but they managed to hit the gun out of her hand. She asked us to shoot her but . . ." Carter glanced at Tali who hung her head shamefully. "They wouldn't give us the shot. We couldn't see where she was. They drug her off before we could do anything else."

Bishop nodded.

Tali finally started crying then grabbed her bag and bolted out the door.

Luke was still sitting in the backseat, so Carter nudged him.

"Come on, man, there's nothing else we can do."

Luke finally got up and handed the file to Bishop. They filtered out leaving Jayce and Bishop alone in the garage. Bishop sat down on a small pile of spare tires and put his face in his hands.

Jayce stood awkwardly, "I know this is difficult. It's hard anytime you lose a recruit, especially one you are close to.

This will be hard on all of us. She was tough as nails but she kind of grew on all of us. Take your time, I can wait outside."

He moved to leave, but Bishop stopped him. "All she wanted was to be left alone so she could survive in peace. And I took that from her."

"You gave her something to fight for, Bishop. She didn't have a reason before, she just survived. We gave her a reason to live here, a reason to fight, a purpose. I saw it in her eyes the morning they left."

"We can't even send a team in to get her out of there. Not even a team to go in and kill her. It's too risky. They'll reinforce their defenses after this. That was our only shot at getting inside."

Jayce nodded. "I think she will find a way to end her own life quick enough. Her biggest fear was being taken captive, she will figure out a way to escape it one way or another. There is nothing else we can do. Come on. Let's go remember your little hellcat over a bottle of my best."

***

Ace groggily opened her heavy eyelids. Her limbs all felt tingly and weird. When she tried to move her fingers it felt like she was moving in thick syrup. All of her motions were slow and weak. She tried to bring her hand up to her face but she couldn't move it. Panic slowly rose in her chest. She looked around to see that she was strapped to a table in a small white room and dressed in a hospital gown. There was a needle in her left arm, pumping something into her veins. Her wrists and ankles were strapped down along with a strap across her chest, preventing her from almost any movement. She struggled and pulled but she couldn't get free.

She had a white bandage around the top of her right arm and she could feel a gauzy bandage on her head and around her midsection, but she couldn't feel any pain from the injuries.

The memory of what transpired came crashing in on her. Ace scanned the room to get her surroundings memorized. She needed to develop a plan even though her thoughts were sluggish.

The room was small, about the size of a horse stall. There were white cupboards all along the wall to her left and behind her. On her right the wall was lined with random kinds of medical equipment on wheels. She couldn't see any obvious weapons, but that didn't mean something in here wouldn't be useful to her. The problem was she was securely strapped down.

Her panic was almost at its height when a door opened in front of her and a man in a white lab coat strolled in with a clipboard in hand.

When he saw that she was awake he raised a brow in surprise. "Interesting. I wasn't expecting you to be awake yet. I will have to make a note in your chart that you are not very sensitive to sedatives." He sat down on a little chair with wheels and rolled over to her side. He held up the clip board and pulled a pen from his pocket.

"So, tell me about your time with the Rebels, Soldier three one two four."

~*~*~*

Meet Our Author

Kaitlyn Leyva

Kaitlyn Leyva

Kaitlyn Leyva (Kait) was born December 25th 1992 in Spokane, WA, child number three to Daniel and Kris Stoop. Growing up she always had a fiction novel in her hand. Whether it was horse competitions, soccer games, baking competitions or just spending time with her family, she always had a book with her. As a teenager, she was homeschooled so there was more time for her horses. Her senior year in high school, Kait started writing her first book. It started when she ran out of books to read in the house and had already spent her monthly book allowance. After two years, her very first book was complete. *The Girl Champion* was roughly published a few years later, but she wanted to write something better. Writing became her passion.

Her mother and three sisters are her closest friends. As a child, she looked up to her father; he worked hard for his family, but more importantly he loved his job. He always encouraged her to aim high, and never quit no matter what obstacles were found in her path. She currently works as a veterinary assistant with her awesome mother-in-law and a fun group of co-workers who make it easy to go to work every day. Her favorite hobbies currently include exploring mountains on her horse, hunting, coaching youth soccer, camping, cooking, and writing. Although she one day hopes to start a family, for now she and her husband are enjoying their first home and raising their hunting dog. Her dreams include continuing to write and one day getting back into three-day eventing with her appaloosa filly.

She is most grateful to her family for always being there to support her dreams and encourage her forward no matter what crazy idea she comes up with next.

www.ingramcontent.com/pod-product-compliance
Lightning Source LLC
Chambersburg PA
BHW051528260626
70CB00003B/843